California
Sunset

by

Casey Dawes

Mountain Vines Publishing

Book cover design by For the Muse Designs
Edited by Jennifer Lawler
Interior design by Concierge Self-Publishing
(www.ConciergeSelfPublishing.com)

First printing 2012.

Published by Mountain Vines Publishing
Missoula, MT
Contact email: info@ConciergeSelfPublishing.com

To all my writing groups, past and present, who have encouraged, goaded, corrected and inspired me to keep going, especially Bill, Caryn, Clare, Grace, Heidi, June, Laurie, Linda, Pam, Rionna, Rosemary, and Susan. For my most faithful reader, my husband, Ken.

In memoriam to Stanley W. Young, Jr., may you finally be in a place to be at one with the peace that passes all understanding.

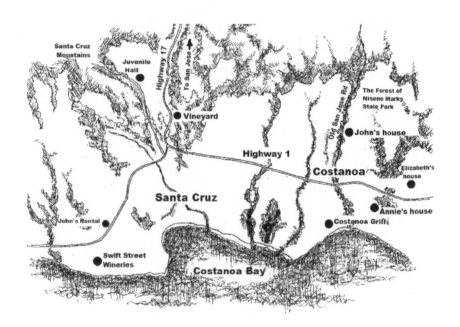

Santa Cruz
Mountains

Juvenile
Hall

Highway 17

To San Jose

Vineyard

Old San Jose Rd

The Forest of
Nisene Marks
State Park

Highway 1

John's house

Costanoa

Elizabeth's
house

Santa Cruz

Annie's house

John's Rental

Costanoa Griffi

Swift Street
Wineries

Costanoa Bay

Chapter 1

Annie strode into her boss's office to answer his summons. *Maybe I'm finally going to get a bonus this year!* It would be great to be able to sock that money away in David's college fund.

She grabbed the printouts off Randy's chair and dropped them to the floor with a thud. "It's going great, Randy," she said. "The next piece of the project is nailed down and we're still on track."

"Close the door, please," he said.

"I'm counting on this project to showcase what I can do for the company." Annie shut the door and plopped down in the chair, her pen poised over her pad as she leaned forward. How should she react? Surprised? Matter of fact?

Randy cleared his throat, his Adam's apple bobbing in his scrawny neck. "I'm afraid the project has been terminated."

"What?"

"JCN needs to cut costs," he started. "Ten thousand people are being laid off from the company."

"There's got to be another project somewhere."

Randy pawed through the papers on his desk. "There is another project you can apply for. You'd be great for one in New Jersey and they could use your skills. It's complex and government-mandated—one of those impossible situations you're good at handling."

"I can't move to New Jersey." She'd been to New Jersey once—boardwalks, billboards, and Bruce Springsteen. Not a place she could ever imagine living. And she couldn't drag her son away from his friends. He was only fifteen.

"C'mon, Annie. Give it a chance. I'd hate for the company to lose you."

She shook her head. *New Jersey may have been fine for Frank Sinatra, but it wasn't fine for her. It had taken so long after her divorce to feel secure again. She had her friends, her home, her cats.*

"There's nothing in the company in this area for someone with your skills. I looked. If you aren't willing to apply for the job, then I have no choice. I have to lay you off. Even if you do apply, there's no guarantee that you'll get the job in New Jersey. You may be laid off anyway."

Her stomach dropped and the bitter smell of Randy's coffee became nauseating. She stared out the window, not really seeing the rain-greened California hills, unable to believe what she was hearing. What was she going to do?

Randy's voice streamed around her, and her mind snagged phrases like "severance package," "layoff procedure," and "resume class." She gripped the arms of the chair as if she was trying to steady a rocking boat.

An ache began in the back of her neck. She needed this job. No one else was going to support David or provide medical benefits. She was going to have to do something to keep a salary coming in. And with the economy the way it was, chances of finding a new job soon would be slim, especially for a thirty-five-year-old woman. Unemployment wouldn't cover her mortgage, much less her other expenses.

Maybe she could learn to like New Jersey. After all, she liked Bruce Springsteen. Boardwalks and billboards might grow on her. There *was* an ocean, even if it wasn't the Pacific.

But what about David? Would her ex fight her for custody if she tried to move their son out of state? Her stomach roiled and she forced back the tears welling in her eyes. *Never cry in the office. Never.*

"You have six weeks before the layoff is final." He gathered papers into a folder. "In the meantime, look these over. Annie?" He held the papers out to her. "I really hope you change your mind."

She took a deep breath, looked Randy in the eye, and took the folder, feeling like the proverbial truck had just slammed into her. But she wouldn't show it if she could help it.

So she threw back her shoulders and marched to her eight-by-eight office. Gently closing her office door behind her, she hurled her pad, pen, papers, and keys on her desk. Damn! She ran her hands through her curls. It would make her already frizzy hair stand out like Young Frankenstein's, but she didn't care.

Tears rolled down her face. She was tired of being the strong one, handling everything by herself. And now this. She'd worked at this company for eight years. How could they lay her off? Or worse, send her to godforsaken New Jersey?

She slid her laptop and Randy's folder into her canvas bag and put on her "gently used" Burberry raincoat. Her head held high, low heels sounding a brisk staccato on the cement walkway, she strode out into the chill March air to the parking lot.

Her mind raced as she opened the door to her Prius. How could she move to New Jersey, leave behind her friends, and abandon the small beach bungalow that had been her sanctuary ever since the divorce? On the other hand, how could she give up a job that provided security and benefits for her child? David was going to go to college soon. Being laid off would destroy the nest egg she'd built for his college fund. Her ex wasn't going to be any help. He could barely take care of himself. She slammed the door a little harder than she meant to do.

What would David think about moving to New Jersey? Could she make him understand? David was doing his part. He kept his grades up and practiced soccer faithfully. She was so proud of him and she couldn't let him down.

She stared out the window, idly watching the moving clouds and changing light patterns as the sun peeked in and out. The recession had hurt Silicon Valley hard. She'd been working long enough to make it to management, the worst place to be during a recession.

She should at least look into the job in New Jersey. *Tomorrow I'll figure out what they're looking for and find out how to apply.*

A small ray of hope filled her. Maybe a move would be okay. She could make a list and see what it would take. She glanced out the windshield. In a cone of sunlight, she spotted a soaring hawk. She trailed its spiral flight on an updraft, its red tail gleamed in the small patch of sunlit clouds. An omen that New Jersey was the right path? Or a signal that she was doing the wrong thing?

Tears threatened again, but she forced them back. She was still in the JCN parking lot and no one at the company was going to see her cry. She pressed the start button and started home.

She drove automatically, oblivious to the towering redwoods fading in and out of low-lying fog as she climbed the mountain highway. Her mind churned over the scene in Randy's office, her emotions twisting and turning with the curves of the road.

"Some choice," she muttered. "Lose my job or go to New Jersey. Start all over again. Find a new place to live. Pack up all my stuff!" Her knuckles whitened as her hands tightened on the steering wheel. "Do you have any idea what it's like to pack up a house?" she yelled at the curve-ahead sign.

She zoomed up the hill, thoughts reeling through her brain, trying to still her emotions with logic. She'd made a good living through perseverance and hard work when no one thought she'd be more than a check-out clerk. This was a little bump in the road;

that was all. No one was going to take away all she'd achieved, even if it meant she had to move to New Jersey. Rapid raindrops pummeled her windshield, forcing her attention back to the road. She didn't need an accident on top of everything else. What she needed was some relief. On impulse, she turned north on Highway 1 instead of south toward home. For years, the Ocean Reads bookstore had been her sanctuary from the craziness of her marriage. A cup of tea and a new romance novel would give her some downtime before she tried to convince David that moving would be a good thing.

She drove into the covered parking garage. Right on cue, a faded, wired-together Volvo pulled out of a space. She swung in with ease, beating out the Volkswagen bus headed for the same spot. At least something was going her way.

Inside Ocean Reads, she shook the raindrops from her coat and glanced around. Everything was as it should be: locals sat on the banquette under the clock, parents and children pored over brightly colored books in the children's section, and patrons hunted through the used book boxes for bargains.

Her shoulders relaxed as she began her usual routine, wending through the sections of the bookstore, her fingers caressing the stories of other people's lives, loves, and imaginations.

She browsed stacks of books on the current fiction table, migrating to the piles of romance novels. The covers showing multi-muscled men made her sigh. Fantasy had been her escape from real life since she was a kid—especially when reality was the pits. Fictional heroes weren't the trouble that real men were, either. One book cover showed a rugged Stetson-topped cowboy posed in front of prairie grasslands; in the distance, snow-capped mountains towered. She stared at the cowboy, imagining herself carried off on horseback to a remote cabin in the Rockies, her worries forgotten. *Perfect.* She picked it up and walked toward the register.

And stopped short.

There he was. Long and lanky, with broad shoulders and slim hips. Thick dark brown hair brushed the top of his collar. Rippling muscles strained against his pale blue shirt as he carried an enormous stack of books to the front of the store. All he needed was the Stetson.

I haven't seen him before. He must be new. I would have noticed. Her eyes drifted down to the curve of his butt cradled by tight blue jeans. *Definitely would have noticed.* She strolled forward, keeping her eye on the man. If she worked her way to the front before he did, she could glimpse his face. Would it be as wonderful as the rest of him?

The clerk turned and caught her staring. Sky-blue eyes burned into hers. His thin lips twitched slightly and he gave her a nod as if he were tipping a hat.

Heat moved up Annie's neck and warmed her cheeks. Jeez, she'd been caught gawking like a schoolgirl. Escaping out of sight to the magazine section, she spotted the latest *Cosmopolitan.* "Fifteen Ways to Spice up Your Sex Life!" No way. She needed something boring, something to tamp down the steam rising within her. Food and flowers—every woman's refuge when she didn't want to think about sex. Her hand skimmed the glossy covers and pulled out one to hide behind.

You're being ridiculous, a voice from the Greek chorus that lived in her head announced. Annie ignored it. Her eyes strayed back to the *Cosmo* cover. It wouldn't take much to spice up her sex life; it had been so long since she'd been with a man she wasn't sure she'd remember what to do with one.

But if the bookstore cowboy was available, she'd be willing to try. She looked at the *Cosmo* cover again. Maybe she should get a copy.

What was she thinking? She didn't have time for sex. *Go home and take a cold shower, girl.* Or did that only work for guys? She peeked around the magazine rack. The coast was clear. She hurried to the counter to pay for her book.

Plunking the paperback down on the worn wooden counter, she looked up. Those same sky-blue eyes stared back at her. The same little smile played with his lips. He took a moment to study the cover of the book and looked up at her with a grin.

Annie felt the flush rise up her cheeks. *Where was that hole in the floor when you needed it?*

"Do you want the magazine, too?" he asked.

"What?"

"*Organic Gardening.*"

She looked down. She still clutched the magazine she'd used as a shield. At least it wasn't *Cosmo.* But still ... she gardened as little as possible—the results were nice, but the work was continual in the temperate California climate.

"Uh, sure," she said.

"Frequent buyer card?"

"Oh, yes."

She searched her wallet for the card and handed it to him.

"My mother gardened," he said. "As soon as the snows left Montana, she'd plant spinach and lettuce. What do you grow?"

"Um, flowers." she said. "Did you move here from Montana?"

"Yep. I bought this place after the Crawfords retired. My name is John Johnson." He put his hand out. She looked at it for a moment before gripping it with her own. His palm was calloused, his hand warm and his grip firm. A spark sizzled up her arm.

"Hello," she said, grasping his hand. She forgot to let go.

He peered down at their joined hands. "This is nice," he said, "but it's hard to ring you up like this." He leaned closer to her. "And there are other customers waiting," he whispered.

"Oh!" She dropped his hand and looked over her shoulder. A dozen people snaked through the stacks, their eyes riveted on Annie.

He chuckled, punched a few keys and glanced at the computer screen. "Thanks for being a frequent buyer ... Annie Renquist."

"No."

He looked up. "No?"

"That's not my name," she said. "I mean, it was. I'm divorced. Now I use my maiden name."

"Let me fix it in our records. What do you want to be called?"

"Annie Gerhard."

John smiled at her and her heart gave a little jump. He stabbed a few more keys, handed her the credit card and slipped her purchases into a bag. Annie turned. The row of eyes stared back at her. For the second time that day, she squared her shoulders and marched out the door.

# # #

John chuckled as he watched her exit. He admired the spunk she showed when she strode past the long line of customers, raincoat flapping, allowing him a brief glimpse of the figure underneath.

When the sales assistant came back from her break to relieve him, he went back to shelving books. The memory of Annie's actions lightened his afternoon. He found himself repeatedly staring at the section of the store where he'd first spotted her, willing her to reappear.

There was something about Annie—a combination of

strength and vulnerability—that he loved. He absently rubbed the stubble on his chin. His wife had had some of those same qualities. Jessica had been gone a long time, but sometimes he felt as if it had only been yesterday. Fortunately, the pain was occurring less and less. But was he ready for a new relationship?

You've got enough problems, Johnson. Don't be adding to your troubles with a woman. Isn't buying a bookstore and finding a house at thirty-nine enough of a challenge for you?

One of the tattooed, pierced, and purple-haired denizens of Santa Cruz approached him.

"Where are your vampire books?"

He led her to the right section and pointed out a few new releases. On his way back to the front of the store, he spotted a boy with mousy brown hair slumped in one of the green wingback chairs scattered around the bookstore. The kid looked like he was about twelve and bored as hell. John squatted down beside him.

The boy glanced at him and then went back to picking at his nails.

"Your mom around?" John asked.

"Uh-huh." The boy gestured in the direction of the mysteries.

"You look pretty bored. What's your name?"

"Ted."

"Don't like to read?"

"S'okay."

"A man of few words. I like that. Got a minute? I'd like to show you something."

Ted shrugged again, but when John stood up, he stood too.

John strode in the direction of the children's books.

The boy stopped. "I'm not going there ... that's lame."

"We're not going there ... we're going past there."

John stopped in front of a cardboard display of books. He plucked one out and handed it to Ted. "This," he said, "is one of the greatest adventure stories of all times."

The boy looked at it, frowning. "There's a mouse on the cover. I told you, kids' books are lame." He held it out to John.

"That's where you're wrong. Adults read these books all the time. I've read these books and I love them. *Redwall* is the story of someone trying to save his home from evil. There are lots of battle scenes and mysteries and adventure. Have you heard of *Lord of the Rings*?"

"Yeah. Everyone's heard of that. I saw the movie."

"Did you like it?"

"Yeah. It was great." Ted grinned, his eyes opening wide with excitement.

John nodded. "Then you'll like this book. Tell you what. I'll give you a discount— half-off. But ..." He raised his index finger. "You have to come back and tell me how you like it." He took a piece of paper from his pocket, scribbled a note and handed it to the boy. "Have your mom give this to the cashier on the way out."

Ted eagerly took the paper. "Thanks!" he said.

That's why I'm a bookseller. If I can keep this old store financially alive, I can get more Teds excited about reading.

He headed up the stairs to the office. It was one of the things that had attracted him to the store in the first place—this aerie where he could survey his domain. He sat in his chair, scanned the view below, and smiled with satisfaction. People dotted the sections, perusing the shelves. Some paused before the displays he'd painstakingly created, several by the list of upcoming author visits.

I wonder if Annie ever attends those.

He could feel his smile broaden.

She'd obviously been interested in him and she'd awakened feelings in him he thought were dead, or at least in a deep freeze somewhere. His one attempt at dating after Jessica's death had been a disaster. Maybe it was time to try again.

The moment he'd seen Annie staring at him, he wanted to pull off the knit cap she wore and release the blond curls peeking out from the edges, surrounding her face with their halo. She'd run off like a startled deer to the magazine section. John grinned again at the memory. He hadn't had that effect on a woman in a long time.

Close up, she'd been even more enticing than he'd thought. Her pixie face was fresh and natural. Brown-flecked green eyes had peered out from under thick, dark lashes. Dark pink lips, with a little bit of a pout. What would it be like to touch her, feel those lips against his? He'd wanted to shut down the register, whisk her away to a dark corner and find out. He shook the fantasy from his head. It would have to wait. First, he had to make this business viable. Second, find a house to live in. Once he'd accomplished those two tasks, he could discover what kissing her would be like. He turned on his computer.

An hour later, he called downstairs on the interoffice phone. "Can I have the invoices from last month?"

"What's up, John?" Sunshine asked when she sauntered into the office. "You've got this silly smile on your face."

He frowned at the soft face of the older woman, pretending he was giving her a stern lecture. "Ah, Santa Cruz. The place where employees have permission to tell the boss whatever's on their minds." With her graying hair in a long braid and feathered earrings, she was living proof that the 1960s counter-culture was alive and well on the Central Coast of California.

Sunshine shrugged. "We were raised to 'Question Authority.' You're authority and I'm questioning. Is there a problem?"

He laughed. His bookstore manager was incorrigible.

She laid a folder of invoices on his desk. "What's her name?" she said over her shoulder before she clattered down the stairs to the main floor.

"Bring me the sales report from last month too, please," he called after her.

"Yes, boss." The answer floated up the stairs.

He thumbed through the invoices. If sales didn't improve soon, he'd have to cut back on book orders. He tapped his pen on the desk. Cutting back on books meant cutting down on service and he didn't want to do that. Maybe he should rethink his marketing budget instead. He leaned back in his chair and laced his hands behind his head.

"You must be thinking about her again," Sunshine said, back in his office with another folder. "Here's the sales report you wanted." She put the papers on his desk and eyed him. "Or maybe you're trying to pretend it's not as bad as I know it is."

He looked up at her. "Sometimes you're too smart."

"Don't get concerned. The store always hits a slump at this time of year. Students study for exams and the tourists haven't arrived. We'll be okay." She patted his shoulder. "We've got loyal customers."

"Umm, do we have a list of our loyal customers?"

"Sure do, boss. I'll be happy to get you one if you promise to tell me her name."

"Not on your life."

"Gotcha!" She whistled and headed down the stairs.

John shook his head. He'd have to work to keep his private life safe from Sunshine.

Chapter 2

"You're late, Mom." David folded his five-foot-nine frame into the Prius.

"Hi, Mom. Love you, Mom. How was your day, Mom?" Annie grinned as she chided her son. She ruffled his rain-drenched hair and started up the car. "I'm sorry I was late. Things came up. How was practice?"

David peeled off his soaking sweatshirt, grunted, and tossed it with his shin-guards into the back seat. He leaned down to unlace his shoes.

Anticipating the smell of teenage male feet, Annie said, "Don't. This is a small car."

David rolled his eyes. "Mom, it's not that bad. My feet are all hot and sweaty."

"Exactly."

Her son sighed and leaned back in his seat. "Practice was okay. Coach is working us hard for the tournament. He thinks we have a real chance of placing."

"Good!"

"He taught me a new trick to get some spin on the ball when I kick it out of the goal. I think I can make starting goalie for the high school team next year, even though I'll only be a junior." David continued to rattle on about saves and plays as Annie drove through the pounding rain. Her heart ached as she listened. How could she tell David he wasn't going to get a chance to try out for his high school team next year, much less be starting goalie?

Sheets of rainwater splashed against the car wheels when she pulled into her driveway. With David on her heels, she dashed to the door.

Cold water from the eaves dripped on her head as she unlocked her bright yellow door. She climbed upstairs to the kitchen of her reverse floor plan beach cottage, while David thudded to his room downstairs. Mindy and Max, the two "used" cats from the shelter, greeted her with protests about the lack of kitty chow. Annie dumped her computer bag and bookstore purchases on the dining room table and knelt down to hug her cats. She buried her nose in Mindy's soft fur. "How would you like to move to New Jersey?" she whispered. Max bumped her hand, demanding his share of loving.

She stood and looked around her home, missing it already. The brightly hued kitchen, dining nook and living room were small, but they were hers. Because the main living area was on the top floor of her home, it was light and airy. She didn't have an ocean view, but large windows on the wall facing west always made her feel as if she did. Her house was only a few blocks from the Monterey Bay shoreline so it was an easy illusion to maintain.

Droplets from her raincoat fell on the kitchen floor while she started the water to boil for pasta and put spaghetti sauce in a pan to heat. The tart odor steaming from the pot made her stomach rumble.

David clomped up the stairs. He had stripped to his soccer shorts and filthy socks.

Annie groaned when he opened the refrigerator door. Why was it teenagers had to stand in front of an open refrigerator door, letting all the cold out? It was obvious they didn't pay the electric bills. "Pick what you want and shut the door," Annie began. "And don't forget—"

"That we're eating dinner, soon. I know, Mom, but I'm hungry now." He grabbed the half-gallon of milk and headed for the cereal cabinet.

"Tournament's on Saturday, right?" Annie asked. She plucked a glass from the cabinet and filled it with tap water. She sat down at the tiny kitchen table, draping her raincoat on the chair next to her. It was good to be home. She loved these times with David, the casual conversation that made up their lives together.

"Yeah—Morgan Hill." David placed a bowl of Cheerios on the table and slouched in the chair behind it. "You taking me or is Dad?"

"I am. Dad will meet you there. Are you the starting goalie? Dad will want to know."

"Mmm," came the response from David's Cheerios-filled mouth.

Annie studied her only child. He'd gotten his father's dark brown hair and eyes, but the smile was all hers. *He's turning out okay.* She said a little prayer for continued grace.

How was she going to tell him? How would it affect him? Right now, he had good grades, solid soccer skills, and his head wasn't turned by girls. Would a dramatic move turn that all upside down?

David set his bowl in the sink. "Do I have time for a shower before dinner?"

Annie listened for the hiss of the spaghetti water. "It's got a while before it boils. Make it quick, though."

David leaned over and wrapped his arms around her. "Love you, Mom," he said. "You're the best."

Her eyes misted. *Will he still think I'm the best when I tell him he's moving?*

After dinner, she went to her home office to check her e-mail. While the machine booted up, she contemplated her garden sanctuary through the office window. The rain had stopped, leaving behind red-orange clouds in the fading light. Her bright pink azalea glittered with raindrops next to a silent water fountain. With the help of her friend Elizabeth and a *feng shui* gardening book, she'd picked each plant carefully for maximum benefit and minimum weeding. The little patch of green was as close to a "room of her own" as she'd ever had. She loved to spend time there, sometimes dreaming of the future, sometimes simply being still, and connecting with the presence of something bigger than she was.

Maybe she'd allow herself some time in her nook this weekend. She could even indulge in a fantasy or two about the new owner of Ocean Reads.

"Don't go there!" she said to herself. *You don't have time to lust after a cowboy from Montana.* Besides, men never turned out to be who you thought they were when you started.

Still ... a quiet voice from her chorus hinted. It's been a long time. *Maybe men from Montana were different. And dating would be nice.*

It would be more than nice.

Annie sighed and dragged her attention back to the e-mail.

Later, snug in her pajamas, she settled in her overstuffed armchair, mug of chamomile tea on the end table, *Mountain Maverick* in her hand. Mindy leapt into her lap while Max took up his perch behind her head. Soon she was caught up in the lives of two people in a small Wyoming town: a new schoolteacher and ranch-owner in the foothills of the Rockies. As she read, she pretended she was the heroine destined for a new life, meeting the man of her dreams who looked an awful lot like the new owner of Ocean Reads.

She wrapped her hands around her mug, sipping the sweet-smelling tea. Why was she so attracted to a man she'd barely met? The twinkle in his eyes and the twitch of his lips had made her feel playful and sexy. She wanted to rub her hands over his back, caressing the rippling muscles she'd seen while he'd been lugging books. She shook her head.

Maybe she was reading too many romance novels. What would it be like to go out with him?

She wouldn't get the chance.

She set down her mug, picked up *Mountain Maverick* and again began to read.

# # #

The drive to the office the next morning was a nightmare. Slick roads from the rain caused a spinout ahead of her, tying up traffic on the twisting mountain highway. It gave Annie too much time to think about what she was going to do all day. Ending a project was dull and took too long. She'd rather be starting a project ... or a new relationship.

Even if she wasn't leaving, would she have the courage to go out with the bookstore owner? Would he even want to go out with her? It had been a long time since she'd been on a date. She hadn't had time to get involved in a long-term relationship while she was raising David. At least that's what she told herself. But the truth was she was afraid she'd get involved with another alcoholic like David's father Fred. Or worse, an abuser.

Once she reached her office, she yanked the envelope Randy had given her from her briefcase. Six months of benefits, a nice settlement that would last her about three months, help looking for a new job—all were standard in her company's "termination package." Piles of papers in triplicate, badge, key, and laptop turn-in forms. She shoved them back in the envelope and tossed it onto a corner of her desk. She wouldn't need it if the job from New Jersey came through. There was no reason why it shouldn't. She took out a pad of lined paper and began to make a list.

1. Tell David
2. Tell Fred (ugh)
3. Find out details from Randy
4. Connect with new boss in New Jersey
5. Start transfer process
6. Call realtor
7. Contact corporate housing for help in finding an apartment in New Jersey
8. Hold a garage sale
9. Pack
10. Move

There. A nice ten-point list. Things were under control.

The rest of the day passed quickly. Annie pretended the layoff hadn't happened and everything was normal. No one asked about her situation and she didn't volunteer the information. Still, it was a relief to have the day end. Sometimes *not* talking about the elephant in the room took more energy than kicking the damn beast.

The commute home was far easier than it had been in the morning. The rain had ended during the day and the roads were dry. It *was* spring, she thought, time for a change in the weather. After months of gray skies, she was ready for the warmth of the sun.

She turned off the highway at the Costanoa exit and drove the few miles to the tiny seaside village for her weekly dinner with Elizabeth. Wednesdays, along with alternate weekends, were Fred's time with David. For Annie, the evenings had evolved into a girls' night out with her friend. A single mom like herself, they'd met when Annie hired Sarah, Elizabeth's daughter, to babysit David.

Annie drove past Crystal Visions, with its tinsel wind sculptures dancing in the breeze and a sign in the window announcing the arrival of Patricia, a new psychic. Should she get a reading some night? No. She didn't want any more bad news and she certainly didn't need a tall, dark stranger.

She continued past the Thomas Kinkade Gallery and the local wine bar and grabbed a parking spot by the breakwater. Dutifully, she emptied her coin purse into the meter. The Costanoa parking police were unrelenting and she didn't need a ticket on top of everything else.

The clack of her heels on the cement sidewalk counterpointed the swoosh of incoming waves. Across the beach, artists had created massive driftwood sculptures that gleamed in the fading sun. Gusts of ocean breezes ruffled her coat and hurried her down the alley.

When Annie got to Beauty by the Bay, Elizabeth was waiting on an older woman. Annie's friend mouthed, "Five minutes," without missing a beat with her customer.

Annie watched her in admiration, wishing she could pull herself together as well as her friend did. Elizabeth's five-foot-two stature was augmented by three-inch open-toed stiletto heels. With dark brown hair piled artfully on her head, antique teardrop earrings dangling from her ears, and luminescent red lipstick, she could have stepped from a Lancôme advertisement.

While she waited, Annie wandered around the shop, sniffing new perfumes and smoothing rich cream on her skin from the sample bottles, loving the sensuousness of the scents and textures. Should she pay more attention to her looks? Even if her fantasy cowboy were unavailable, there'd be men in New Jersey. David only had two years of school left. It was time to start thinking of her own future.

But where to begin with her makeover? Small pots of lotions

competed for her attention. Special selections of nail colors nestled next to lengths of beaded necklaces and exotic earrings. She grabbed one of the silken scarves from its rack and draped it over her arm.

The customer paid for her purchase and left. Elizabeth hurried over and embraced her.

"What's up?" she asked. "Is it that obvious?"

Her friend nodded.

"Nothing much. I'm moving to New Jersey, but other than that ..."

Elizabeth rolled her eyes. "That's crazy. Why would you do that?"

Annie played with the blue paisley scarf she still had in her hand, debating how much to tell Elizabeth. "It's for the best, really. A great opportunity to show them what I can do. Maybe I'll finally get that bonus I've always tried for."

"You never were a very good liar. Let me close up and you can tell me the truth about what's really going on." She took the scarf that dangled over Annie's arm, clipped off the price tag and wrapped it around Annie's neck. "It's yours. Somehow I think you need it."

"Thanks. That's sweet. Anything I can help you with?"

"No, it's faster if I run around and do it myself."

Elizabeth hit a few keys on the register and ripped off the tape that spewed forth. She disappeared into the back room and re-emerged in a few minutes, pulling a sleek leather jacket around her.

"Brr," Annie said buttoning her coat closed as they walked to the restaurant.

"Yep," said Elizabeth. She picked up the pace.

A minute later, they arrived at Costanoa Grill, their favorite local haunt—at least in the off-season before hordes of tourists descended on the town.

Two adjoining rooms made up the restaurant. A curved redwood bar anchored one corner while potted ficus threaded with twinkling lights provided accents to the stucco-covered walls and red-tiled floors. Behind the bar, a patio nook with intimate tables and a fireplace provided a view of the beach and one of the many coastal rivers.

A willowy waitress with a diamond stud in her nose and a purple streak at the front of her hair detoured to Annie and Elizabeth's table on her way to the kitchen. "The usual?" she asked. They nodded.

"Thanks, Mandy," Elizabeth said.

"On its way." Mandy scuttled off to rear of the restaurant.

Elizabeth turned to Annie. "Now what's all this nonsense?"

"I'm being transferred to New Jersey."

"What if you don't go?"

"I'll lose my job."

"That's not a transfer, that's blackmail. Any other options?"

Annie shook her head. "They gave me the severance package yesterday. If I don't take the job, that's it."

"I hope it was a good package. That will give you time to look around here for a new job."

"I'm not going to look for a new job. I'm going to apply for the transfer. That way I keep all my benefits and my salary. It can't be too bad in New Jersey."

The waitress slid the glasses of chardonnay in front of them. "New Jersey?"

"My company is moving me there," Annie said.

"You won't like it," the waitress said as she took out her order pad. "I grew up there. It's like, totally different from California."

"But they both have oceans," Annie said.

"Like, totally different." Mandy poised her pen over the pad.

"What would you ladies like this evening?"

Elizabeth ordered the pasta special. Annie sighed and ordered spinach salad with dressing on the side.

They clinked their wine glasses. "Okay," Elizabeth said. "Start at the beginning and tell me the whole story."

Annie took a deep breath and began. She described the scene in Randy's office, giving Elizabeth the details of her compensation for being laid off.

"Wow," said Elizabeth. "All that money for not working?"

"It's not 'all that money.' It could last me maybe three or four months if I'm very careful."

"Still, that would give you enough time to find a job here."

Annie shook her head. "I've thought this all through. The economy's iffy right now. And I've got a lot of seniority at JCN. If I left, I'd lose vacation time, pension, and stock benefits. I'm better off sticking with the company and moving. It's the practical thing to do."

"I don't think you should go."

Annie twirled the stem of her wine glass. Then she leaned forward. "I really need your support right now. I feel I need to go. I've made my decision and nothing is going to change it."

"I'm sorry. I didn't mean to question your decision. What can I do to help you? What did David say?"

"I haven't told him."

"He's not going to be happy."

Annie shook her head. "No. But he'll adapt. Kids do, you know."

"Not teenagers," Elizabeth said.

"I'll make sure he understands that I'm doing this for him. It can't be too bad," Annie said and sipped her wine, releasing the taste of buttery lemon into her mouth. "The Atlantic Ocean can't be that different from the Pacific. We could take in some

Broadway shows." She took another sip. "Maybe a change in job is the jolt my career needs. A promotion would mean more money for David's college and my retirement."

"Money isn't everything," Elizabeth said.

"It is when you don't have it."

"I wish you had more faith that things would turn out okay."

"I wish I did, too. But in my life, things that are left to chance never turn out well."

"Annie, it doesn't have to be that way."

"It does for me. I'm not you, Elizabeth. I didn't grow up in a boisterous Italian family with too many siblings and more than enough love. It was me and my mother in Michigan and that's it." Annie's words came out clipped.

"Ouch."

"I'm sorry," Annie said. "The uncertainty has me stressed out. Too many years living with Fred, never knowing what was going to happen. Was the call going to be from the police or the hospital? When was he going to be in a fatal accident because he was driving drunk? I need security. Money is security."

Elizabeth started to say something.

Annie held up her finger to stop her friend from commenting. "I don't know if you can understand what it's like not having anyone to depend on. You have a great family. Your dad had a good job and so did your husband. When you grow up without money, things get bad ..." Her voice trailed off. She tried again. "I don't want to lose my friends," she said as she looked up at Elizabeth. She could feel her eyes fill with tears threatening to spill from behind her lashes. "This is my home. I love this town and these people. But I won't go backwards. I won't."

She took a tissue from her purse. "Can we stop talking about it?"

Elizabeth nodded. "Sure." She put her hand on her friend's

arm. "You know, I really admire you, Annie."

"Why?" Annie dabbed her eyes.

"No matter what happens, you keep moving forward. You know what needs to be done and you do it. You're so organized about it, too."

"Want to know the secret?"

"Of course."

"Lists. I make lists. Then all I have to do is check off what needs to be done. Just like Santa Claus."

Elizabeth smiled.

Mandy plunked their pasta and salad on the table. "Enjoy," she said and whirled around to take an order from a nearby table.

Annie dumped the entire container of salad dressing over the greens and sloshed her spinach leaves around the bowl.

"I don't know why you bother," Elizabeth said.

Annie looked up quizzically.

"Getting it on the side, I mean. You always put all of it on anyway."

Annie grinned at her friend. "I like the illusion that I'm doing the right thing."

Elizabeth grinned back. "Any new men in your life?"

Annie felt a betraying heat crawl up her neck. She shook her head. "You're sex-crazed. Me, I'm done with men. I'm never getting involved with one again."

"You just haven't found the right one."

"Yeah, right." The image of the cowboy rose in her mind. She smiled at the memory.

"So what's that smile about?"

Annie forked a piece of hard-boiled egg from her salad. "It's not important. Besides, I'm hungry and this is delicious, as usual."

"Nice try. Who is he?"

Annie put down her fork. "I went to the bookstore yesterday.

The new owner was there."

"I've heard he's gorgeous. And single."

"How do you know?"

"I run a beauty store. I hear everything." Elizabeth filled Annie in on what she'd heard about the new owner of Ocean Reads. Then she moved on to stories of other people in the area. Annie was grateful for the distraction. She didn't want to think about moving *or* men.

Elizabeth was in the middle of a story about a young girl who wanted her to wax off all of her eyebrows, when she stopped. "Mmm, mmm," she hummed, her eyes on the entryway. "I wonder who that is."

Annie turned to see intense blue eyes focused on her. His smile was broad. She felt the warmth on the back of her neck creep up her cheeks. He put his finger to his forehead as if he was tipping his hat. She waved. And immediately felt ridiculous. She did not need to encourage the man—she was leaving the area. Nonetheless, the warmth stayed in her chest.

"Let me guess," Elizabeth said. "That must be the new owner of Ocean Reads. The rumors about his looks are definitely true. Let's invite him to have dinner with us."

"Oh, no," said Annie, but her friend was already waving him over.

# # #

John recognized the mass of blond curls and compact figure immediately. He felt the same pull of desire he had when he first saw her staring at him in the bookstore. Tonight Annie had on a green sweater that drew his eyes to the luscious curve of her breasts. When the woman with her waved him over, his heart beat a little faster.

His boots thudded on the stone floor as he followed the hostess to their table.

"Hello, again," he said to Annie, smiling. Her thick-lashed hazel eyes looked back at him steadily. He forced his gaze to the other woman.

"Hi, I'm Elizabeth," she said, holding out her hand. "Annie says you're new in town. Won't you join us?"

"John Johnson." He shook her hand. "Thank you for the invitation." He sat down in the unoccupied chair next to Elizabeth, giving him a good view of Annie. She grinned at him and her smile was beguiling. "Hi," she said.

"You're from Montana, right?" Elizabeth asked. "How did you wind up in Santa Cruz?"

"Drove south."

Annie chuckled at his joke and another loop snaked around his heart. Only Jessica had ever laughed consistently at his stupid jokes.

He turned back to Elizabeth.

"I managed a bookstore in Missoula for about five years. Everyone in the independent book association knows about Ocean Reads. So when it came on the market, I knew it was a great opportunity."

"California is a long way from Montana," Annie said.

"It was a big step."

"How could you leave?"

He sensed there was something behind the question, but he wasn't sure what. "I took a gamble. Sometimes you have to. You can't control everything—for some things, you just need to trust that it will turn out okay. You go forward even though you can't see the ending. An independent bookstore with the reputation of Ocean Reads doesn't come on the market often. It was an opportunity to make a difference in people's lives, help them find books that made them think, maybe even change their lives. I had the money—I'd just sold my ranch. I made an offer, the Crawfords accepted, and we hit the road."

"We?"

"My horse and me."

"You're not married?"

"No." He paused. "I was, but Jessica died a little over three years ago. Cancer."

"I'm sorry." Annie rested her hand on top of his and he felt her warmth travel up his arm and touch his heart. He looked into her hazel eyes, staring so intently at him. There was no guile there, simply concern and caring.

"Thank you. She was a wonderful woman, but she's gone and I've gotten used to it, as much as you ever do, I suppose."

"Any children?" Elizabeth asked.

He shook his head. "We were trying, but then she got sick. I always wanted them; I still want them. It's in a Montana rancher's blood—big strapping sons to help out with the work when you get too old to toss bales of hay around." He laughed at the image in his mind and rubbed his thumb on Annie's hand.

She snatched her hand away, leaving cold air behind.

A waitress with a purple streak of hair added a place setting to the table. What was it with this area? Couldn't women leave their hair a natural color? His eyes strayed to Annie's curls and he wondered if she was a natural blond.

"Whenever you're ready, I'll take your order," the waitress said.

John glanced at the menu and selected the steak special. "Enough about me. Tell me about you."

Elizabeth spoke up first. "I own a business here in Costanoa—skin care."

"And you?" John looked at Annie.

31

"Me?" Her eyes widened and she looked like a deer caught in the headlights. "Um … I'm a project manager."

John cocked his head. "I'm not sure I know what that means."

She licked salad oil from her lips and John felt his blood quicken as the tip of her tongue circled her mouth. "It's a bit like being a mother. You make sure people know what they're supposed to do and when it's supposed to be done. Then you make sure they do it." She leaned forward and grinned. "I'm really good at it."

"I bet you are." He drew out the words slowly and smiled.

A red blush crept up her neck.

"How's your business going?" Elizabeth asked.

He wondered how he could get Annie alone and have a more intimate conversation.

"I've got my work cut out for me with the bookstore. The Crawfords built an institution, but I think they were getting tired at the end. Maintenance slipped a little and they bought too many books that didn't sell. It was still in the black when I bought it, but barely. The popularity of Amazon isn't making it easy."

"What are you going to do?" Annie asked. Lines of worry crinkled her forehead. She'd be a terrible poker player.

"Fortunately, I've got loyal customers." He grinned. "Like you."

"I'll have to prove my loyalty more often," she said. "Do you spend all your time at the store?" she asked.

"The store, my novel, and the house search take up a lot of time. But I'm sure I could squeeze in one more activity."

"You're writing a novel?"

"Not a very good one, I'm afraid. It's gotten twenty-five rejections from agents so far."

Her luscious lips turned up in a smile and her eyes focused on his. "I'm sure it's good. You just haven't found the right person."

Were they still talking about agents?

Annie took another bite of salad, once again licking the oil from her lips. He watched, fascinated, until the waitress plunked his plate in front of him.

"Where are you looking for a house?" Elizabeth said. "There's an agent in town who's really good at finding the perfect place. Lots of my friends have used Beth Brighton and they rave about her. I think there's a stack of her cards on the hostess stand."

If only he could get Annie alone.

As if she heard him, Elizabeth stood up. "I'll be right back." She headed toward the restroom.

"I need to do something," John admitted to Annie. "I'm living in a dump. And any time I want to see Starfire—that's my horse— I have to drive from Santa Cruz to Soquel. With the traffic you folks have around here, it can take a long time to get from one place to another." He cut into his steak. "I took the first thing I could find when I got here, figuring I wouldn't have to stay in it too long. But with the bookstore—"

"And the novel," Annie interjected.

"And the novel," he added, "I haven't had time to look."

"Maybe you should make a list," Annie said. "Write down what you want in a new place, like number of bedrooms, and give it to a realtor. Finding a home is important— probably more important than other activities you could squeeze in."

"I don't know about that. Living alone is hard—no matter how nice your place is. No one to share news with at the end of the day. I suppose I haven't looked hard for a house because I'd rather complain than face the fact that no matter where I go, I'll be alone."

"Sometimes it can be lonely. No one else to depend on. I'm sorry about your wife. You must have loved her very much."

He looked intently at Annie and longed to take her hand in his, to feel her soft skin next to his again. "You're right. I loved Jessica a lot, but enough time has passed. I'm ready to date again." *At least, I hope I am.*

Leaning forward, he asked, "Would a woman consider house-hunting a real date? I could use someone to show me around."

A shadow crossed Annie's face and her smile disappeared. Damn! He'd gone too far too fast.

Chapter 3

Annie had to tell him. Flirting was one thing, but leading him on wasn't fair.

"Do you work 'over the hill'?" He picked up his knife and cut another piece of steak. "I love that expression. You can pretend that it's an easy drive to San Jose, rather than the white-knuckle commute that it is."

"Yes, I work for JCN in South San Jose."

"But not much longer," Elizabeth added, returning from the restroom.

"Well, not much longer in San Jose," Annie corrected. She looked at John, suddenly reluctant to tell him about the move. It'd be fun to date, even if it was only temporary. Maybe they could have one of those commuter relationships she'd read about.

"I'm taking a transfer to New Jersey," she blurted. And immediately regretted it.

"Oh." He frowned.

"It'll only be for a year or two. Then I'll be back!" She smiled.

"A lot can happen in a year or two," he said, frowning more deeply.

"Yes, it can!" Annie called on every perkiness gene she owned—all three of them. She pushed her salad plate toward the candle in the middle of the table.

"I've never been to the East Coast," he said. "I know nothing about it. What's it like?"

"Well, it will be a change, that's for sure. But there's a lot to do and I'll be able to take my son to museums and events in New York. It'll be good for him."

"Isn't there something around here you could find, rather than New Jersey?" he asked, his eyes staring at a spot somewhere over her left shoulder.

Her determination to be in control wavered for an instant. "No," she said. "I have too much in seniority and benefits to leave. I ... I ... have a teenage son that I have to think about. When you're the only support of your child, sometimes you have to do things that you don't want to do. I'm sure you can understand that."

John nodded slowly. "How's your son taking the idea?"

"She hasn't told him yet," Elizabeth said.

"Oh." John looked thoughtful. "What is New Jersey like?" he asked again.

"It's industrial in parts—that's what everyone always thinks about—the New Jersey turnpike. The corporate offices for JCN are down near Princeton. I was there once and it's much more rural. Very pretty with a whole lot of history."

"Doesn't Springsteen come from New Jersey?" he asked.

Annie nodded. "Bon Jovi, too."

"And 'Old Blue Eyes.'"

"Who's that?" Elizabeth asked.

"Sinatra!" John and Annie answered together. They glanced at each other and grinned.

"Seriously," John said. "I do understand. When you have responsibilities, you can't always make the fun choices. I wish you weren't going, though. It would have been nice to get to know you."

Annie's heart thudded to her stomach. She looked into his eyes for a few moments, wishing that life were different, that she wasn't moving. He held her gaze. Finally, she looked away from him.

He stood up. "It's been entertaining, ladies, but I've got to go." He waved for his check. "I'm still sorting out the best way to keep Ocean Reads in the black. I have some reports I need to read tonight." He glanced at the check and put a number of bills on the tray. "That should cover it."

"See you again, I hope," he said to Elizabeth and turned to Annie. "When will you be coming back to the bookstore? I want to make sure I treat my loyal customers well."

"Um, I'm not sure," Annie said, feeling the heat rise in her cheeks.

He looked at her steadily. "I'll be watching for you. And if you decide not to move, I'll buy you a cup of coffee in celebration." He waved and walked out of the restaurant, his boots ringing against the stone floor. Annie stared at his back, feeling emptier than she had before they sat down for dinner, as if her happiness was walking out the door.

Mandy whipped by their table to collect the dishes. "Who was that?"

"New bookstore owner," Elizabeth replied.

"He's ..."

"Uh-huh," Elizabeth and Annie said at the same time.

"Pie?"

"Uh-huh," the women repeated. Mandy rapidly reappeared with a generous slab of strawberry pie covered with a dollop of whipped cream.

"He could be right for you, you know. He seems interested," Elizabeth said as she took a bite of pie. "I know you don't want to discuss it, but are you sure that moving is the right thing to do?"

Annie laughed. "You're always an optimist! I just met the man. And I'm not going to make life decisions based on a guy I've met twice." Annie savored a bite of pie. "Remember, 'a man is not a plan.' I need to run my own life."

"Didn't you ever believe in the knight in shining armor rescuing you?"

"My knights don't look so good when they take off their armor." Annie chuckled. "Remember when I tried online dating? The 'five-foot five-inch forty-five-year old' who was really a five-foot one-inch sixty-year-old? And he smelled like baby powder. That's the kind of knight *I* get!"

"They do background checks of knights now. You can x-ray the armor and see what's under there before you go out with him. That way you can be sure he's a real knight."

Annie laughed and shook her head. "It would be nice to live in a world where wishing made everything come true." She took another bite of pie. It really would be nice to believe in pixie dust and magic wands again.

"This is great pie," she said. "But I have to stop eating it, or I'll need to do another hour of exercise tomorrow." She sat back. "Now that we've dissected my love life to bits, how's Bobby?"

"Bobby's great. I wish he'd get off this marriage kick, though."

"Why not marry him and make him happy? You could get free pizza at George's place if you were part of the family."

George was one of Bobby's brothers. His mother had taken the church's words about procreation to heart. There were seven children—all boys who doted on her.

"I already get free pizza. And I like things just the way they are. Bobby and I have our time together and I have my time alone. Why can't he be satisfied with that?"

Annie shrugged. "Beats me." She glanced at her watch. "I need to get going. Fred should be dropping David off about now."

"What do you think David'll do when you tell him?"

Annie twirled her fork. "He's a lot like me. He figures out what needs to be done and then he knuckles down and does it. It's what makes him such a good soccer player and why he's getting straight As. I think he'll be upset at first, but then he'll make the best of it."

"I hope you're right."

Mandy stopped at the table, a black folder in her hand. Elizabeth reached for it. "My treat."

# # #

"Damn!" A bright pink envelope was tucked under the wiper blade of Annie's car. "I could have sworn I put in enough quarters." She grabbed the parking ticket and tossed it on the front seat. Ugh! One more thing to add to her list: 11. Pay parking ticket. Reality was back with a vengeance.

Wouldn't it be nice to hope that love was possible? Could someone like John be as good as he seemed to be? That would be a true knight—someone who was exactly what he appeared to be. No lying, no game-playing. And good-looking on top of it all. She shivered as she thought of the touch of his hand, his thumb rubbing on the top of hers, sending electricity to the marrow of her bones.

The waves crashed beyond the breakwater. Annie stared out the car windshield at the inky blackness beyond the shoreline. What would it be like to date a good man? Could life actually turn out like one of her favorite novels? Or was a solid relationship only an illusion—smoke and mirrors at a carnival show?

She'd never find out. John didn't seem interested in seeing someone who was leaving. He'd definitely chilled after she told him she was moving. Besides, she knew what she had to do. Her life was in her control. If everything went the way she planned, they'd be in New Jersey by summer.

And John would still be in California.

She pushed aside the fantasy and started the car.

The thump of loud bass greeted her when she opened the front door to her house. Annie went straight to David's room and pounded hard on door. The thud of sneakers hit the floor. A second later, the stereo volume fell to an adult level. She grinned. David always cranked up the music when she was gone, just as she'd done when she was a teen. She rapped on the door and heard a faint, "Come in."

David was sprawled on his bed, studying a labeled diagram of a human body in a thick textbook.

"How was your night?" she asked, stroking his head with her hand.

"Okay," David replied.

"Where'd you and Dad eat?"

"Usual place."

"Hungry?"

"No."

"Okay. If you are, I think there's still some Top Ramen left. You have a biology exam?"

"What's with all the questions, Mom? It was a normal Wednesday with Dad. I'm full. Yes, I've got a test tomorrow. I'm fine."

And testy, Annie thought to herself. The moodiness was new. Elizabeth had told her that teenagers exhibited some strong emotional swings. All those hormones. This mother-of-a-teenage-boy stage of life was not going to be easy.

"If you need anything, I'll be in the kitchen," she said. "Love you."

"Love you, too, Mom," David mumbled.

She quietly closed the door. She missed the days when words spilled out of him, when he couldn't wait to tell her every detail of his life.

When she got to the kitchen, she checked the message machine. No blinking light. No handset, either. Where could she have left it? She hit the retrieve button and listened for the answering beep. Silence. Maybe David had it. If he was studying for an exam, he didn't need to be on the phone.

She trotted back down the stairs.

The rumble of David's low voice came from behind his closed door. She rapped and heard him say, "Gotta go," followed by, "What?" Taking that as a signal to come in, she opened the door.

"I was looking for the phone. Who were you talking to? I thought you were studying for a biology test."

"I was talking to Larry. I'm done studying."

"It's a little late, isn't it?"

"Mom, everyone talks on the phone all night. I'm not a baby anymore, you know."

"Do I know Larry?"

"Mom, what's with the inquisition? You've met him."

Annie thought about David's friends but couldn't come up with anyone named Larry. "Which one's he?"

"You met him at the mall last week."

"The one with the grungy shirt and big pants?"

David nodded.

"Isn't he a little old for you to be hanging out with?"

"He's fun to be with."

"How old is he?"

"He's nineteen. He's in a band and sometimes he works at the mall. He's okay, Mom." He stood up, handed her the phone and gave her a hug. "G'night, Mom." Carrying the phone, Annie slowly closed his door and walked back to the kitchen. The move to New Jersey was sounding like a better and better idea.

# # #

The following Saturday, Annie roused David early for the soccer tournament. He sprang out of bed, but the energy disappeared the moment he flopped into the car. He clicked the seat back and closed his eyes.

She took the southern route over the coastal mountains, climbing the switchbacks to Hecker Pass on Highway 152. The road always soothed her, even though its twists and turns required concentration. Glimpses of Watsonville's morning-lit strawberry fields framed by the curve of Monterey Bay lifted her heart as she ascended. The early spring air was clear, washed clean by the rain of the previous two days.

The landscape abruptly changed from sunlit ocean edge to secretive forest when she crested the summit. She always felt as if she was entering a fairy forest. Maybe this was where the mountain knights lived. Maybe that wasn't a patch of dogwood in the trees, but a white steed, ready for battle. *Song of India* played on the car radio and she could almost believe in dreams coming true.

Almost, but not quite.

But it didn't matter. She peeked at David. No matter what the difficulties, she was glad she'd had him. He was growing up so quickly. Every moment with him was precious.

He was stirring by the time they got to Morgan Hill. She was starving and figured he was, too; he always seemed to be hungry these days. She dropped him off at the soccer field to register and then went to the nearby Safeway to stock up on Starbucks, lunch items, a cardboard flat of water, and bag of oranges for the boys.

By the time she got back to the acres of soccer greens, David's team was warming up on one of the fields near the tree line. She left the food in the bags and the cooler in the back of the car, grabbed her folding chair and "boredom bag," and strolled toward the cluster of parents on the sideline. A few of the other parents smiled at her as she set up her chair. They'd been together with the team for years. She chatted briefly with them, settled down in her chair and pulled her "to do" list from her bag.

1. Tell David

When was she going to do that? Maybe after the soccer game if they won. Or would that be the wrong time? He'd hate to leave a winning team. Maybe she should tackle something else on her list.

2. Tell Fred

As if to answer her summons, her ex-husband plopped his lawn chair beside her and settled his bulk in the protesting object.

"When do they start?" he asked.

"I'm not really sure."

"Why not? Didn't you ask David? What about the play sheet? Did you look at that?"

"Not yet. There are always some last minute changes, so I figured I'd wait."

"Hmmm. Someone else must know," Fred said.

Annie drank her coffee and looked at her ex-husband, who was already scanning the other parents for enlightenment. *His beard is going gray.* She caught the smoky sweet odor of alcohol and cigarettes as a breeze drifted past. *Must have been a fun night. Thank God I don't have to deal with it any more.* She took the last sip of her coffee and put it down next to her chair.

Fred lurched to his feet and ambled over to the referees' trailer and she went back to her list.

Skip telling Fred.

She scanned the rest of her list. Most things would have to wait until Monday. She supposed she could begin sorting things in the garage when she got home—figure out what to put into a garage sale and what to take with her. Who knew what she'd find there? Even if she didn't get the job, it would be nice to have a clean garage.

She folded the paper and stuffed it back in her bag. Fred reappeared with two cups of coffee. He handed her a cup. "With milk, like you like it. First game starts at nine-twenty. David's the starting goalie."

"Thanks," she said.

"I'll be back." He pulled a cigarette pack out of his shirt pocket and walked toward the other smokers huddled at the end of the field. Annie dug through her bag and picked up the news magazine. It was going to be a long day. She'd settle back and enjoy the warmth of the early California spring for a while and gear up to cheer David to victory.

The day passed as most soccer tournament days did—long periods of boredom punctuated by moments of frenzy. She screamed every time the ball came close to the end zone. The parents chorused long groans when the ball flew into the net inches from David's outstretched glove, their cheers lifting when he threw himself on the ground to block a goal. At the end of the day, his team came in second in the overall tournament.

"Great job!" Fred gave his son a bear hug. "I'm really proud of you." "Thanks, Dad." David beamed in his father's praise. "I'm really working hard with the coach." Annie hugged her son, too. "You're terrific," she whispered in David's ear. Fred helped them load up the gear in the back of the car. "See you Wednesday," he said, giving David a pat on the back. Then he turned to walk back to his car.

She hopped into her seat and began the long drive home, with David snoring gently in the back seat. What was the best way to tell David about the potential move? When he woke up about halfway home, she thought about saying something before they got there. Before she could start, however, he began reliving the game for her, his arms gesturing as he explained the plays, his voice animated as he reenacted his saves.

She couldn't burst his bubble.

Once they got home, he went straight to the shower. Lugging the leftover groceries upstairs by herself gave her a few more minutes' respite before she broke the news. She paced the kitchen, opening cupboards, staring at the contents, and closing the doors again. Picking up a used envelope, she began to write a shopping list. After "milk," she couldn't think of another thing she needed.

She had to get this over with. Sooner or later, Elizabeth would let something slip and then David would be angry with her for keeping secrets.

Once she told David, the next thing on her list was to tell Fred.

Annie sank into a chair. How would Fred react? Would he fight her? Try to take David away from her? No way. Her ex could barely support himself in this town of high rents and even higher house prices. He wouldn't be able to support a growing teenage son. But Fred loved his son. His reaction would depend on how much he'd had to drink.

I'll pick my time carefully. But is it better to approach him when he's a happy drunk or when he has a miserable hangover?

Her son walked into the kitchen a few minutes later, filling the small room with his presence. He wasn't extra tall or overweight, but over the last few years, he'd reached five-feet nine-inches and filled out. His broad shoulders and thin waist reminded her of how her dad had looked, although her dad had been at least six feet tall.

David grabbed a pot and two plastic bags of Top Ramen from the bin where Annie kept a large supply. She bought it by the box load. It was a cheap supply of nourishment that he and his friends

45

were willing to cook.

She drank in every aspect of her son as he moved about the kitchen, knowing she was about to rock his safe world. There wasn't going to be a good way to tell him.

After he filled his bowl, David sat down and looked at his mother. "What's up?" he asked, slurping a spoonful of noodles. "You look funny."

"How would you like to move to New Jersey?"

"Huh?"

"You know, one of those small states on the East Coast."

"You're kidding, right?"

"No, I'm not."

"I'm not moving to New Jersey. I'm not moving anywhere. Are you crazy?"

"Watch your tone, young man," Annie said automatically. Maybe a different tack would work. "David, there's trouble at my work. They can't keep as many of us employed as they did. The economy ..."

He interrupted. "They fired you."

"They didn't fire me. There's another job in New Jersey."

"What if you don't go?"

"They'll lay me off."

He let his spoon plop back into the broth. "I don't get it. How can they lay you off? You've worked there for years."

How could she explain the workings of Corporate America to David? There were times she didn't understand it herself.

"I don't know," she said honestly. "But unless I go to New Jersey, I won't have a job. And that's a problem."

Scooping another spoonful of Top Ramen, he said, "I'm not moving. I've got a good shot at varsity soccer next year, maybe even starting goalie. I've done really well at the rec league this spring. We'll have to figure out something." He leaned back and thrummed his spoon on the table, droplets of soup scattering across the top.

Suddenly, he bent forward. "I know! I can get a job and help out. Summer's almost here. They always need help at the Boardwalk in the summer. You don't have to do it alone, Mom. I'm grown up now. I can help."

Annie smiled. If only it were that simple. Kids had no idea how big a mortgage for a beach house really was. To David, cutting back on expenses meant a McDonald's hamburger without the fries. Not nearly enough for the few thousand a month it took to live where they did.

"Thanks, kiddo. You're the best, but I need to stay with the company. That way, I can keep my benefits and the salary I've got. And ..." She paused to make sure she had her son's full attention. "... I'll be able to help you when you go to Berkeley in two years."

David went back to shoveling soup into his mouth without answering. The silence lengthened as Annie waited for the reaction that she knew would come. Like her, he needed to chew on something in his head before giving his opinion on anything important.

He stopped eating and looked at her. "I already told you. I'm not moving to New Jersey. You have to do something different. I'm sure you can find another job. A company would be stupid not to hire you."

"David, it's not that easy," she said. "There aren't enough jobs right now."

"But you can find one. I know you can. We can't move to New Jersey. All my friends are here. I'm on a good rec soccer team. You'll ruin my life if we moved to New Jersey." His voice ramped up. "You don't understand. I'm not going. I'll stay with one of my friends if I have to, but I'm not moving to Nowhere, New Jersey!"

David stood up and tossed his spoon in the sink; the dish

clattered after it. He stomped toward the stairs, stopping at the edge of the kitchen.

"I'm going over to Chris's," he announced, glaring at her. "Okay?"

Annie hesitated before answering. Chris was a soccer friend who lived a few blocks away. The walk there and back would probably do David good. "Just be back by ten," she replied.

"Yeah. Whatever." David thudded down the stairs. A few minutes later Annie heard the front door slam.

Well, that didn't go well. Annie got up to load the dishwasher. She thought about the next item on her list. Tell Fred.

She shook her head and put David's bowl in the top rack. Not happening today.

Besides, she needed to find out more about the job and when everything was happening.

Fred would be annoying and want all the details. She'd talk with Randy about the job in

New Jersey on Monday.

Then she'd talk to Fred.

Chapter 4

John leaned back in the nubby brown recliner and closed his eyes for a moment. Images of Annie filled his mind. The green sweater she'd worn at the restaurant, her high cheekbones, her eyes ... But it was her mouth that attracted him the most ... that damn kissable mouth.

He suspected there was also a great personality behind those hazel eyes and pert lips. She reminded him of his mother—the determined attitude and strength a single mom had to have to keep everything together. His mother had shown the same character after his dad had died, handling the ranch chores and bills, managing the household and helping him with school work, but she still found joy in the little things in life—crocuses coming up in spring and the birth of new puppies. Jessica had shown the same strength when she was dying.

He sighed. He still missed her, and he probably always would, but perhaps he was ready to love again. Real love, like he'd had with Jessica, not the desperate loneliness that had driven him to propose marriage to Deborah. He'd lost both women, one to cancer and one to a new job. If he risked his heart again, would he wind up breaking it for a third time?

Annie intrigued him, but she was moving to New Jersey. It would be foolish to pursue her.

The bell from the nearby Catholic church rang out its call to Sunday Mass. In Montana he'd been a regular attendee at St. Paul's Lutheran until Jessica had died. God had given up on Jessica, and he had given up on God. He'd lived on autopilot until he bought the store in Santa Cruz. The move to California had given him new purpose, made him feel alive again. Maybe it was time to give God ... and love ... another chance.

He snapped the footrest to the floor. Did Annie go to church? He remembered seeing steeples from the highway near Costanoa, where she lived, according to the store's loyalty program records. Right now, any church would do. Maybe he'd get lucky and see her. If not, he could take his horse out for a short ride after the service.

He threw a corduroy jacket over his button-down shirt, switched from jeans to khakis and left the house. As he drove down the highway, he paid attention to the scenery— verdant mountains to his left and house-crowded lowlands leading to oceanfront on his right. Where should he look for a house? Anyplace with more room than he had right now, which probably meant the foothills. He was ready to get away from the densely populated university area where houses with small yards overflowed with twenty-somethings and discordant music.

When he reached the Costanoa exit, he picked the first church he saw, St. Andrew's Episcopal. The service was beginning and he settled in a back pew where he could see most of the faithful. All eyes were focused on the priest as he intoned the initial prayers. Sun poured through the windows, intensifying painted silk banners. John settled in a seat and sensed the strong feeling of connection in the community. It was part of what he'd been missing. After Jessica's death and Deborah's betrayal, he'd pushed everyone away, not wanting any form of companionship. Hell, he'd pushed everyone so far away he was now a thousand miles away from his friends.

Time for a change.

During the first hymn, he distinguished a voice soaring above the awkward chorus of enthusiastic, if off-key, singers. The powerful contralto rose from the other side of the aisle, its beauty sending a message directly to his heart, cracking it open a little more. There'd always been music in his house with Jessica. Silence reigned after she died. It was time to change that, too.

When the song ended, he scanned the congregation for Annie. It was a long shot, he knew, but there was always a chance. With everyone else sitting, it should be easy to spot her.

An older woman to his right cleared her throat loudly. He looked down.

"Sit down," she mouthed, playing with the cane in her hand.

He sat.

The rest of the service could have been in Greek. He stood, sat, and knelt with the congregation, but his mind drifted. Ever since the move from Montana, he hadn't had a moment to catch his breath. Owning a business was a full-time rush of things to be done, people to manage, and fires to put out. There was no time to think and he'd wanted it that way—no time for dark memories. But somewhere in all that busyness, he'd started to find his footing again. Now for the next step.

What would it be like to kiss her?

"Peace be with you," the priest intoned.

"And also with you," the congregation chorused.

People began shaking his hand and welcoming him to the church, driving all thoughts of kisses from his head. He tried to keep a pious mental state for the rest of the service, an attempt that was hampered by his eagerness for it to end. He was ready to saddle up his horse and enjoy the quiet connection to Starfire and nature.

But when the service was over, he found himself trapped, tradition and courtesy allowing the front pews to empty first. He shifted his weight from side to side, barely restrained by politeness. Finally making it through the throng of well-wishers, he told the priest he'd be back again soon. He scanned the courtyard for a quick exit.

A woman in a large-flowered dress and an impossible hat plowed toward him, her hand extended. "Hello," she said, pumping his hand vigorously. "You must be new. My name is Doris."

"John." He extricated his hand.

"You must come to coffee hour so I can introduce you. I'm in charge of the welcoming committee and it's my job to make sure you get to meet everyone."

He endured an hour of earnest parishioners introducing themselves and asking him where he was from. At one point he was backed against a wall by two divorced women vying for his attention.

"Excuse me, ma'am," he said to the nearest woman. "I've got a date with a horse."

Minutes later, he was traveling up the mountain to Starfire.

Did Annie ride? Would she be a good companion? Did she even like the outdoors?

Like it or not, he was becoming fixated on the woman and he'd just have to see it through until he got it out of his system.

# # #

Planting flowers wasn't on Annie's list, but she was selling her house and curb appeal was important. With her plastic garden tote in hand, she began by checking the connections of the drip irrigation system she'd put in the year before. Then she freed up irises from choking weeds, noting with pleasure the emerging gladiola stalks. Once the roses were dead-headed, she dug holes for her new bright gold marigolds and yellow and purple pansies.

Her mental Greek chorus began to chatter.

Why don't you stay here and go out with John? It's hard to find a nice man, particularly at your age. A husband would make your life so much easier. Yeah, right.

That was her mother's drum song. A woman needed a man to be complete. It didn't matter how good or bad the man was, it only mattered that he married you. She'd given up arguing with her mother years ago. In spite of all the horrible things her father had done, her mother had hung onto her beliefs that a man was an answer to all of life's problems. Of course, *she* hadn't remarried after her father's suicide, but she never stopped pushing her daughter toward the altar.

Annie wasn't following that path. Her father and her ex were all the proof she needed that men couldn't be trusted.

Still, something about John felt different. She pictured his strongly etched face, blue eyes, and easy smile. His guileless eyes had never left her face instead of darting everywhere like Fred's did when she was talking with him. Maybe she could trust him. It would be nice to have someone else to lean on once in a while.

She thrust her trowel into the moist dirt, trying to free stubborn roots as she tugged while she imagined strong masculine arms wrapped around her. Suddenly, the weed gave way and she fell flat on her butt, dirt from the roots showering her body.

She laughed out loud. That's what she got for fantasizing about a man. She flung the weed into the pile. Better keep her mind on reality.

But her mind didn't want to stay in the real world. She replayed their conversation at the restaurant while she tackled a new patch of weeds, sobered as she remembered the sorrow in his eyes when he talked about his wife. What would it be like to have someone you love die of cancer? She wished she could do something to erase the pain she saw. *Impossible.* She'd never been able to ease her mother's pain ... and no one had ever been able to fill the empty hole that had been inside of Annie as long as she could remember.

Whenever her father came home in one of his moods, she'd huddle in her room, door locked, chair under the knob while the storm of her parents' marriage raged in the kitchen. In the morning, after the front door slammed behind her father, she would pick up broken dishes, brew the coffee, and fetch ice and bandages for her mother's bruises.

Aching inside, she'd never let anyone see her feelings and never told anyone about her father's rages. Friends didn't come over. She couldn't let them see how she lived. Her mother cried a lot and Annie learned to take care of herself.

Enough memories.

She stood, brushed herself off and admired her handiwork. Pansy petals fluttered in the soft breeze and daffodils patrolled her walkway. Smiling, she put her tools back in the tote and headed inside.

David would be home from soccer practice soon and he'd be ravenous. Maybe if she fed him his favorite dinner, he'd change his mind about moving. *Fat chance.* He'd been giving her one word answers since he returned from Chris's the night before.

She was heating up homemade chili when she heard the door slam.

"Hi," she called out.

David grunted and stomped downstairs. A few seconds later, she heard the shower start. She had dinner on the table by the time he appeared. "Chili, your favorite."

"Good." He sat down and waited for her to sit before he started eating.

"How was soccer?"

He chewed and swallowed. "Okay," he mumbled and immediately stuffed another spoonful of food into his mouth.

Annie took a tiny bite of her own meal. "Any new tournaments coming up?"

He shook his head and continued eating.

She was running out of questions. "When's your next practice?"

"Tuesday," he said between mouthfuls.

She gave up.

"I'm going over Larry's," he said when he finished. He dropped his fork in the dishwasher and slid his plate into the rack.

"Be back—"

"Mom, I'm almost sixteen. I got it. Be back at ten. Yeah, my homework's done. I can take care of myself." A few minutes later the front door slammed again.

She should have made an issue of his attitude but didn't want an argument. Maybe he'd work out his anger with his friends.

He was barely out the door when the phone rang. She eyed it suspiciously, in no mood to talk to Fred. On the fourth ring, she picked it up.

"Hello?"

"Is this Annie?" a male voice asked.

"Yes. Who is this?" She really should get caller ID.

"John Johnson, the bookstore owner."

A thrill went through her body and she smiled. "I remember who you are, but I don't remember ordering any books."

He chuckled. "This isn't about the store. I was riding my horse today and I wondered if you rode."

"A long time ago—when I was twelve or thirteen—but not since."

"Would you like to try it again?"

She thought back to her few years of riding, the freedom and power of controlling a thousand-pound animal with her hands and a few bits of leather. "I think about it once in a while, but lessons are expensive."

"I have a deal for you. The Wiggins, who own the barn where my horse is stabled, have a mare they need exercised. Come with me some day and I'll show you a few pointers. It's like riding a bike. You'll pick it up again in no time."

"That would be nice, John, but ..."

"I know, you're moving. If you like riding, it will give you something to do after you move. I hear they have horses even in New Jersey."

"I believe you're right. But I think they're thoroughbreds and I don't see horse racing in my future." She laughed at the image.

"I think you'd make a perfect jockey—especially in those bright colored silks." He paused a moment, as if he'd realized he might be crossing a line. "Seriously, I'd really like some companionship on my rides. No strings attached. Can you find a few hours?"

Her heart screamed, *Yes!* But she said, "Let me think about it."

"Fair enough. I'll check in during the week. Have a good evening."

She thought about his offer while she cleaned up the kitchen, imagining them riding into the sunset like Roy Rogers and Dale Evans singing "Happy Trails." She laughed out loud at the crazy image. She'd loved Roy and Dale when she was ten years old, but it was a fantasy. No one could have a life that romantic.

Could they?

After she finished the dishes, she called Elizabeth. Her friend answered on the first ring.

"David's mad at me," Annie announced.

"Did you really expect him to jump up and down for joy when you told him you're taking him away from his friends?"

Annie suddenly realized that she'd expected him to do just

that. "I suppose I was unrealistic. He was so easy when he was younger. Everything was a big adventure. Now I suppose waking up in the morning and finding out how your body changed during the night is the big adventure."

Elizabeth laughed. "Give him time. It's a lot to adjust to. How are you doing? Seen any more of the bookstore owner?"

"He called me about an hour ago."

"Wow. He's interested. What did he say?"

Annie told her about the invitation.

"You're going, of course," Elizabeth said.

"It's not fair to encourage him. Not when I'm going away. And … the truth is … I'm scared."

"Why?"

"You've got to admit, the men in my life haven't been very nice. And … I'm never sure what they want—are they going to be like my dad who made my mother stay home and serve his every need?"

"Most men don't expect that these days."

She chuckled. "No, they expect more. I think we women messed up when we said we could do it all. Men believed us!"

Elizabeth laughed. "You've got that right. But you've got a lot going for you. You're pretty and smart. A good mother …"

"Stop it," Annie said lightly. Her friend was the best—always boosting her spirits. "I don't feel like a good mother at the moment." She told Elizabeth what had happened during dinner. "He's barely talking to me and he's borderline rude. What am I going to do?"

"Wait. There's not much more you can do right now. You're a fierce mama bear when it comes to your son. Right now he needs to go climb his own tree. He'll come down when he's ready."

"I hope you're right. How are things with Bobby?"

"The same. He wants to get married and I don't. He tried to

have a serious discussion about it at George's last night."

Annie laughed. "George's? That restaurant is so loud you can barely discuss the weather, much less getting married!"

"He tried, but he gave up."

"What are you going to do?"

"Wait. He'll get tired of asking and we can go on like we were before."

"Are you sure that's what he'll do?"

"Totally. We love each other. That's all that matters. We don't need a formal ceremony to seal the deal."

Annie was thoughtful when she hung up the phone. She hoped Elizabeth was right.

David returned by curfew, and even spent a few minutes chatting with her about soccer practice. She felt herself relax. Maybe Elizabeth was right about that, too. He just needed to be on his own for a little while.

Chapter 5

John stared at his reflection in the mirror and brushed back his hair. Maybe it was time to get a haircut. The cuffs on his denim shirt were getting frayed, too. Mentally, John went through his closet. His other shirts weren't much better. He was going to need a serious upgrade to go courting. He smiled at the old-fashioned phrase his mother had been fond of using.

He shook off his memories, popped a slice of sourdough bread in the toaster and grabbed a cup of black coffee. Would Annie agree to a ride? If she did, would he feel the same easy companionship that he had with Jessica? *I hope so.*

The toast popped and he slathered it with butter and jam. Standing at the counter, he ate his breakfast and remembered rides with Jessica along the banks of the Bitterroot River. It had been one of their favorite outings before she'd gotten sick five years ago. They often rode in silence to encourage birds and small animals that lived near the water to show themselves. Losing her had left a hole in his life.

I miss you, Jessica, but it's time to fill that hole.

Glancing at his watch, John put the empty plate in the sink, poured the rest of his coffee in his travel mug, and went out the back door to his truck, ignoring the overgrown lawn on his way. He needed to find somewhere of his own to live—or buy a goat. He'd call a realtor today.

"Hi, boss," Sunshine called out from behind the register when he walked into the store fifteen minutes later. "Glad to see you finally made it."

"Staff meeting in a half hour," he snapped and strode to the stairs leading up to his office. He didn't want to have a long conversation with his store manager. She was too good at figuring out what he was thinking.

A stack of mail sat on his desk. He recognized his handwriting on the top envelope and tossed it in a corner with annoyance—probably another rejection of his novel. He'd been really hopeful this time—the agent had taken a long time to get back to him.

John concentrated on his paperwork, thrusting all thoughts of novels, women, and goats from his head until he heard the clomp of Sunshine's boots on the stairs.

"I thought you'd want the next week's schedule before the meeting. Jamie has exams next week and she's asked for time off. We'll need to find someone to cover."

He pawed through his papers and picked up the phone. "Thanks." He stared at the receiver, not remembering why he'd picked it up.

Sunshine perched on a stool and tossed her gray braid over her shoulder. "So, are you going to ask her out?"

He flicked a glance at her that should have telegraphed, *It's none of your damn business.*

She didn't get the message. "Well?"

He sighed. "I already have."

"And?"

"She'll get back to me."

"Give me a break. That's polite-woman speak for 'no.' You need to call her again."

"Not everyone is as pushy as you are." He looked at his watch. "Why don't you get everyone together for the meeting?"

"Yes, boss." She paused. "But I still think you should call her again."

He looked at the phone that was still in his hand. Maybe he should.

# # #

During the commute to work that morning, Annie spotted signs of spring around her. The towering redwoods sported new growth while Scotch broom announced the change of seasons with bright yellow flowers. Lexington Reservoir glinted with the morning sun as scull boats glided effortlessly across its waters.

She divested herself of her computer bag and raincoat when she reached her office. Time to tackle Number 3 on her list—find out the job details from Randy. His office door was closed. She took a deep breath and rapped.

"Come in."

She opened the door and gazed at the paper-strewn mess. Sitting down wasn't an option. "Can you tell me about the job in New Jersey?"

Randy looked up from his computer. "I'm glad you've come to your senses. I'd really hate for the company to lose you." He dug through his papers. "It's a project management job for a new release—make sure the software is compliant with Common Criteria—you know, government stuff." He handed her the paper and went back to his screen.

She scanned the job posting.

He clicked a few keys and looked up. "Sorry, Annie, I really need to get this presentation out. Anything else?"

"Do you know the reporting manager?" She looked back down at the papers. "Jim Borzetti? Have you heard anything about him? Will the company pay for relocation?"

Randy gestured at the paper in her hand. "That's all I know about the job. Contact the manager who posted the job and ask him. I'll be happy to give you a good reference. He might want to see you for an interview. Those East Coast managers are big on _face time.' Can you handle that?"

"I suppose." Damn! She hadn't been on an interview in years. What if she flubbed it?

He rubbed his temples. "I know change is tough. Until the economy turns around, it's going to be like this for a while. Be glad you have a shot at a job." He turned back to his screen.

"Thanks, Randy." She put her hand on the doorknob.

"Annie? One more thing. I know doing interviews is tough, but you can handle it. You know your field and you're good at what you do."

"Thanks."

"Good luck." The click of the computer keys restarted.

When she got to her office, she took out her list, carefully crossed out "Randy" and put in "NJ Director Jim ..." She glanced at the papers Randy had given her. "... Borzetti."

She plugged in her hot pot for tea, brought up a browser on her computer and searched for "Common Criteria." A quick scan of the organization's website told her why the project was a problem. Documentation was needed—lots of documentation. And one thing that programmers hated to do was documentation.

Ugh.

While the tea brewed, she composed an e-mail introducing herself to Jim. She finished it and read it over and over, making minute corrections until it was as perfect as she could get it. She pressed Send.

She put a squiggle next to item Number 3 on her list. Started, but not finished. She spent the rest of the day cleaning out her office, tying up loose ends of the project that was ending and going to meetings. At the end of the day, there was still no response from Jim.

David wasn't home when she got there. A note on the refrigerator said, "Out with Larry. Be back later."

Her stomach gave a queasy lurch. She had a bad feeling about Larry. He hadn't been able to look her in the eye when they'd met. Instead, his eyes had darted everywhere, as if he were on the lookout for an opportunity—or trouble. Should she forbid David to see him? What reason could she give—that she didn't like the way he dressed? He had shifty eyes? And would forbidding him really change what David did when she wasn't around? She sighed. Time to start dinner. She'd make spaghetti *carbonara*, another of David's favorites. The pasta water had started to boil when the phone rang.

"Mrs. Renquist?" a male voice asked.

"Ms. Gerhard, but yes, I used to be Mrs. Renquist. Who's this?"

"This is Detective Ramos at the Costanoa Police Station. We have your son in custody."

# # #

Annie found the police station with no problem.

"You have my son, David Renquist," she said to the woman in the glass information booth.

The woman flicked a look at her computer and hit a few keys. "Have a seat in the lobby. Detective Ramos will be out to get you."

In the background she could hear the sound of steel doors opening and closing. At every clank, her stomach turned.

A middle-aged Latino in a light brown jacket and slacks bustled into the lobby. He ran his finger around the inside of his shirt collar, loosening it against a constricting tie as he walked toward her. "Ms. Gerhard?"

"Yes."

"My name is Detective Ramos." He thrust his hand out and she shook it quickly. He gestured toward the door in the rear of the lobby. "Let's go in the back."

"What's my son supposed to have done?"

"He stole some liquor and CDs from a drug store."

"David wouldn't do that."

"We'll discuss it further in the back, Ms. Gerhard." He thumbed a button by the side of a solid metal door. A loud buzz and click signaled a lock release and he pushed the door open.

The detective led her to a small room with a metal table and four chairs. He waved at a chair on the far side of the table and she sat down, her muscles clenched.

"I'll be right back," the detective said, closing the door behind him.

Alone in the room, she tried to gather her wits about her. What was she going to do? What had David been thinking?

The door jerked open and David came into the room. She leapt to her feet and took a step toward him.

"Sit down, Ms. Gerhard," the detective said. She obeyed.

David sat, gave her a brief glance, and then focused his eyes on the table between them.

"I understand you and David's father are divorced," Ramos said.

She nodded.

"Do you have sole custody of your son?"

"Yes."

"Then you're legally and financially responsible for him." The detective opened a folder he had in front of him and perused the papers. "David was caught shop-lifting from the L and L Drug Store by the store manager shortly before five p.m. Your son had a small bottle of vodka and a couple of CDs in his pockets."

She started to protest, but the detective held up his hand.

"We have it on the store surveillance camera," he said. He turned to David and said, "You want to tell us about it?"

David looked at his hands, glanced at the detective, and looked back at the steel gray table. "I was with these guys. They said it would be really easy for me to get something out of L and L 'cause I was a kid." He paused. "They said they'd give me money to get a bottle of vodka. It'd be easy."

"Who were they?" the detective asked.

"I don't know," David replied. "Some random guys I met downtown."

"I thought you were with Larry," she interrupted.

"I ditched him. He got into playing chess in front of Starbucks. It was way boring, so I took a walk."

"And then you met these guys ... these strangers," the detective prompted.

"They weren't exactly strangers. I'd seen 'em with Larry. They knew my name and everything."

"Why?" Annie asked. "Why did you do this?"

David shrugged.

She hated it when he shrugged. "Why?" she repeated.

"I dunno. I guess I wanted to see if I could do it. I guess I wasn't thinking."

"I guess not."

David opened his mouth to say something and closed it again.

She looked at her son in bewilderment. It was as if she were seeing a stranger; someone she didn't know at all.

"Is there anything else you want to tell us?" Detective Ramos asked.

David looked down at his hands and shook his head.

The detective shuffled the papers in front of him. "Because your son is a juvenile and this is his first offense, we're going to release him to your custody. You'll need to bring him back to court in two weeks at four p.m. on the twenty-first."

He scribbled on one of the papers in front of him and pushed it across to David with a pen. "Sign there. You're not acknowledging guilt. You're saying you'll be in court at the appointed time to face the charges against you." He looked at Annie. "His signature's a formality. Because he's a minor, the only one that counts is yours."

David signed the papers and pushed them over to her. She scanned them and signed.

Detective Ramos put the signed papers into his folder and stood up. "I'll take David back for processing and then he'll be released to you in the lobby."

They left the concrete room and she went to wait.

Now what? Would it be worth hiring a lawyer, or should she use the public defender? Waiting for David to sort things out on his own hadn't turned out well. She wished she had someone to talk with. A man's point of view would be nice.

Forty-five minutes later, David walked through the door with the detective behind him.

Ramos handed her the release papers and looked at David. "Stay out of any more trouble." He turned and walked away.

She stared at her son.

"Let's go, Mom," he said and walked out the front door. She followed, her mind racing as she tried out all the things she might say. *Were you out of your mind? This could go on your record! You could have been hurt!*

She said nothing.

When they got home, David slammed into his room. She went right after him.

"No you don't," she said, her voice cold with anger and fear. "You aren't going into your room and closing the door without having a conversation with me first." "What do you want me to say, Ma?" he asked. "Fine. If you want to lecture me, get it over with and let me get some sleep. I'm tired." "I don't care if you're tired, young man. I want to know what you think you were doing."

He continued to glare at her with his arms crossed for another minute before slumping onto his bed. His skin had a gray hue and dark circles underscored eyes bloodshot from lack of sleep. Annie felt the tension begin to seep out of her body.

"I'm sorry, mom. I don't know. I feel crazy. When we lived with Dad, you were angry all the time. You split us up and it was better, I guess. But now you want us to move to nowhere New Jersey. If I don't go, I lose you. If I do go, I lose everything else. It's not fair."

She sat next to him on his bed.

"No, it's not fair. I know you want to stay here. I wish we could. But I'm thinking of you. I'm thinking of the money it's going to take to get you through Berkeley. Even living here is expensive."

"It's always about money with you. What about our lives? What about my friends? I don't have to go to Berkeley if it means I can stay here."

She started to stroke his head, but he pulled away.

"Honey, I'm trying to keep you safe. I worry about you. No matter how big you get, you'll always be my kid. What you did is bad—it could screw up your future. Promise me you won't do anything this stupid again." She hugged his stiff body and said, "You're grounded, you know. Probably for the rest of your life." She smiled at him, her heart aching.

"Okay. Can I sleep now?"

"I'll see you in the morning."

The sooner they moved, the better.

She trudged up the stairs and thought of the next item on her list.

Call Fred.

Tomorrow would be soon enough.

# # #

Annie shook coffee beans into the grinder and whirled them into submission. Too bad her problems couldn't be ground into tiny bits as easily. While her coffee brewed, Annie's thoughts scattered. *Maybe I should repaint before I put the house on the market.*

I could put David in a boarding school while I'm in New Jersey. A military boarding school.

Should I go out with John?

I need to clear out the garage.

She shook the untidiness from her mind and dug her original "to do" list out of her handbag.

1. √ Tell David
2. Tell Fred
3. ~ Find out details from Randy NJ Director Jim Borzetti
4. Connect with new boss in New Jersey
5. Start transfer process
6. Call realtor
7. Contact corporate housing for help to find an apartment in New Jersey
8. Hold a garage sale
9. Pack
10. Move
11. Pay parking ticket

Hopefully, she'd hear from Jim today. She could call him to make sure he received her e-mail, but that might make her seem desperate.

Who was she kidding? She *was* desperate.

She looked at the clock and listened for the shower. No noise. She padded down the stairs and rapped on David's door.

"Get up. You're going to be late for school."

"Stop nagging, Mom. I'm on it."

"Just do it," Annie said and stomped upstairs. She hadn't slept well last night, images from every prison movie she'd ever seen haunting her. What would David get as a first offense? Realistically, he'd probably get community service.

The coffee pot gurgled as she pulled two cereal bowls and a box of cereal from the cupboard and a carton of milk from the refrigerator. Would David have a record? Weren't juvenile records sealed? Too many questions. She needed to call the public defender.

Grabbing a cup of coffee, she added Number 12 to the list: Call public defender. Her eyes traveled back up to the second item: Call Fred.

Ugh.

She looked at the clock again. Good. He was already at work so she could put that off until later. Everything else, except Numbers 11 and 12, needed to wait until she heard from Jim. She'd call the lawyer later.

Although if she was going to have a garage sale, she'd better clean the garage. Carefully, she added Number 13, "Clean garage."

A mockingbird jabbered on a tree outside her window. Maybe she'd have time to take a walk today, enjoy nature. A horseback ride might be even better. She flipped her list to the blank side, drew a line down the middle of the paper and wrote PROS on one side of the line and CONS on the other.

Under PROS she wrote: get exercise, admire a good-looking man, have fun.

Under CONS: don't want to lead him on, might not like him if I get to know him.

The fantasy was always better than reality, wasn't it?

On the other hand, John would be someone to discuss David's problem with. She added that to the PROS side.

She took a sip of coffee and stared at the chart, knowing she wasn't being entirely honest with herself because she'd left off the biggest CON of all.

She was afraid.

The downstairs shower went on. David was up—good. Time to get moving. She'd get him off to school, and start to work on the presentation for the project wrap-up.

Four hours later she was tired of trying to get graphs, statistics, and bullet points to behave. Her son was easier to control. And she still hadn't gotten a return e-mail from New Jersey.

She needed a break.

You could clean the garage, the puritanical voice from her chorus said.

Leave one ugly chore for another? No thanks.

Bread. She'd bake bread. Rye bread would be perfect—sticky and difficult to work with—like the rest of her life. The pungent combination of yeast and caraway seeds would clear her head.

She looked in the freezer for her stash of rarely used flour. Packages of whole wheat, spelt and kamut stared back at her. No rye. The spice drawer revealed a lack of caraway seeds. A dilemma.

Five minutes later she was speeding north on Highway 1 toward Grenaldi's Market. She flicked on the classical station and thought of the curried chicken salad she planned to buy for lunch. Traffic was light, the sun was shining, and the tension left her body.

As soon as she walked through the old-fashioned market door, the distinctive scent hit her. Chain groceries smelled sterile.

Here, ripening fruit and yeasty flour tantalized her nose. Sweet and spicy odors wafted from the other end of the store from the deli and bakery sections.

She filled plastic bags with rye flour and caraway seeds and strolled toward the deli counter, her mouthwatering in anticipation of sharp curry and succulent raisins. When she was close she recognized the tall figure placing an order.

John.

Drat! She wasn't ready to give him an answer. She considered going somewhere else.

As if sensing her presence, John turned and smiled. "You look nice today, ma'am."

Liar. I look terrible and you know it. "Could you stop calling me that?"

"Ma'am?"

"Yes. It makes me feel older than dirt."

His grin deepened. "You don't look old." A shiver went up Annie's spine as John studied her. "Nope, not old at all. Not a day over twenty-five. I was thinking about a picnic. Care to join me?"

Annie moved to the counter to order her chicken curry salad, her lips turning up at the corners. Twenty-five. It was nice to have a good-looking man take a decade off her age. But she was curious. "Why did you come all this way for lunch? Zanotto's is a few blocks from the bookstore."

"I was in the mood for a thick roast beef sandwich today and asked my store manager for the best place to get it. She said Zanotto's was good, but nothing could beat Grenaldi's." He stepped closer and leaned down to talk with her. "Actually, I think she wanted me out of the store for a while. She hates the boss hovering. How about you?"

She flicked him a glance. "I hate the boss hovering, too."

He grinned. "Difficult when the boss likes hovering."

"But you're not my boss."

"I could be."

"I already have a job, thank you." She frowned. Actually, she didn't.

A clerk handed him his paper-wrapped sandwich while a second clerk handed her a filled plastic container, a fork, and napkin.

"Your lunch?"

She nodded.

"Perfect. Let's eat together. There's a picnic table nearby."

"But ..."

"Annie, you need to eat lunch. I don't bite. Promise."

She looked at his warm smile and her heart broke its steady rhythm. It *was* only lunch.

"Okay."

His grin widened.

Chapter 6

Annie and John crossed the side street to a small green park where daffodils' cheerful heads gathered at the edges of flowerbeds. Finches and starlings chattered about the best branch for nesting.

Settled on opposite sides of a picnic table, they unwrapped their lunches.

He took a large bite from his sandwich, slowly chewed, swallowed and sighed. "*That* is truly a wonderful roast beef sandwich."

Her eyes on his, she took a forkful of her salad, savoring the splurge of creaminess, the curry's nip and the sweet bit of raisin.

"You've got some sauce on your lips," he said.

She licked the corner of her mouth. "Did I get it?"

"I can't stand it when you do that."

"What?"

"That licking thing you do. You were driving me nuts the other night with that damn salad dressing."

"Like this?" She slowly licked her lips again.

He groaned.

A sizzle of sexiness made her shiver.

"Cold?"

She shook her head. What was she doing? Heat raced up and down her limbs, responding to his flirting. What was it about this man?

You're leading him on, the nagging chorus member intoned.

She leaned back and picked up her fork. "Where did you grow up in Montana? What was it like?"

"Like nowhere else in the world." John looked over her shoulder, as if envisioning Montana in the eucalyptus trees behind her. "They call it 'Big Sky Country' and it feels like the sky really does go on forever. I grew up in Choteau, a small town on the Rocky Mountain Front. The plains butt right up against the mountains—golden brown wheat colliding with icy gray granite."

"Sounds like you miss it."

"Uh-huh."

"How could you leave it if you loved it so much?"

He shrugged. "It was time to make a change. I was stuck living a life that I no longer had."

"Will you ever go back?"

He looked at her intently. "It depends."

"On?"

"On how my life turns out here. If I meet someone and fall in love, and her life is here, I'd stay here. Eventually, I hope, we'd get a small cabin in the Bitterroot Valley and spend our summers and retirement there."

"You've got it all mapped out."

He focused his eyes on hers. "All except the girl."

Her body went into overdrive again. "I hope you find someone."

He put down his sandwich, propped his chin on his folded hands and stared at her. He was making her nervous. "What about you? How did you wind up in California? Or were you born here?"

"I was born in Michigan—Ann Arbor."

"And ..."

"And I decided to come to UC Santa Cruz."

"Instead of the University of Michigan?"

"Yeah, seems crazy, doesn't it? But I wanted to leave Michigan ..."

"Let me guess, there was a man."

She took another bite of salad and chewed. After she swallowed, she said, "Yeah, there was a man ... Fred. His name was ... is Fred. He was accepted in the philosophy program at UC Santa Cruz. I saw it as a chance to get out of Michigan." *And away from horrible memories.*

"So you followed him here."

Annie nodded. "We moved in together and I applied to the university in the music program. I had to drop out when I got pregnant."

"Must have been tough."

"We married, but it didn't work. We divorced about five years ago."

"So you've been on your own for a while. Fred giving you any support?"

She shook her head.

He put down his sandwich. "Why not?"

"He does the best he can. He doesn't have a good job, barely makes enough for himself."

"Maybe he should get a better job."

Her temper flared. "We've worked it out. It's okay and David is doing fine."

Or he was until last night.

John raised his hands in a gesture of surrender. "Sorry. I overstepped my bounds. I guess I've seen too many single mothers struggle while fathers move on with their lovers."

"It's not like that."

"I'm sure it's not." The tone of his voice said otherwise.

They chewed in silence.

"Tell me more about David," he finally said.

She took a deep breath. "He's fifteen, a good student, and a goalie on two soccer teams."

"Two?"

"He plays in a rec league in the spring and on the high school varsity team in the fall."

"Sounds like you're doing a good job, Mom."

She shook her head. "I thought I was, but ..." There was no good way to say it. "He was arrested last night."

"I'm sorry. What happened?"

She told him about her trip to the police department.

"Any idea why he's acting out?"

"I'm not sure. But it's probably because of the move."

John leaned back and looked at the picnic table, as if there were answers in the bug-eaten wood. "That might be. What are you going to do?"

"Keep a close eye on him until we move. Getting him out of Santa Cruz is probably the best thing I can do for him."

"There are bad kids everywhere." He took another bite of his sandwich. Silence lingered for a few moments. "I'm probably going to overstep my bounds again, but I'm not sure taking him away is the best thing. Teenagers have a tough time as it is." He stared at the table again and then looked up at her, his sharp blue eyes focused on hers. "My dad died when I was in high school—heart attack. I tried to take his place on the ranch and go to high school at the same time. When I did get time for myself, which didn't happen often, I did wild things to let off steam."

She leaned forward, looking at him intently. "What happened?"

"Fast girls and fast cars. We all must have been crazy back then. One night the driver of the car I was in lost control. He and a girl were killed. I was the only one wearing my seat belt, so I survived. They had to pry the wreck apart to get me out, but amazingly enough, all I had were a few scratches." His eyes watered. "But my friends were gone." He took a swallow of his drink and stared at the table.

"I'm sorry." She put her hand on his arm. "You've had a lot of death in your life."

He nodded. "Straightened me right out. I had a second chance at life and I took it." He put his hand on top of hers and her fingers warmed at his touch. "My point is that teenagers do crazy things when they feel their world is falling apart. Have you considered taking David to a counselor?"

"I hadn't thought about it."

"It might be helpful—and good for you, too."

She shook her head. She was done with shrinks. "Thanks, I'll think about it for David." She reluctantly pulled her hand away and glanced at her watch. "I need to get to Santa Cruz, pay a parking ticket and get back to work. Thanks for the company. I enjoyed it."

John stood. "I need to get back, too." He picked up his empty wrapper. "Have you had a chance to think about a horseback ride?"

She snapped the lid closed on the empty salad container. "I don't think that's a good idea. I really am moving in a month." *If everything goes right.*

He looked at her steadily. "Somehow I don't think that's the real reason, Annie. What are you so afraid of?"

"Nothing," she said automatically. "I just don't think it's a good idea." She scanned the table for crumbs.

He shrugged. "If you change your mind, I'd like to see you. You know how to find me. Well, so long." He took her hand in a strong grip, quickly released it, and walked away.

Her eyes teared up, blurring her vision as she stared after him.

# # #

Thwack! Annie threw the dough on the board, causing it to skid across the countertop. She poked the lump on the breadboard with gluey fingertips, testing for consistency. In order to rise correctly, it had to be balanced between too sticky and too dry. *It would be nice if you could knead your life into shape as easily as dough.*

Baking bread had been the only activity Annie had been able to do in peace with her mother. They'd worked in silence interrupted only by the slap of dough on the counter.

She focused on the taffy texture and yeasty odor of the bread. Push. Pull. Heels of her hands coaxing the gluten to form. Shaping the bread. Shaping her life.

Stand up straight. Bring home a good report card. Don't be too smart or boys won't like you. Don't like boys too much. Her mother's litany played in her mind in rhythm with her work. Other words crept in. *Don't talk back to your father. Good girls are seen but not heard. Don't upset your father. Your father isn't well. Hide in here when Daddy gets mad.*

Annie pushed thoughts of her parents back into their assigned compartments in her head. No use in thinking about the past, she had enough to do. Her mind drifted as she fell into the cadence of the bread.

She spent the next few hours alternating between working on the presentation and reshaping bread between rises. After she put the loaf in the oven, she checked the kitchen clock. Fred should be done with his shift as an orderly at the nursing home. She picked up the phone and dialed his number.

"What's up?" he asked.

"David's in trouble."

"Did he break an arm or something? Where is he? I'll be right over."

She took a deep breath. "Legal trouble. They caught him

shoplifting at L and L Drug Store."

"David? You've got to be kidding. Is this some kind of sick joke?"

"I wish it were. They've got him on tape."

"Why did he do such a stupid thing?"

"I don't know. He's not talking to me. At least he's not saying anything that makes sense."

"Anything happen to upset him? He's always been so damned sensitive—like you."

She bristled. Everything was always her fault in Fred's eyes. "Well ..."

"What, Annie? What's going on that you aren't telling me?"

"I've been offered a job in New Jersey and I'm going to take it." The words came out in a rush.

"Why the hell are you going to do that?"

"It's either take the job in New Jersey or become unemployed. They're doing layoffs."

"So find another job. You're a bright girl."

She stiffened, but bit her tongue. There was no point. "It's probably only for a couple of years. If I leave JCN now, I'll lose years toward my pension and health benefits. I can't afford to do that."

"It's always about money with you, isn't it?"

"You don't seem to have any trouble cashing your alimony check." *Ouch. That was below the belt.*

"I put ten years into our marriage. While you were out gallivanting around the world, I was home dealing with David. I earned that money."

"Someone had to earn it first."

"There you go again, blaming everything on me."

This time she didn't answer. None of the retorts she had on the tip of her tongue would help the situation.

"Why don't you leave him here, if it's only for two years?"

"With who? You live in a room."

"What about Elizabeth? Couldn't he stay with her? You could come back once a month to see him."

She began to pace the small kitchen. "I'm not leaving my son behind. He'll be fine in New Jersey. In fact, it'll be good for him. Get him away from the losers he's hanging out with here."

"You're going to take him away two years before he finishes high school with the kids he grew up with? That's cruel, Annie."

Fred was right. It was cruel. But so was being laid off in a jobless economy.

"We'll talk about this later. I wanted to let you know what was up, that's all."

"We're not done discussing this, Annie."

"I've got things to do. I can't talk about it now."

"You mean you don't want to," he said. "Look, I'll pick up David up from soccer tonight. See if I can get something from him about the shoplifting."

"I can get him."

"Annie, David's important to me, too. I love that kid. Let me talk to him."

She sighed. "All right. See what you can do. I'm grateful for the help."

"Yeah."

Fred hung up.

She went back to her office and put a check mark next to "Tell Fred," on her list. It hadn't gone any better than telling David, but it was done. She tapped her pen on the desk and scanned her e-mail for a message from Jim. Nothing. She'd call him tomorrow. She had to get an answer so she could go on to the next item. Once she did that, everything and everyone would fall into line.

Fred brought David home from soccer practice as he'd

promised, following him into the house. While their son went to his bedroom to change his clothes, Fred came up to the kitchen.

"Do you mind?" he asked, already grabbing a coffee cup. He gestured toward the round loaf cooling on a metal rack. "Looks good."

"Thanks. Did David say anything?"

"I couldn't get anything out of him. All I got were those stupid one-word answers that you and he always give me when you don't want to talk." He took a slurping sip of coffee.

God, she hated that noise. She took a deep breath. *Calm down. He was just being Fred ... except he was being Fred in her kitchen.* She scrubbed her already spotless counter. "I guess we'll have to wait and see what happens at the hearing in two weeks. I'll call the courthouse tomorrow and find out which public defender he has."

"Public defender? He needs a real lawyer. Do you really want him stuck in jail at his age? It's a terrible place."

"You should know." *Shit. I'm really tired.*

"Aw, Annie, don't go there."

"Sorry. I'm upset. I can't afford to get him a 'real lawyer.' Fred, a public defender *is* a real lawyer. It's David's first offense. They aren't going to throw him in jail. They'll give him community service and probation." Her voice tightened.

"Oh, yeah, you're an expert on this, too. You always know everything. What if you're wrong?" Fred's voice grew louder.

"I'm doing the best I can, Fred! I work, keep house, run David around, make sure he gets his homework done, and now I have to move to New Jersey! What do you ever do besides pick him up from soccer once a week and watch movies with him on the weekend? Why don't you go home and back to that bottle you love more than anything else?"

"Shut up!" David stood in the doorway of the kitchen. "Stop

yelling at each other! I can't stand it anymore!"

He glared at them for a minute, shook his head in disgust and then stormed back down the stairs to his room. The door slammed.

The ugly words reverberated in the tiny kitchen. They looked at each other silently. Annie's breath slowed. "I'm really sorry, Fred. That was out of line, stress talking. But, still, I think you'd better leave."

Fred nodded and put his coffee cup in the sink. At the top of the stairs he paused. "I'm sorry I hurt you so much, Annie," he said softly. "I didn't mean to."

And then he was gone.

# # #

While Annie waited for the computer to start up in her office the next morning, she stared at her list. She hadn't gotten around to calling the public defender yesterday; she absolutely needed to do it today. Somehow the checkmarks next to the first two items didn't give her the satisfaction she usually got from ticking things off. She'd told David and Fred, but the after-effects weren't quite over. What should she do next?

She got out her pen and made some additions:

14. Convince Fred that David's place is with me
15. Convince David that he'd be better off in NJ

A list. Her life was in control again. Wasn't it? A flicker of worry wisped through her brain.

Exercise. That was it. All this sitting around and stewing weren't getting her anywhere. She pulled on her walking shoes, grabbed her company badge, strode out the side door, and marched to the Par-Course track.

She took the long loop, pushing herself around the dirt path that circled almond trees and hay fields to a small rise on the edge of the company property. She'd miss the passing of the seasons, the odor of newly grown hay tickling her nose in the spring, followed by the dusty tang of browning fields. California smelled different from any other place she'd been.

Winded, she slowed down at the top of the hill to catch her breath. Hands on her hips, she looked down on the scene below, the office building cube huddled between still-green hills. It hadn't been her ideal job, but it was comfortable. She knew what to expect—or at least she'd thought she had. She sighed, picked up her pace, and returned to the office.

Finally.

"Sorry for the delay," Jim's e-mail said. "I wanted to talk with Randy before I contacted you and we've had a hard time connecting. He highly recommends you. Can you come for an interview next week? It's short notice, but it's the only space in my calendar. I want to make sure you get a good idea of what you'll be stepping into if you take the position. Besides, our corporate director likes to meet potential candidates face to face. You can come to the annual corporate dinner and meet everyone. Let me know as soon as possible."

Next week! That was impossible! The week after? No, I have to be in court with David. Later? No, they wouldn't like that.

She cradled her weary head in her hands, resting her tired eyes in her cupped palms.

Maybe if I cover my eyes, no one can see me. No one can ask for anything. I won't have to uproot my life.

She sighed, dug into her resolve, and lifted her head. There were things to do—talk to David's attorney, make sure David could stay with Elizabeth while she took a quick trip to New

Jersey. She'd reply to Jim tomorrow.

After a few more hours of work she headed home, but instead of going south on Highway 1 when she got to Santa Cruz, she went north.

Maybe she could blame her car: *I was going home, but when I got to Highway 1 the car refused to go home. There wasn't a thing I could do about it.*

No one would believe it. She didn't believe it. The truth was she wanted to see John again.

What the hell was she doing?

Annie sauntered into the bookstore, automatically taking her normal route to the travel section. The Montana shelf had been expanded. She idled for a while, browsing books to learn more about where the man came from. Curiosity finally got the better of her and she inched her way to the front of the store.

Hips swaying slightly, she sidled to the new fiction table. A quick scan of the high-level office and the front of the store showed no sign of the new owner.

Disappointed, she picked up the new novel by Debbie Macomber. It would be wonderful to be one of the women in Debbie's books, find someone to share some of her burdens, a partner in love and life. But wasn't she walking away from that very opportunity? Could John be the one? She didn't have time to find out.

Book in hand, she went to the cash register. If she couldn't have the man, she'd have the fantasy. She started reading the book and was soon caught up in the life of a cat-loving knitter in Seattle.

"Hi, Annie," John said. "Let me ring up your book." She dropped the book with a clatter on the counter. "Are you free for a cup of coffee?" she blurted.

He shook his head. "We're short-handed today. I need to be

by the register. Maybe some other time."

Annie watched his capable hands scan the book, slide in the free bookmark and ring up her total. *She should never have come here.* Their fingers brushed when he took her charge card, and she felt the familiar spark that touching him brought.

He handed her the book. "Thanks for coming in. I—"

"I'd love to go riding." She watched the grin spread across his face.

"That's great. How about Friday?" He touched her hand. "I'm glad you've changed your mind."

She took a deep breath. "So am I. Friday would be great."

Chapter 7

Driving to work the next morning, Annie was oblivious to the white mists ascending from the narrow mountain valleys, and the red-tailed hawk peering down from the Summit Road highway sign. Had she been insane to agree to ride with John? Probably. But going horseback riding seemed so, well, *normal*. There wouldn't be time for drama.

Did John drink? He'd had a glass of wine at dinner, but did he drink more than that?

Another reason that riding would be safe. Not a lot of opportunity to belly up to the bar.

She pushed thoughts of John out of her mind to concentrate on her upcoming business trip and made a quick mental list: Tell Fred and David where she was going, make arrangements with the cat sitter, book a flight and hotel, pack her laptop with its extra battery, and repack her standard travel bag. Elizabeth had already okayed David's stay at her house when she called to invite Annie to Sunday brunch the previous evening.

What was up with Elizabeth and Bobby? Why couldn't her friend simply marry the man? He was kind, he had money, and they loved each other. They didn't know how lucky they had it.

She went back to her trip preparation. She'd make her flight arrangements when she got to work and call Fred when he was busy at work, cell phone off, and leave a message.

Coward, the critical member of her internal Greek chorus jibed.

Yep.

The cat sitter could be e-mailed from work and she'd talk to her son tonight. Everyone taken care of.

Except you.

I'm going riding on Friday, she announced to the chorus. *Isn't that enough?*

We'll see.

I must be going crazy. I'm talking to myself.

As soon as Annie got to the office, she booked her flight. A small boutique hotel in Princeton, priced within corporate limits, was a pleasant option. She e-mailed her current and future bosses with her arrangements. Both responded that they were delighted she'd taken action and she felt like she'd been patted on the head and told she was a "good girl." Only a few more years and she'd be able to get out of Corporate America.

# # #

Friday afternoon, John paced the driveway in front of the small barn as he waited for Annie to show up. Starfire picked up his nervousness and ran restless circles in the corral next to him.

Right on time, a Prius turned cautiously off the road and came up the rise. After it stopped, he opened the car door and gave Annie a hand.

"Good to see you," he said as he checked out her clothes. The lavender sweater she wore accented her figure nicely.

"Do I pass your approval?" she asked with a smile.

"Sorry. Too many people have no clue. They show up in fancy new clothes and sneakers." He looked pointedly at her jeans and small-heeled boots. "You knew better." *And you've got a great butt in jeans.*

"I told you. I took lessons." She gestured at Starlight. "Your horse?"

He nodded.

She walked slowly toward the horse standing by the fence, eyeing her cautiously. John watched with a smile as she offered the back of her hand to the mare, just like she would to a dog to sniff. Starfire snorted and nodded her head up and down. Annie stroked the mare's face and soon the mare was nudging her with her head in friendship.

"She's gorgeous."

"Thanks." He walked to the gate and grabbed the lead hanging on the fence. Starfire trotted over, head held high in anticipation. He murmured to her, fastened the lead, and led her out the gate. Glancing at Annie, he said, "Follow me into the barn and I'll get you set up with Mathilda."

"Who?"

"The Wiggins horse. Named after a great aunt or something."

"I wonder if the aunt was flattered."

"It's a nice horse."

"Hopefully, it was a nice aunt."

John chuckled and led Starfire to the saddling stall. He handed Annie a lead. "You want to get Mathilda ready? There's another stall over there and her gear's already set."

Her eyes widened.

"You have saddled a horse before, haven't you? I'm happy to do it as soon as I finish here."

"No, no, that's okay. I can do it. It's just ..."

"I'll check the saddle when you're done, to be sure the cinch is snug."

"Thanks." She approached Mathilda, going through the same routine she'd used with

Starfire to introduce herself before taking her to the stall to saddle her. John watched her movements with approval. She was tentative, but appeared to know what she was doing. He wondered why she'd been so nervous.

"Do you date much?"

"What? No. It's tough being a single mom and dating. I didn't want a lot of men coming in and out of my son's life."

"But you made an exception in my case."

She paused in her brushing and looked at him. "I guess you feel safe."

He grinned. "Safe? Not handsome and daring?"

She stared at him seriously. "Trust me. In my world, safe is a lot more important than tall, dark, and handsome." She turned away.

He heard the clunk of the brush as she tossed it in the gear box. What had happened in her life to make safe more important than anything else? He thought back to the few times he'd seen her before. She'd been flirty, but cautious, like an animal that had been abused and didn't quite trust humans.

"I'm ready," she called out.

Ten minutes later, they were traveling down John's favorite trail in silence. Coos of mourning doves and the chatter of mockingbirds accompanied the rustling of wrens and sparrows in the brush. The clop of the horses' hooves and occasional snorts were the only sounds announcing their presence.

The woman knew how to ride.

They reached his favorite spot by Soquel Creek forty-five minutes later. He slid off Starfire, and Annie followed suit.

"Good," she said. "I needed a break. It's been a long time since I've ridden and my muscles are feeling it."

He dug in his pack for the water bottles and snacks he'd prepared and gestured to a large rock overlooking the rushing stream. They settled down and he was amused to see that she left a good amount of space between them.

They chattered for a while about local news and international politics before John felt comfortable introducing a more private topic. Still, he approached it warily. "I suppose it's none of my business, but I'm curious. What made you finally decide to get divorced?"

She took a long swig of water before she answered. "I think the beginning of the end came when Fred was arrested for DUI. He had to go to jail for four days and pay a fifteen hundred dollar fine. Of course, he wasn't bringing in much money, so I had to help out. I resented every penny of it."

John leaned closer, wanting to wrap his arms around her and erase the pain in her voice, but she gave him a quick glance, her eyes wide open like a startled doe. She looked back at the rushing stream, but he doubted she was seeing the water. Her breath shuddered and she continued.

"Things went from bad to worse. He always seemed to be drunk. I'd come home from work every night, take care of David, clean up the mess, and try to sleep until he came home. One night I simply had enough. He fell into bed next to me with his clothes on, stinking of alcohol, fell asleep and started snoring."

The disgust in her voice was agonizing to hear. He hoped no woman ever talked about him that way.

She took another sip of water. "I got up, got David and myself dressed, and went to Elizabeth's to live. I never went back to Fred. We were divorced six months later. Fred didn't fight for anything, so it went fairly quickly.

This time he touched her hand. "I'm so sorry," he said.

She pulled her hand away, stood up, finished the water, and gave him a sad smile. "It's over. That's the important part. But I'm sure you can see why I'm a little reluctant to date."

He stood and took her hand again. "I would never treat any woman that way. I have a beer now and then, and I enjoy a good glass of wine with my dinner, but that's it. You said it yourself. I'm safe. Let me prove it to you, Annie." He looked steadily into her eyes.

"I'd like to believe you, really I would. But it will take time. And time is the one thing we don't have."

"Maybe you'll find a job here."

She shook her head. "I don't want to talk about it. Can't we just have a nice day and let it go at that?"

"Sure. Ready to go?"

She nodded. They saddled up and rode back to the barn.

Once they'd taken care of the horses, she left so fast that there was no time for any more conversation. She sure was skittish. He wondered if there was more than a bad divorce in her past.

# # #

When Annie and David got to Elizabeth's for brunch after church the following Sunday, Elizabeth was pulling biscuits out of the oven. "Sarah and her new boyfriend Ray got here a few minutes ago from Berkeley. They're in the living room." Elizabeth dumped the biscuits into the linen-lined breadbasket and handed it to Annie.

"Mmm," Annie said, sniffing the ambrosia of warm butter and yeast. She snagged a crumb from the edge of the basket. "Is there anything you don't do well? I thought bread-making was my gig."

Elizabeth pointed to the stainless steel garbage bin in the corner. The edge of a bright blue wrapper peaked out from under the lid. "You remain queen of the bread." She picked up a glass casserole containing a kaleidoscope of cheese, eggs, and bright green chiles.

Annie followed her out of the kitchen with the breadbasket, David trailing her. "Yum, *huevos rancheros*, my favorite."

"Come and get it," Elizabeth said as she placed the bubbling dish on a long wooden trivet at the end of the oak dining room table set with Italian blue, white, and yellow Fiesta plates perched on blue woven placemats.

Elizabeth's daughter, Sarah, walked in from the living room, towing a reluctant Ray. "David!" Sarah said, rushing toward the teenage boy. "You get bigger every time I see you! I'd never be able to babysit you now!" She gave him a strong hug; David patted his hands on her back. In spite of his awkward attempt at a hug, he had a large grin on his face.

"What's this nonsense about you getting in trouble with the law?" Sarah asked. "You know better than that!" She shook her finger at him and then turned to Annie, giving her a quick hug before plopping into a chair next to Ray. "And why is Mom telling me you're moving to New Jersey? You're not moving anywhere. What would my mother do without you two ... she'd start showing up in Berkeley! No, you need to stay here to protect me."

"Enough with the inquisition," Elizabeth admonished her daughter with a smile. "I'm not going to invade your life in Berkeley. I've got too much going on here."

"R-i-i-ght." Sarah looked around. "Where's Bobby?"

"He couldn't make it this morning." Elizabeth glanced at Annie.

"This is Ray," Sarah announced, kissing the young man on his cheek. He immediately reddened, raising his hand in a brief wave, mumbling something that sounded like, "Hi."

Elizabeth held out her hands to Sarah and Annie. When the circle was completed, she bowed her head and began the well-worn prayer, "Bless us, O Lord ...." The chorused "Amen" gave the signal to dig in.

Elizabeth dished the eggy custard onto passed plates as the biscuits made their appointed rounds. The clatter of serving spoons and dishes served as the counterpoint to Sarah's recounting of her latest lab failure. She was getting a degree in environmental science—if she could ever pass organic chemistry.

Elizabeth turned to Ray. "So how are *your* classes going?"

"Ray's a political science major," Sarah said. "He's a member of the Young Republicans, too."

"They allow Republicans in at Berkeley?" Annie asked.

"I wanted to understand their point of view," Ray said. "Last year I was a member of College Democrats of America. So far, I haven't seen much difference. Everyone's talking and no one's listening."

Out of the mouths of babes, Annie thought.

Tension at the table eased as Ray enthusiastically described his classes. In spite of his tendency to blurt everything that came into his mind, he was entertaining.

"Why do you want to move out of California, Annie?" Sarah interrupted Ray. "They've got snow for months in New Jersey. I think it even snows on the beach." Sarah looked at David. "Are you moving too? Or are you staying here until you graduate from high school?"

David glanced over at his mother and mumbled, "I told Mom I'm not going." He shoveled eggs into his mouth.

"Of course you're going," Annie said. "They've got good schools in Princeton. Soccer, too. It'll be tough in the beginning, but you'll be fine. Nothing to worry about." She sounded like she was trying to convince herself.

After brunch, Sarah and Ray drove off to see some of Sarah's friends, taking David to drop him off at soccer practice, while Annie and Elizabeth cleaned up. When the last pot was dried, Elizabeth said, "I have two more cups of coffee and a *Sunday Chronicle*. Want to sit in the garden?"

"Sounds heavenly. Need help with the coffee?"

"No, go on out. I'll be right there." She handed Annie the

paper.

Annie settled into the blue-cushioned wicker chair with the entertainment section on her lap. Iris and gladiola stalks were intermingled with bright daffodils while pink and red cyclamens and silver-leaved Dusty Millers edged the jade green lawn.

Elizabeth placed a painted metal toleware tray on the glass-topped garden table.

"How do you make the garden look so beautiful all the time?" Annie asked.

"Hard work and lots of water," Elizabeth settled down into her own chair with the financial section.

"How come Bobby wasn't here for brunch?"

Elizabeth folded her paper down. "I left him a message. I've been leaving him messages all week and he hasn't answered one of them yet."

"You guys have a fight?"

"Not really."

"What happened?"

"It's the same old thing, Annie. He wants to get married and I don't."

"I've never understood that. You had a good marriage with Joe. Bobby's perfect for you—you're great friends and everyone can see the electric sparks between you. He's stable financially. Love, money, and sex—what more can you want?"

"Freedom. Annie, I went from my crazy Italian household to marriage with Joe. Everyone was always telling me what to do— my parents, my brothers, tons of Italian relatives who came every Sunday for dinner—even Joe. We had a great marriage, but I never really knew what it was like to live on my own, be my own person. I love Bobby, but I like my time alone, too. I can run my own life and I'm not willing to give that up for twenty-four hours every day with anyone, not even Bobby."

"Does he understand that?"

"I explain, and he nods his head, but I don't think he's really listening. We're good for a few weeks and then he asks again. He's so stubborn that he figures if he keeps asking I'll give in."

"There's got to be some way you guys can make this work."

"I don't know. I'm tired of trying." Elizabeth snapped open her paper and buried her nose in it.

Chapter 8

John spent his weekend with Beth Brighton, the real estate agent Elizabeth had recommended, looking for a place where there was enough room to stable Starfire and set up his welding equipment, which was still in storage after the move from Montana. He'd tried welding in college, using the class to fulfill an undergraduate requirement.

Surprising himself, he'd taken to it, enjoying the process of pulling broken shapes together.

During his marriage to Jessica, he'd maintained the ranch equipment and structures on their small spread in the Bitterroot Valley south of Missoula. As his wife had become sicker, and even more after she'd died, he'd begun to weld odd sculptures together, using the physical labor to sweat out his sorrow, littering the lawn with angry bits of metal.

By five o'clock on Sunday, he still hadn't seen any properties that suited him. The houses were either too close together or too expensive. Brushing off dinner with the Beth, John climbed into his truck and headed back to his temporary home.

Why in hell did Annie have to leave? She had said she felt safe with him. Truth was, he felt safe with her, too. He was pretty sure that what he saw was the true woman, but there was something she was hiding. The skittishness he'd seen on Friday ran deep. There was more to her story than a bad marriage with Fred. Was that she why she was sticking with a company that was ready to lay her off? What had happened to her that made her afraid to take a risk?

Could he offer her a job? Would it be enough to keep her

close?

More importantly, could he keep his hands off her if she worked for him?

He smiled and shook his head. Probably a bad idea.

It was after eight o'clock when he ran out of chores around the house. He stared at the phone for five more minutes before he picked it up to call her.

"How are you feeling?" he asked after she answered the phone. "Any soreness from Friday?"

"A little, but not bad at all."

"I was thinking about getting together for coffee. Are you free tomorrow afternoon?"

"Really, John, I don't think we should."

He began to pace his living room. "No strings, just a cup of coffee. I got the message. You're intent on leaving. But I'd like to spend time with you while you're still here. How about it?"

He could feel her hesitation over the airwaves.

Finally she answered. "I can make time around three. Shall I meet you at the bookstore?"

"Getting away from prying eyes would be better for me. How about Peet's in Soquel?"

"I'll see you at three."

John got to the coffee shop fifteen minutes early, giving him time to choose a fair-trade, dark-roasted espresso and a Pacific Cookie Company sugar cookie. At the last minute, he made it two. He settled himself outside at a metal table in the sun and kept an eye out for Annie.

He spotted her as soon as he sat down and waved at her as she approached the coffee shop, admiring her figure as she sauntered toward him. A bright pink tee-shirt accented her blond hair, fuzzed by ocean humidity and the faint spring breeze. Unfolding his body from the low chair, John pulled out a chair for her. "Thanks for coming. Have a seat. Can I get you something?"

"Medium-sized coffee with milk will do fine."

John gestured toward the brown paper bag on the table. "I hope you like sugar cookies."

She looked up at him, a faint smile on her face. "That was nice. Thanks," she said, pulling out her wallet.

"No, my treat."

She settled back in her chair and lifted her face to the sun as he went back into the dim coffee shop to get her order. He felt like a teenager on his first date, instead of a thirty-nine-year-old man who had buried a wife and survived a broken engagement. He glanced through the tinted window and saw Annie stretch her arms over her head, forcing the taut tee-shirt fabric over her breasts. Blood pumped more quickly through his veins.

Returning, he placed the coffee in front of her and sat down. "How's the situation with David?"

"I called the public defender last week. He said since he's David's lawyer, he needs to talk with David directly. We made an appointment. I pushed a little harder, though, and he confirmed what I thought. Most likely David will get a fine, community service, and probation."

"That's probably as good as it's going to get. I'm sorry you have to go through this. It must be tough."

"It is."

They sat in silence for a few minutes before she asked, "How's owning a California bookstore coming along? Do you ever want to dump it all and move back to Montana?"

Definitely skittish. She was keeping conversation neutral. He'd follow her lead.

"I miss Montana almost every day, but I'm here for good. The big sky never really gets out of your soul, so I'm sure I'll go back now and again. Maybe sometime you could come with me." He waited for her reaction.

She grimaced. "Montana is a long way from New Jersey. Besides, I'm not even sure we should be seeing each other at all. Planning a long trip with you is definitely not on my radar screen."

He sipped his coffee. Should he push her a little or wait? Silence won out—it worked with nervous animals, maybe it'd work on humans, too.

"I'm sorry," she finally said. "That came out harsher than I wanted it to. I guess I'm torn, knowing that the right thing is to go to New Jersey, keep my job, and give my son some new surroundings. But then I think of all I'll miss here, especially my friends, and ..." She looked up from her cup, her hazel eyes glinting with unshed tears. She took a deep breath. "And an opportunity to get to know you better."

"What are you so afraid of?" he asked softly.

"Nothing. My life is in control, like I told you. I don't have to like it, but I'll do what needs to be done. I always have."

The defenses were up again. He went back to neutral territory.

"I loved Montana, but I knew it'd be tough to stay. After Jessica died, I saw our lives together everywhere. We'd met at the university and our lives as a couple were there." He broke off a piece of the cookie and savored the soft sweetness before continuing. "Jessica had been gone a little over a year when I got involved with a friend of hers."

"What happened?"

He shrugged. "We were both still hurting and it seemed natural to comfort each other. One thing led to another and we started going out. I didn't think I'd ever find the love I had with Jessica again, but we learned to care deeply for each other. At least I thought we did. I'd asked her to marry me when a job came through for her in Bozeman at Montana State. Deborah was a biology professor—non-tenured—and it was the perfect chance for her. We figured we could make it through the first year—see how it panned out—and then I could move down there and find a job."

"And ..."

"And ... it didn't work out. She became involved with someone else and that was the end of that."

Funny, the betrayal still got to him in ways that Jessica's death didn't. He picked up his coffee cup. It was his turn to put up some walls. He looked at her.

She stared at the table, her mouth turned down, and a wrinkle furrowed the spot between her eyebrows. He could fall in love with that wrinkle.

"Oh, John, I'm so sorry that happened to you." She raised her head. "Why on earth would you want to get involved with me? Especially when I'm planning on moving?"

That was an excellent question. One he didn't really have an answer for. He sat in silence for a few moments, sipping his coffee. She let him be, drinking her coffee and staring at the traffic in the parking lot.

He put down his coffee. "I don't really have an answer to that. All I know is that you stir something in me, something I haven't felt since Jessica died. I never felt this way with Deborah. It seems important to me to give it a chance to blossom."

She put her hand over his. "I really am leaving, John. I have to."

Placing his hand on top of hers, he looked into her eyes. "Why? Silicon Valley must be filled with opportunities for you, even in this economy. Take a chance with me, Annie."

She shook her head. "You don't know much about the valley. When the economy goes down, there aren't any jobs anywhere—except maybe contracting jobs. And they don't give me the medical benefits I need." She paused. "And what happens if it doesn't work out between us, John? What do I do then?"

He didn't have an answer to that, either. He knew in his heart of hearts that it would work out. He just had to make her believe that.

She withdrew her hand from his. "Why did you want to own a bookstore?" she asked.

They were back to neutral territory.

"I always wanted to write, but it's a hard slog. So I worked odd jobs, including working at Fact and Fiction, our local bookstore. I was there so long that they finally made me manager—took pity on me because they could see no one was ever going to publish the drivel I wrote." He finished off his cookie. "At some point I realized that I wanted to be my own boss. So I started looking for a bookstore to own. This one came up and here I am."

"I wish you well with it." She swallowed her last sip of coffee. "Look, John. I wish it were different. I like you, too. But it doesn't look like it's going to work out for us, so why don't we leave it alone?" She glanced at her watch. "I have to pick up David. Thanks for the coffee." Her voice hitched. "See you." She walked toward the parking lot. At the corner of the building, she turned and gave him a weak smile and a small wave.

He could swear he saw a tear on her check.

Damn.

# # #

Even the chirpy greeting from the flight attendant couldn't lift Annie's mood. Grunting a hello, she staggered down the narrow aisle with her heavy carry-on bag banging her knees in front of her. She jammed the bag in the overhead bin and sidled to her window seat. Strapping her seatbelt around her, she grabbed the water bottle and thick book she'd purchased at the only open airport kiosk. A thin, balding man sat in the aisle seat, gave her a brief smile before stabbing at his Blackberry with a stylus.

The airplane was almost full when a tall gray-haired woman in a soft purple blouse strode through the cabin to stand at the end of their row. Annie groaned inwardly when the woman settled in the middle seat beside her.

"Carol Eos," the woman said. "It's going to be a long flight in cramped quarters—may as well get to know each other." The broad smile on the woman's face reached her sparkling deep blue eyes.

"Annie Gerhard. Nice to meet you."

She turned, rested her head against plastic fuselage and closed her eyes, hoping the woman would take the hint. Six-thirty in the morning was too early to be on a plane, and definitely too early to be that cheerful. She shifted to get more comfortable, propping her head up with her sweater. Soon the murmur of voices around her lulled her to sleep.

The engine's roar during take-off brought her back to consciousness. Half-awake, she rehashed the previous evening.

David had been moody the entire night, barely saying a word while they finished dinner and loaded his bags into her car. When they'd gotten to Elizabeth's, he'd slammed the passenger door, yanked open the rear door, and grabbed his stuff, slammed that door, too, and stalked toward Elizabeth's front door.

She caught up with him on the doorstep. "What's wrong with you? Stop acting like this!"

"I'm not moving to New Jersey."

"You'll do what I tell you."

"I'll sleep on Dad's floor. I'll run away. I'm not moving."

The door opened. Elizabeth looked at each of them.

"Something wrong?" she asked.

"No," David and Annie chorused.

"I can see that. C'mon in."

"Thanks for letting me stay," David said, plunging past Elizabeth toward the spare room he always used. Annie poked her head into the room. "David, I'm leaving now."

"Bye," he said without turning away from his hand-held video game. She walked over to his chair, putting her hand on his shoulder.

"David, don't be this way. I love you. I'm trying to do what's best for both of us."

"Then stay here."

She took a deep breath. "We'll talk some more when I get home. Give me a hug. You know I can't get on a plane without a hug from you."

He'd stood and thrown his arms around her in a half-hearted hug. "I love you, too, Mom."

She'd said her good-byes to Elizabeth and hurried home, tears once again stinging her eyes. Life was getting to be too many good-byes.

She opened her eyes and stared out the plane window, shifting to relieve the stiffness in her neck. "Want anything?" a voice thundered in her ear.

"What?" Annie asked.

"Food. It's eight dollars," Carol, the woman sitting next to her said, gesturing to the aisle. A flight attendant was leaning over holding a paper box.

"I guess." She fished out a ten-dollar bill from her purse, exchanging it for the box and change.

"Anything to drink? That appears to be free."

"Oh. Coffee."

"Good thing they don't charge us for going to the bathroom

... yet."

Annie chuckled. "Actually, I just read that Ryan Air is going to charge to use the toilet."

"Really?" Carol gasped. "Obviously the airline is run by a man with a big bladder."

Annie's chuckle turned into a laugh. She managed to get the tray table down before the attendant handed her the hot coffee. She opened the box and poked at the skinny egg burrito.

"I'll try mine first," Carol said. "If I don't gag, you'll know it's safe."

Annie had to grin. "Okay." She watched as Carol unwrapped the paper from the burrito and took a bite.

"Safe," she declared after she finished chewing. "I suppose now that we have to pay for it, they have to give us better food." Annie bit into her own burrito.

"Why are you flying to Philly?" Carol asked.

"Job interview."

"Opportunity or necessity?"

God, this woman was nosy. "Necessity."

Carol's laugh startled her. "Sorry. Occupational hazard. I'm a life coach—we're trained to ask lots of questions. I should start every conversation by saying, _I ask too many questions. You don't have to answer me!'" She laughed again.

"What's a life coach?"

"Someone who asks lots of questions to help you realize that you have to do some work if you want to change your life. Then we hold you accountable for doing it."

"Sounds tough."

"Sometimes it is, but I love it. Watching people change is quite amazing. I guess I love it so much that I never quite leave it behind. I've become sensitive to people who hedge what they're saying, trying not to reveal too much."

"Like me."

"Could be. We've got a long flight. What's the story?"

Annie glanced over at the man in the aisle seat, who was engrossed in the latest best-selling business book. After a few moments of silence, she began, telling the total stranger in the seat next to her everything about her transfer and David's reaction.

"Wow," she said, finishing up the last sentence. "I usually don't dump like that. Sorry."

Carol waved her bejeweled hand. "It sounds difficult. I'm glad you felt safe enough to 'dump.' The economy's been a bear. Many of my clients have experienced layoffs ... they all react differently. The ones who do the best are the ones who use the opportunity to take a look at what they really want to do, regroup, and try something new."

"More coffee?" the attendant asked.

"Sure," said Carol, passing both cups for refills. When she handed a cup to Annie, she said, "I'd love to be able to help you, but this isn't the time or place. I do most of my coaching by phone. If you want to talk about this more, give me a call." She handed Annie a business card.

Annie put it in her purse.

The next hour of the flight passed quickly as Carol told Annie stories about her small town of Surf City on Long Beach Island, a smaller East Coast version of Santa Cruz, complete with tie-dye shops, surfers, and a lighthouse.

Somewhere over the Rockies, the drone of the engines, drama of the last few weeks, late night, and early morning trip to the airport caught up with Annie and her eyelids began to droop.

"I've taken up enough of your time," Carol said. "I'll let you get back to your book, or take a nap."

"Thanks. And thanks for listening."

She stared out the window at the snowcapped mountains for a long while and tried closing her eyes, but sleep wouldn't come. Carol's words echoed in her head: *The ones who do the best are the ones who use the opportunity to take a look at what they really want to do, regroup, and try something new.*

What did she really want to do?

When she'd become pregnant with David, Annie'd stayed in school long enough to finish the spring semester. Fred had been in his sophomore year working toward a philosophy major while she'd been a freshman music major. At night she'd sung folk music in small clubs and house concerts in the area; she'd begun to build up a following and began to write her first songs, until pregnancy forced her to give that up. No room for both a baby and a guitar on her lap.

After David was born, Fred used it as an excuse to drop out of college. He spent most of his days hanging out with surfers, travelers, and other tellers of tall tales while she worked as a temporary secretary to pay for necessities. When he got a night bartending job at a local beach hangout, he started drinking more heavily. Each night he came home later, heaving himself up the porch steps to their apartment, loud groans accompanying every heavy footstep. In the beginning he came right to bed; later a clinking glass, the slam of the refrigerator door, and the low drone of the television announced his homecoming.

After a few months of waking up to him sprawled on the couch, dirty dishes everywhere, she reached her first breaking point. "It's like my dad," she told him. "Drinking every night. You're going through half a gallon of vodka a week. It can't be healthy. Maybe you should see someone."

Fred's face turned red. "You're always on me about something. First it was finish school, then get a job. Now you're bellyaching about how much time I spend relaxing. You're not my mother. Hell, you're sounding like *your* mother. You don't get to tell me what to do." He'd slammed out of the apartment, coming home even later after work that night.

She was not going to be like her mother. She'd hired her first babysitter, begun night classes at the local college, and upped her exercise routine, believing if she worked harder, he'd stop drinking. She'd been sure of it. Maybe he'd even love her again.

It hadn't worked. No matter what she did, he'd continued to drink. The only affection she'd gotten from him was a slobbery alcoholic kiss after groping her breasts in the kitchen. When he had come to bed, he'd passed out snoring the moment his head hit the pillow. She'd learned to be grateful for the loss of consciousness.

An ache that threatened to engulf her opened in her chest. *I lost myself. It was his insanity and I bought into it, believing his version of the truth. It was lies, all lies.* Piercing pain brought tears to her eyes. *Not now. Not on a plane. Later.* She slammed the door shut on memories, using the napkin to wipe the dampness from her eyes.

"Tears are okay," Carol said. "It's the ones we don't shed that cause us problems." She patted Annie's arm. "Call me. We'll talk."

Annie gave her a wan smile. She spent the rest of the trip reading her book, staring out the window, and napping. Her mental door remained tightly shut. Carol must have sensed her need to be quiet, because she stayed immersed in her own book or chatted with the man in the aisle.

"Coffee cups?" asked the flight attendant as the head attendant droned on about arrival times, transfer gates, and baggage locations.

At baggage claim, Carol said good-bye. "I travel light. Good luck with your trip. Please call me if you think I can help you. I'd really like to do that." Giving Annie a brief hug, she whisked off to the exit.

Budding trees crowded the soft rises between the airport and the Delaware River. Driving her rental car over the bridge from Pennsylvania into New Jersey, Annie looked at the broad stretch of water coursing to the ocean, no other bridges in sight. *It probably looked the same when Washington crossed it.*

Her easy trip continued for another half hour, before she got to a construction zone where signs announced the conversion of one of the highway's rotaries into an overpass.

Roads went every which way, concrete dividers leading the jammed traffic through the maze of bright yellow construction trucks, piles of dirt and ditches. Her breath shortened as she tried to concentrate on finding the right path through stop-and-go traffic. Horns blared around her; cars zipped past.

From her right, a silver sports car cut in front of her and stopped. She slammed on her brakes, praying they'd take. Tires squealed. A horn blared behind her.

"Don't honk at me!" she screamed. "That jerk cut me off."

The rental skidded to a stop, inches from the sports car bumper, before stalling out. Shaking, she rested her head on the steering wheel. Gathering her breath, she looked up to glare at the driver in front of her.

Blaring horns sounded behind her. She turned the key. Nothing happened. She tried again. The noises behind her got louder. One of the construction workers came to the side of the road, signaling her to move ahead. She turned the key again. Nothing.

A tap on her window made her jump. She looked up to see a short, thin man in a business suit, shirt unbuttoned, tie hanging down. He pointed at her gear shift. "Put it in Park," he mouthed.

"What?" she asked, trying to roll down the window. It didn't budge. Damn electric everything. She looked up again, concentrating.

"Put it in Park."

"Oh."

She shifted into Park. Turning the key, she was rewarded by the beautiful hum of a starting engine. The construction worker wildly gestured for her to move. She shifted to Drive and moved ahead.

Chills ran through her body. That was too close. True, it would have been minor, but still ... *What am I doing driving through this mess in New Jersey?*

Clearing the congestion, she obeyed the GPS voice, turning down a two-lane road through rolling countryside. She could see colonial farms with sprawling fieldstone and clapboard houses, mismatched extensions hanging like poor relations on a wealthy landowner. She felt her racing pulse slow with the more peaceful drive. The soothing green of great lawns, sprinkled with sleek-looking horses and miles of white fences, entranced her. *It won't be too bad.*

The easy ride let her mind drift. She wondered what the corporate dinner would be like. She hated functions like that, all the posturing and eagerness of the corporate climbers.

When she'd heard of the event, Elizabeth had hunted through her own closet for the right dress and shoes to send with her. "I can't wear that!" Annie told her when her friend had held out the green silk spaghetti-strapped cocktail dress and strappy sandals. "It's too ... too ..."

"Chic?"

"No. Clingy. Besides, it'll never fit me."

"Ah, yes. You need this." Elizabeth pulled a spandex tube from one of her drawers. "Put this underneath. It hides everything."

"I'm still not wearing this dress. It's unprofessional—

inappropriate. What about a bra?"

"You don't wear one."

Annie laughed. "You can get away without wearing a bra, I can't."

Elizabeth stared at Annie's well-rounded chest and shook her head. "Don't you have a strapless one?"

"I think I have one in the back of a drawer somewhere."

"Well find it. Or get yourself a new one. You'll knock 'em dead in this dress. It's the perfect color."

"I'm not looking for a date. I'm looking for a job."

"Believe me, honey, the process is the same."

Annie had taken the dress to stop her friend from hounding her, but she had no intention of wearing it. One of her business pantsuits would do fine.

She breathed a sigh of relief when saw the church spires vying with the tree line on a small rise ahead. The road took a final dip through trimmed grass athletic fields before crossing a stone bridge over a narrow lake to reach the town. Ivy-covered walls lined the sidewalks where historic signs pointed to the gates of Princeton University, founded in 1746, well over a hundred years older than the oldest California university. Prompted by her GPS, she turned down Nassau Street. Quaint shops with colorful awnings lined the right, while the high Princeton wall continued on the left. A few more turns brought her to her hotel.

After unpacking, Annie grabbed her coat and purse and headed out to explore the streets of town. She slipped into the Ma Chérie Boutique, which boasted a unique blend of clothing, jewelry, and accessories, and found an inexpensive but classy set of earrings that she knew would please Elizabeth as a thank-you gift.

Around six, she found an attractive-looking restaurant on Hullfish Street. Mediterra's looked like her kind of place—casual with a good menu and wine list. She grabbed a newspaper from the foyer and followed the waitress to her table.

She was finishing the last of her broiled chicken when she spotted the advertisement. She called for the check and the waitress assured her that Walnut Lane was only a fifteen-minute walk. After she slipped into the restroom to freshen her make-up and run a brush through her hair, she left the restaurant and stepped briskly up the hill to the church.

Chapter 9

Craggy-trunked trees laced with snowy white blossoms glowed under street lamps on Wiggins Street, softening the stern lines of solid brick buildings with formal white trim. The buildings marched up the slight slope giving way to colonial clapboard homes determined to protect the privacy of the families within. In an odd way, the place reminded Annie of her younger years in the car-factory towns of Michigan and a slight chill swept through her in spite of the hint of warm spring in the air. No wonder she'd escaped to the pale stucco and flamboyant foliage of California.

As she emerged to the top of the hill, she saw her destination. The A-frame church, gleaming glass windows reflecting the evening sun, looked like it had been plucked from the ski slopes of Vail, a conspicuous act of defiance against the conservative Presbyterian town fathers.

She followed the sidewalk around the building and headed down the flight of steps to the basement, anticipation heating her body. It had been a long time since she'd done this.

She paid her small fee to the attendant, selected a folding chair by an aisle, and settled in. The utilitarian hall was set up like every other church coffeehouse she'd seen: mikes, stands, guitars and assorted electrical equipment scattered across the platform that stood in for a stage. She remembered the restlessness before a performance, her nerves showing up in meaningless pacing and fidgeting fingers followed by the total peace of beginning, connecting with the audience, the give and take of voices reminiscent of a choral antiphon. Maybe someday she'd have the courage to step on a stage again.

The aroma of coffee drew her to a table on the side of the room. Homemade oatmeal cookies with plump raisins compelled her to forget her dietary resolve. Returning to her place, she opened the newspaper she'd carried from dinner and bit into the sweet confection, savoring the melting sugar on her tongue. She'd finished her forbidden treat and was absorbed in the local gossip when her arm was jostled, tossing her empty paper plate to the floor, scattering cookie crumbs across the linoleum.

"Tight in here, isn't it?" The man sat in the chair in front of her, glancing at the floor. "They'll get it later. Kick it under the chair." He turned back to the front and snapped open his newspaper.

She bent down to get the plate, although she couldn't do much about the crumbs. Putting her paper and coat on the chair to hold her seat, she dumped her garbage in the trash and looked around for somewhere else to sit. The room had filled up fast; the singer must be popular. Short of clambering over dozens of knees to a center seat, she was stuck where she was. *Maybe he won't be a jerk through the entire concert. Maybe pigs can fly.*

When the performer began plucking the guitar strings for the notes of the opening number, she let go of her angst about the incident. The mid-twenties singer spun a story in the air, drawing her into his vision. The song crept into her soul, whispering to a part of herself she had long forgotten. More than anything in her life, singing went right to the heart of who she was.

The vision expanded and she closed her eyes, feeling the ghost of guitar strings beneath her callused fingertips. Her chest vibrated with unsung songs. From thin air, she created the fantasy of a small studio of her own amid Monterey Cyprus trees and acres of wildflowers bordering a rocky coast. She'd create a CD, selling it from the back of the room. Her technical skills would make selling it online easy. With each song, she built her dream, the joy of touching souls around the country, maybe even abroad, in places like this.

She brought herself back to reality. Dreams were for the innocent, women who hadn't had their spirits wrung out of them by circumstances and bad husbands; people who didn't need to make a living. She'd chosen the right path—the only one open to her. No matter what anyone said, no matter what her heart whispered, she would continue to do what she'd done since she left Fred. It was the best way she knew to make sure she was secure.

When the concert ended, the sense of the dream remained, like the aura before a migraine, creating a well of sadness within her. She sat in her chair absorbing the beauty of what she'd heard, reluctant to return to the loneliness of her hotel room, no matter how comfortable it was.

Gathering his things, the man in front of her stood up. "What drivel," he said.

"Oh. You perform?" She stood.

"No, but I know good music when I hear it. That wasn't it."

"It's easy to be a critic. Not so easy to get up there and sing."

"What makes you an authority, lady?"

"Been there. Done that. Got the damn tee-shirt," she announced, stunning herself with her reaction. *Where the hell had that come from?*

She spun around when she heard a slow clapping start behind her.

"Bravo," said a good-looking man in a navy blue tailored jacket. "I've been waiting for someone to take Walter down for a long time."

"Yeah, right, Mark," the offender said. "Why don't you go back to academia where you belong?" Walter shoved his way down the aisle.

"Hi," said the man behind her, extending his hand. "My name is Mark Hopkinson. Did you enjoy the concert?" He wore rimless glasses perched on a patrician nose and his broad smile displayed whitened teeth. A starched Oxford shirt and pressed khaki pants showed off a trim body.

"Yes, I enjoyed the concert very much," Annie replied, shaking his hand before picking up her coat. "My name is Annie, Annie Gerhard."

"We've spent the evening in a coffeehouse, but I'd love some decaf. Would you like to come with me?" he asked.

She should go back to her hotel room and prepare for her grand entrance in the morning. On the other hand, maybe this was an opportunity to meet someone who might be as nice as his appearance. "Sure," she said, stifling a momentary whisper of caution. "Good. I know a place not far from here."

The two walked out into the chilly air to the tiny coffee shop a few blocks from the church. A couple was leaving when they arrived, providing a place to sit in the crowded café. Mark slipped the coat off her shoulders, hanging it on the hook at the end of the booth. Declining the offer of a sweet from the waitress, he ordered coffee for the two of them. "Have to watch our waistlines, y'know," he said, glancing at her. She started to object, but thought of the cookies she'd had at the concert. *Maybe he's right. I could stand to lose a little weight.*

After the waitress left, Mark began a running commentary on his exploits. Once he found out she was from California, he focused the monologue on his time in the state. He knew many of her favorite places, including Yosemite and Big Sur. "I've even climbed the back of Half Dome," he announced halfway through his coffee.

"Wow. That must have been amazing. I've never felt strong enough to handle that trek."

"It's a matter of training. I'm sure you could do it if you got in shape. It's best to get up really early to beat the crowds, but the view is spectacular. Climbing the cables to the top can be a little scary the first time—not a problem the second or third time. I make a point to do it every few years."

"You must be in really good shape."

"I have a really good trainer. I'll give you his name. When you move out here, you can get started right away. As we age, it's best to maintain our fitness level."

Why is everyone always trying to change me?

As the time wore on, she relaxed into her role as a good listener. He was an entertaining storyteller, but it felt like something was missing. He certainly was different from John. She felt a small pang of yearning for the quiet Montanan, but quickly pushed it away. That relationship wasn't possible.

When she finished her cup of coffee, she glanced at her watch, startled to see how late it was. "I need to get back to my hotel."

He picked up the check, glanced at it and left some bills on the tray before standing to get her coat. "Where are you staying?"

She told him.

"I'll walk you there," he said.

"You don't have to bother. I'm used to walking alone."

"Yes, but I can't retain my chivalrous reputation if I let you."

She really wanted to walk by herself, to clear her head before going to sleep, but acquiesced. It would be rude to turn down the gentlemanly gesture. She rethought her decision when he followed her into the lobby of her hotel. Did he expect to be asked up?

"I know an amazing Italian restaurant. You'll love it," he said as she turned to face him. "Can I make a reservation for Wednesday night?"

"That'd be nice." The words were out of her mouth before she

116

could stop them. She didn't really want to go out with him. There was something about him that was a little bit off, nothing she could put her finger on, simply a slight tinge of fear. *Oh, well, too late now.*

"Good. I'll pick you up here. The dress code is East Coast Casual." He smiled. "I know you Californians are used to a more laid-back life, but this is Princeton. We're a little more formal here."

"I see. So what exactly *is* 'East Coast Casual'?"

"No jeans, no shorts, and for heaven's sake, no flip-flops. You know—a nice skirt and sweater set, or something like that."

She forced a grin. "No flip-flops in my luggage! I get the picture. See you Wednesday."

She waved good-bye and headed for the elevator. *Skirt and sweater set? I thought that went out with the 50s.*

That night she dreamed she was on an island she'd never been on before. The landscape reminded her of Maui, verdant grasslands contrasting with deep valleys of intense foliage. She followed a narrow path through rainbow eucalyptus trees, allowing the sacred silence to seep into her bones. As she walked, she became aware of a deep thrum in the distance, disturbing the birds that nested in the tall trees. She followed the path to a clearing, where she saw a gang of men with chainsaws ripping through the grove. One of the workers spotted her and pointed her out to the man with a clipboard next to him. The boss man turned, a red flush of anger covering his face. Her father's face.

She started to run.

In her dream, her father chased her down, turning into a loud bee, buzzing in her head.

She had to escape. She had to make that noise stop. She had to ... wake up.

Shuddering, she turned off the alarm and dragged herself

into the shower. She let the warm water sluice over her, nudging her to a form of awakening and banishing her father's ghost to the distant memory where it belonged.

She drove to the JCN offices and waited at the lobby desk for Jim to come get her, her company badge not yet programmed for the facility. A flushed, round man in a traditional business uniform of white shirt, striped power tie and dark slacks bustled into the lobby with his hand outstretched. "Jim Borzetti," he said. "You must be Annie."

"Yes," she replied. "Glad to meet you."

"I'm sure you're anxious to see where you're going to be working," he said, leading her up a ramp to the second floor of the building. "We have a great team here. Management is anxious to get the Common Criteria project up and running. There's a great deal of competitive advantage to completing the certification."

Jim's office, nested in a line of similar offices, actually had walls and a door, unlike the maze of cubicles downstairs. He ushered her into the windowless space, closing the door behind her.

"As I said, this project is vital to us. We need a strong project manager, like you, to pull it off. What I'd like to do over the next few days is to have you look over the work the previous manager did, talk with some of the team and give me your plan to complete the project. I've also arranged some interviews with a few of the managers you'll be working with. Based on their input and our opinion of your plan, we'll decide whether or not to extend the offer."

He leaned forward. "Randy highly recommended you," he said, looking pointedly at her. "This is a very visible project in a highly political environment. We need someone who can make things happen without ruffling any feathers, not someone who's going to cause trouble. Do you think you can do that?"

"Of course I can," she replied. "I know I will do a great job for you and your team."

"Okay," Jim said, seeming to be satisfied with her response. "Sounds good. Oh, one more thing," he added as he stood. "You got the e-mail I sent about the corporate dinner tonight?"

She nodded.

"Good. We can put you to the test there tonight."

As she left the building at the end of the day, she knew two things: the project wasn't going to be simple and the help was going to be non-existent. Everyone had too much to do already; providing documentation for her wasn't going to be high on anyone's priority list. Still, she'd completed other difficult projects. She could do it again. The work would be frustrating and time-consuming, but hopefully her success would allow her return to the company office in California.

A half hour later she slid the green silk dress over her bare shoulders and strapless bra. She watched it settle around the spandex cylinder restraining the lumps and bumps of middle age, then forced her feet into three-inch stilettos, more strap than shoe. She felt like a hooker.

Studying herself in the full-length hotel mirror, she shuddered. Elizabeth's borrowed dress clung to her curves, the thigh-high slit revealing her stocking-encased leg. Her friend had been right. Jim had insisted that she come to the managers' dinner dressed appropriately—a cocktail dress, not a pantsuit.

"These are the people who'll decide whether or not we offer you the job," he'd said. "First impressions count. Do it right."

Tossing her coat over the dress and grabbing the slim evening bag Elizabeth had provided, she clicked her way to the elevator. After a short trip, she followed a drive through rolling golf greens. The white columned club looked as if it belonged in a remake of *Gone with the Wind*, with its large chandeliers gleaming over tuxedoed valets.

After surrendering her car, she made her way through a spacious rotunda with inlaid wood floors. She hesitated at the door of the dining room, gazing at the white-clothed tables with their centerpieces of silver tapered candles and vases of spring flowers. Silver-rimmed plates sparkled in the candlelight. Tight clusters of people dotted the room, cocktails in hand, earnest faces in place. On her left, an angular man in a dark business suit brightened only by a vibrant red necktie gestured dramatically at a corpulent fellow in a gray suit. She skirted past them.

She spotted Jim in a group near the heavily curtained floor-to-ceiling windows at the back of the room. She wove her way through the tables to greet him, passing one of the few women in the room on the way. Like her, the woman had on a slim-fitting cocktail dress, heels and glittering earrings. A quick scan of the room showed her that the rest of the females were similarly outfitted.

Jim looked her up and down. "You look fabulous. Good job."

She withdrew her hand from his. "Thank you."

"Are you going to keep her all to yourself, Jim?" a short, balding man asked. The suit may have fit him once, but his current girth gapped his dress shirt where it met his pants, revealing a ribbed undershirt beneath.

"No, Conrad, I'm not. I've mentioned Annie to you. She might take over the Common Criteria project. We've invited her in for a few days to get her opinion on the project. Annie, Conrad Wilkins, Director of IT."

"Very good. Very good. It's very important work, young lady. I hope you're up to it."

"I can handle it," she said quietly.

He patted her arm with his beefy hand. "It's a tough job. We've already lost a few project managers over it. They were all men, so we decided to see what a woman could do. Be sure to save a place for me at dinner. I want to hear what you're going to do differently."

Oh, great. Someone in power who thinks women don't belong in business. She'd need to please him enough to get the job, while keeping her distance as much as possible.

The cocktail hour dragged on and, true to his word, Conrad plopped himself next to her at dinner. "They serve the best rib-eye steak here. Comes with baked potato, sour cream, the works. My favorite. We've been having our corporate dinners here since the company opened this division. My idea. It's a good way to get folks together in an informal setting. Greases the wheels, you know." Conrad launched himself at his blue cheese-laden salad. "Dig in," he said.

Annie was spared from laying out a project plan by Conrad's running monologue about his experience with the company, punctuated by "accidental" touches of her hand and arm. The tight seating around the circular table brought his porcine leg into close contact with hers. When she thought she'd put in the time required to make a good impression, she pushed away her half-filled plate and stood up.

"Lovely meeting you," she said to Conrad. "I've had a really long day. I need to get back to the hotel to get some rest so I can lay out a good plan for Jim tomorrow."

Conrad stood, his shoe coming perilously close to crushing her toe. "I look forward to seeing you around. I think you'll be perfect for the project." He patted her on the arm again, fingers lingering a little too long. Thanking him, she turned to leave, allowing her stiletto heel to land on the soft leather of his dress shoe.

"Ow!"

She stopped, a little amazed at her own action. "I'm so sorry!

I guess I wasn't paying attention."

Red-faced, Conrad glared at her. "It's all right. I'm sure you didn't mean anything by it."

"It was an accident. I'm so sorry," she repeated.

"Not a problem," he said, once again putting his hand on her arm. This time his squeeze was a little too hard.

She pulled her arm away, said good night, made her excuses to Jim, and rapidly left the dining room.

In spite of her concern about the consequences of her action, a small smile of satisfaction twitched her lips as she handed the valet her parking voucher.

# # #

Annie's satisfaction ended early the next morning.

"Conrad's a good ally to have in this company," Jim said after they'd exchanged greetings. She stilled. Did the director report her shoe-stabbing incident? What if he had? *I'm so tired of men behaving badly and thinking they can get away with it.*

"Too bad you couldn't have stayed later."

"Was it a problem that I left early? I was exhausted. Traveling takes a lot out of you. I couldn't keep my eyes open a minute longer." She flashed her best simpering Southern belle smile—a tough job for a hard-working girl from the Midwest.

It didn't work.

"I'm not sure if it's a problem or not. I thought Conrad was enthusiastic about you early in the evening. But he didn't mention you at all when the evening ended. Did something happen? He's an important player in this division and it would help if you stayed on his good side."

"Nothing happened that shouldn't have."

"What's that supposed to mean?"

Oops. "Um, nothing. Conrad and I had a nice chat over dinner and I left. That's about it."

Jim looked at her for a long minute. She went for boldness and continued to look him in the eye. *I'd do it again in a heartbeat.*

"What I'd like you to do today," he finally began, "is talk to the managers who you'll be working with on the project." He handed her a list. "I'll be gathering their feedback before I make my final decision about the job offer. Oh, and I'd like a preliminary report telling me your views on the project."

Her day didn't improve.

Every manager she talked to about the project told her that he or she didn't have time for it. Continual layoffs meant that programmers and analysts were overworked and there was no sign that cuts wouldn't happen again. Producing the documentation that she needed for Common Criteria was not a high priority.

Before she left for the hotel, she wrote the report that Jim wanted. It had to be good enough to show him she could do the job, in spite of the obstacles. It was simply a matter of persistence—keep going back to the managers until they gave her the material she needed.

As she drove to Princeton, she mulled over her upcoming dinner with Mark. *I'd rather have a bath with a book and a glass of wine.* But, she'd made a promise and she'd keep it. Besides, he probably knew a place with good food. He'd been an okay companion the night before, not all over her like Conrad. *I'll enjoy myself.*

By the time she changed into an azure-blue silk blouse and black skirt and freshened her makeup, she'd begun to feel better.

When she walked into the hotel lobby, Mark stood up to greet her. Dressed in a tailored dark blue blazer and slacks, he looked more like a Wall Street investment banker than the history professor he was. His silver hair was neatly combed and he was freshly shaved. He took her hand with both of his and shook it warmly.

"There're some great restaurants nearby. I hope you like Italian," he said. "One of my favorites." "Let's go, then," he said, motioning toward the hotel door and letting her lead the way.

Once they were outside, he put his hand on the small of her back to guide her to the right. She tensed at the gesture. *Why is it men always feel they have the right to touch?* Relax. He's only old-fashioned. It was the cool night air whisking under her thin raincoat that was making her shiver.

"Are you cold?" he asked. "I forgot that you were from California. Your blood isn't used to this. It's only a short walk and it will do you good to get some fresh air and exercise after a long day at the office. Spring nights in Princeton are too pretty to waste in a car."

He looked down at her and smiled. Automatically, she smiled back. I suppose he's being nice, but I wish he didn't always mention exercise.

You're being over-sensitive, her mother's voice intoned. You always were too sensitive about how you looked.

Maybe it's because everyone always harped on it.

We were only trying to help. We wanted you to look your best, being a girl and all that.

"Chilly?" he asked.

"I'm sure I'll get used to the temperature."

"How was your day?"

"Tiring. There was a lot to wrap my head around. I'm not even sure—"

"I had a tough day, too," he interrupted. "Sometimes I think the kids are in high school, not college. They force me to teach one section of history for dummies. I hate it. If I'd made dean last year, I wouldn't have to put up with this crap.

"Imagine," he continued. "There was a kid today who didn't even know the first sentence of the Declaration of Independence. I mean, how could you forget, 'When, in the course of human events, it becomes necessary for one people to dissolve the political bonds which have connected them with another ...'"

Annie wondered if he was going to recite the whole thing.

Mercifully, he stopped quoting the Declaration after the first line. As they closed the remaining distance to the restaurant, he regaled her with stories about his revolutionary ancestor, Francis Hopkinson, who'd signed the Declaration of Independence.

At least I don't have to think about anything to say.

The restaurant fit right into the 1700s scene that Mark had woven: darkly stained pine tables decorated with candles flickering behind hurricane lamps, electric wall sconces softly glowing, and heavy forest green homespun curtains. It was authentic, dark, and small. Everything was impeccable. Annie began to relax—it was going to be a lovely dinner.

"Bet you don't have anything like this in California."

"No, not really. That's the fun of travel, seeing different places, especially older ones like this. In fact, if I look closely, I can almost see your relative over in that corner."

The host arrived to show them to their table.

"Since you like Italian, you'll really like the food here," he said when they were seated. "The chef is from New York. He graduated from the Culinary Institute of America in Hyde Park. I don't know how the restaurant snagged him, but they must have made him a really good offer. The prices certainly reflect it."

He chuckled and she forced a smile. Both her dad and Fred had always commented on restaurant prices. It was a covert signal that either someone else should pay, or payment of another kind would be extracted later. *Stop it! You're over-reacting. He's a nice man taking me out to dinner. Nothing threatening about that ... is there?*

"I'm on an expense account," she said. "I can pay for my own meal."

"And have my mother turning over in her grave?" he said. "Perish the thought. I can certainly afford it."

She gave him a quick smile as she picked up her menu. Based on his recommendation, she ordered penne with salmon and vodka sauce, preceded by a baby green salad, while he chose a heartier chicken Alfredo. He selected a Pouilly-Fuissé from the wine list.

"You seem to know your wines," she said.

"Yes," he said. "I enjoy picking the right varietal for the meal. I'm something of a connoisseur, more of French wines than your California stuff, of course."

"Of course."

"In fact," he continued, oblivious to the slight sarcasm in her voice. "I often use stories about European wine when I teach history. Did you know that some French winemakers risked their lives to protect their wine in World War II?"

"No, I didn't."

"It's fascinating how the Germans and French lied, cheated, and stole from each other during the war. Some French winemakers sprinkled carpet dust into their wines before they bottled it. Made it seem like fine aged wine when it was swill made with their worst grapes!" He laughed. When she didn't join in, he gave her a pointed look. She quickly gave a brief chuckle, even though she couldn't see the humor. But her father and Fred had trained her well. Going along made a man happy and happy men weren't dangerous.

He continued. "I was going to write a book about it, but some

126

wannabe historians beat me to it. Wine journalists. How they ever had the gall to write a history book, I'll never know. I'd have written a far better book than they did. Let me tell you how I would have done it differently."

The long explanation was interrupted by the delivery of their food and the ritual of serving the wine. Mark made a great show of sniffing the cork, examining the label, swirling, smelling, sipping the wine, and giving the waiter a curt nod when he was done.

"This is wonderful," she said after tasting the amber liquid.

He swirled the golden wine around, stuck his nose below the rim of the glass and drank slowly. "Nice balance of acidity and fruit," he said after he swallowed. He held the glass up to the candle light and murmured, "Perfect."

Eating occupied the next ten minutes. Fortunately.

"You're very pretty," he said, putting his fork down. "And you have the most unusual eyes. What color are they, hazel?"

"Yes. Sometimes they're …"

"You're a wonderful listener." He grinned and shrugged his shoulders. "I've been told I talk too much, but I get caught up in the story, and want to share it all, especially with an attractive woman." He put his hand on top of hers.

She gave a slight shiver at the same time she felt the heat rise to her cheeks. "Thank you."

"I'm serious. We can have a marvelous time together when you move here … and get to know each other better." He caressed the top of her hand, but she didn't move.

She knew the dread in the pit of her stomach. She'd felt it every time her father came home from work, impeccably dressed, his drunkenness revealed by his precise movements and slight slur in his speech. She'd learned to pick up the clues to her father's moods quickly, mimicking her mother's soft speech. In reality, it

Casey Dawes

only kept them safe for a while, but the habits were deeply ingrained.

That's what her intuition was trying to tell her. He was another man who looked good, but he had a rotten core. She needed to get through this dinner safely and never see him again.

The waiter replaced the cleared dishes with dessert menus. Annie took the opportunity to move her hand back to her lap.

"They make the best tiramisu here," he said. "You must have some."

"I don't think so," she said. "I'm satisfied. It's been a long day and I need to get back to the hotel."

Mark put up his hand. "Two tiramisus."

"Very good, sir," said the waiter.

"But ..." she protested.

"I know best."

She let it go. She would do what it took to keep him content, at least until she got back to the safety of the hotel lobby. *I can push it around my plate.*

After the waiter set their desserts on the table, she took a small bite and then put her fork by her plate. It was all she wanted.

"That's all you're having?" he asked. "You must finish it. It's the perfect ending to the perfect meal." He covered her hand with his. She slipped her hand away and picked up her fork to finish her dessert like an obedient child. *No use causing a fuss in the restaurant.*

The meal finally finished, they began the walk back to the hotel. The temperature had dropped and she shivered from the cold.

He moved closer. "Do you mind?" he asked. He didn't wait for an answer before he slipped his arm around her waist.

Chapter 10

Annie almost pulled away, but the street was dark. She decided to go along for a little while longer. It wasn't far to the hotel and she could dump him in the lobby.

They were almost there when Mark stopped next to the long brick wall bordering the Princeton campus. His hand slid from around her waist to her arm and he turned her toward him.

He was too close. Annie took a step backward, pressing her back against the rough-hewn brick.

"I had a wonderful time tonight," he said, running his right hand down her other arm. "You're special. That ex-husband of yours was a fool to let you go. When will you be coming back to New Jersey to stay?"

He took a step closer, trapping her. Talk. Ask questions. Men like him always like to talk about themselves. What had he'd asked?

"I leave tomorrow for San Francisco," she said, the citrus smell of his cologne turning her stomach. "When I come back depends on whether or not Jim offers me the job."

"Of course he'll offer it. You're a really smart lady. I can't wait until you get back. There are so many things I can show you. I'll treat you like a queen."

He moved closer. "We'll be great together," he said, leaning in to kiss her.

At the last moment she turned her head and his mouth landed on her cheek.

"Well, that didn't turn out right," he said. "Let's try again." He leaned down again, his breath hot on her face, the sweet scent of wine entwined with the sharp odor of the mint he'd chewed after dinner. "Let's not."

She blocked him with her hand, pushing him far enough away so she could duck under his arm and walked rapidly toward her hotel, heels clicking loudly in the soft spring night. Could she make it to the bright lobby lights?

He caught up with her and tried to reclaim her elbow. She shook his hand off and walked faster, finally reaching the lobby. Mark trailed behind.

Once inside, she turned toward him. "Thank you again for a very nice evening."

Mark ignored her. "I'd like to have your phone number in California."

Annie took out a business card and handed it to him. She could get the company to block his calls.

"I don't want your business number. I want to be able to call you at home," he said and gave her a slim pen from his shirt pocket.

"You can get me here," Annie said, gesturing with the card.

"I want to have your home phone. Annie. Don't be so difficult. What are you afraid of?"

You.

He put up his hands. "I planned a lovely evening at an expensive restaurant. I thought you'd appreciate it. Apparently I was wrong." His voice grew louder.

"No, no," she said. She needed to calm him down and get him out of there. "I had a lovely evening, too. Don't be upset. I don't like to give out my home number to anyone. Single mother, you know." She scribbled a number on the back of her business card, a number that bore no resemblance to her home number. She silently said her apologies to whoever got Mark's call.

"Here you go." She handed him the card.

"You won't regret it," he said, leaning forward.

Oh, God, is he going to try to kiss me again? She stepped back, glancing at the front desk. A staff member saw her look and came around the desk to walk toward them.

"Annie," Mark said. "It's only a kiss."

"I don't want to be kissed." *At least, not by you.*

"Is there a problem?" the staffer asked her.

Mark looked down at the clerk. "No. I was only saying good night to the lady."

"Good night," Annie said.

"Good night."

In her mind, she imagined the click of his heels as he turned and walked out the door. "Thanks," she said to the hotel clerk.

"We don't allow our guests to be harassed," he said. "Are you okay?"

"Yes, thanks."

"Have a nice night."

"Uh-huh." Annie was grateful, but her mind was already on a tub full of hot water and bubbles. An hour later, she called Elizabeth.

Her friend picked up on the fourth ring. "Sorry I missed you last night. I had to run some errands. How did the manager's dinner go over last night? Were they wowed by the dress?"

"A little too wowed. There was an older guy—probably missed the memo on sexual harassment. Unfortunately, he was also a corporate director and politically connected."

"What'd he do?"

"He touched me ... constantly. Everything was 'accidental,' so I couldn't say anything. But after a while it was too much to take and I did something I'll probably regret."

"What?" Elizabeth's voice rose in excitement.

"I stilettoed him with my spiked heel."

Her friend burst out laughing. In a moment, Annie joined her, Conrad's astonished face clearly etched in her memory.

"I shouldn't be laughing," Annie said when she finally calmed down enough to breathe. "He wasn't pleased."

"Annie, can you do the job?"

"Of course I can. It's impossible. No budget, no staff, and a short deadline."

"Right up your alley. Then you'll get the job."

"I wish I was sure. But I also wish I could find a politically correct way to make men like Conrad keep their hands off me."

"Can you talk to someone?"

Annie's laugh was bitter. "No. Men like Conrad know exactly where the line is. They're high enough in the organization that they're protected. Fortunately, they're a dying breed. Younger men have been indoctrinated."

"What about your dinner date? Did that go better?"

"Not really."

"Oh. Don't they have any *nice* men in New Jersey?"

"I'm sure they do. Actually, dinner was fine. Mark likes to talk too much, but the restaurant was classy and the food was amazing."

"Did you stiletto him, too?"

"No, I shoved him."

"Annie, you really need to find a gentler way to say, 'No,'" Elizabeth said, her voice kind.

"I'm not sure I know how. I try to be nice and then all of a sudden it gets to be too much and I do something rash."

"Do you try something other than saying nothing and bashing them over the head?"

Annie laughed and then quieted as she thought about the question. "I think I do. I know I did with Fred and he never heard me until after I left."

"Maybe you need to find a better man."

"I sure know how to pick them, don't I?"

"I don't know. John seems nice."

"He does, doesn't he? I wish it were an option, but I can't risk losing my job if I stay in California. And I certainly don't want to get involved with a man hoping he'll support me. That's not fair to him. Besides, there's always a price to pay for being dependent."

"There's also a price to pay for being too *in*dependent."

"Then why won't you marry Bobby?"

Elizabeth laughed. "Touché! Would you like to talk to David?"

"Nice change of subject, but I'll let you get away with it this time."

David sounded upbeat. He'd made, in his words, an "awesome save" during his soccer game and led his team to victory. *The mercurial moods of teenagers—you never know what you'll get.*

It was so much easier when David was talkative. All too often these days their exchanges were a few short words said in passing when they weren't arguing about school, homework or chores. His excitement over the save reminded her of the wide-eyed little boy he'd been, bringing home bugs, toads, and the occasional snake.

"I'll be home tomorrow night," she said, wrapping up the conversation. "I can't wait to see you."

"Love you, Mom."

"Love you, too."

After she hung up the phone, Annie trolled through her purse to find Carol Eos's business card. She pulled it out, threw on some clothes, and headed for the lobby computer.

# # #

Annie spent her time the next morning interviewing reluctant managers and time-pressed engineers to understand what she'd need to do to make the project successful. By the time she met with her potential boss to discuss the project, she was prepared.

"While I don't know much about Common Criteria, I do know how to manage a project," she said to Jim. "And this one has disaster written all over it unless you're willing to free up a little more time from the programmers and analysts."

"That's impossible," Jim said. "We have deadlines."

"Then the deadline for Common Criteria won't be met."

"It has to be."

"Look," she said. "I get that times are tight and everyone is working to full capacity. How about this? I'll get all the information I can from existing documentation. That way I can keep team interruptions to a minimum. I'll create an interview schedule of the people I need to talk to and clear it with the appropriate managers so everyone is aware of what's required."

"That might work," he said.

They spent another half hour working out the details of her transfer. Jim reminded her that it was contingent on Conrad's approval. As she left to catch her plane back to the West Coast, he handed her an orange book called *Trusted Computer System Evaluation Criteria* for a little "light reading."

"We're looking forward to getting started," he said, pumping her hand vigorously. "I hope there won't be any problems with this transfer."

She should have felt good that things were falling into place. Why didn't she?

Two hours later, Annie sank into her window seat, novel in hand. Everything had gone smoothly; even the airport security lines had been mercifully short.

As the plane took off, she thought about what she'd learned from Carol Eos's website the night before. She'd had been so impressed that she'd filled out the form to request an introductory session. Something needed to change. She couldn't keep stabbing obnoxious men with stiletto heels or shoving them away when they went too far.

Once they landed at San Francisco airport, she grabbed a cup of coffee at a kiosk, picked up her bag from baggage, and caught the shuttle to the long-term parking lot.

Annie began to relax after she merged onto Route 280. The road was familiar and traffic minimal. Her mind drifted to the concert in the church basement. For the first time in years, she thought about the guitar sitting in her garage. It would need new strings at least, if it wasn't beyond repair from the fluctuating temperatures. She'd picked up the second-hand instrument at a garage sale in Michigan, attracted by its mellow tones and polished wood.

Maybe it was time to resurrect it.

A blaring horn made her jump. She'd drifted too close to a merging black BMW as she passed the Route 92 interchange. After the close call in New Jersey, she'd better pay attention. She reached over to turn up a local rock station and began to sing along with Stevie Nicks.

Annie was still singing when she pulled into Elizabeth's driveway after eight. Her friend greeted her at the door with a big hug. "You look exhausted."

"Gee, thanks. Some friend. But you're right. These quick trips across the continent wear me out ... and all the stress of auditioning for a new job. All I want is my own bed." "David's finishing up homework. I've got a glass of wine for you while we wait."

"Sounds perfect."

Elizabeth went to the kitchen while Annie went down the hall to check in with her son. When she returned to the living room, she sank into the couch and picked up the thin crystal wine glass her friend had left on the gleaming end table. The first sip of chardonnay radiated through her body, dulling the effects of the mega-doses of coffee she'd drunk to stay awake on the drive home.

California wine tastes best in California.

Elizabeth came back into the room, cheese plate in hand. She positioned the dish on the redwood coffee table and sat at the other end of the couch.

"Still planning on going?" There was a hopeful note to her voice. "Sounds like the job's tough."

Annie looked at her friend out of the corner of her eye and slowly chewed the brie on crostini. She took a small sip of wine before answering. "I don't think I told you about the concert I went to."

"We're not going to talk about the job?"

"No, we aren't."

"You started to tell me about the concert, but we got distracted by the creep story."

"I knew there was something wrong with him, but I didn't trust myself."

Annie felt Elizabeth's eyes on her. From long experience, she knew her friend wanted to say something, but didn't want to hurt her feelings. "Go ahead," she said. "Say what's on your mind."

"I think that's the problem, Annie. You don't listen to your instincts. You've always let other people, usually men, talk you into doing things against your better judgment."

"Maybe you're right, but it's hard to sort out the right voices— there's a chorus in my head! Mom's voice is always telling me to

_Go along to get along.' Dad's telling me the man is always right and it's all playing over a tape loop of someone singing, _I am woman, hear me roar,' in the background. It's very confusing!" She looked at Elizabeth and they giggled. "I'm a mess, aren't I?"

"I think there's hope yet. Annie, why don't you sing anymore?"

Annie shrugged. "I don't have the time. It's really too bad, because I think I was beginning to find my style. More people were coming to my coffeehouse gigs. I even had a concert lined up at Don Quixote's in Felton. I never did it, though. Fred pitched a fit about the time I was spending on my music, not tending to David. He went on and on about how he had a job, too, and it wasn't babysitting. Blah, blah, blah. I put the guitar in the garage."

"Maybe it's time to dig it out."

"I'm thinking about it. Oh," she said, taking Carol's card from her purse and handing it to her friend. "You'll be pleased. I met her on the plane and I made a phone appointment with her for tomorrow morning."

"Carol Eos, Coaching for Life," Elizabeth read aloud. She looked up with a smile. "I've heard about life coaches. Good ones can really make a difference in your life. Sounds like a good idea."

Annie took the card back and finished the remaining swallow of wine. "I'd better be going. I can work from home tomorrow, thank goodness. Thanks for everything." She gave her friend a big hug. "David," she called down the hallway. "Time to go."

The ride home was easy. David was talkative and she didn't bring up either the impending trial or move.

The next morning she put David's dirty laundry in the washer as soon as he left for school. The rush of water echoed in the hallway as she walked to her office. In spite of the fact that she was an official "short-timer," Annie was still getting a few hundred e-mails a day, and plowing through them took time.

Regardless of how the company treated her, she'd do her job to the best of her ability.

With e-mail answered, laundry put away, and a pot of spaghetti sauce simmering on the stove to make into quick meals for the following week, Annie was ready for Carol's call.

The phone rang promptly at ten.

"Annie Gerhard?"

"Yes"

"Carol Eos. I'm glad you called. How was your flight back?"

"The flight was okay. It's my life that's messed up. All I do is attract every loser around and this time I attacked two of them. One was a director. I think I screwed up my chance of going to New Jersey because I stabbed him with my stiletto heel. I don't even know why I called you." Whew! What possessed her to dump all of that in the first breath?

"I see." Carol said.

"How do I make everyone around me leave me alone and let me do my job and raise my kid? Isn't that enough?"

"Yes, it's certainly enough. The only problem is that the only person you can change is yourself."

"Why do I need to change? My ex is an alcoholic, my son's in trouble with the law, and my company is laying me off. My changing isn't going to change those facts one bit!"

"You'd be amazed. Tell me more about those _losers' you attacked."

Annie told Carol about the dinners with Conrad and Mark. As she talked, she calmed down. It wasn't Carol's fault her life was a mess. Maybe she could have handled Conrad and Mark differently, too. "I feel a little ashamed about what I did. I guess I overreacted."

"Perhaps. But the fact that you reacted at all to bad situations means a lot. Were your parents alcoholics?"

"My dad. He drank right up until the day he died."

"That would explain a lot. Many active alcoholics need to blame others, to keep the focus anywhere but on themselves. They change facts to suit the story they tell themselves. And they convince everyone around them that they're the sane one. It's tough on a kid, very confusing. Do you remember a time when you thought something was true and your dad told you it wasn't?"

Annie chuckled. "Lima beans. He was from the South and loved them. We had them every Sunday. Every Sunday I'd tell him I hated them and every Sunday he'd tell me he didn't understand because I'd loved them the last week. Finally, I gave up and ate the damned things."

"Anything recent remind you of that?"

"The tiramisu!"

"Yes?"

"I didn't want it, but my date ordered it anyway. I ate it simply to keep the peace."

"Given your history, it would be hard for you to do anything else. You don't have good boundaries."

"What do you mean?"

"Most people, in the same situation, would have said, _no,' even if it meant telling the waiter not to bring you tiramisu."

"But Mark would have gotten angry."

"That would have been his problem."

"He would have made it mine," Annie said.

There was a pause on the line. "Annie, did your father hit you?"

She wasn't ready to go there. "I can't really remember."

There was another pause. "Okay. I'll let that pass for now."

"So, if I'm such a doormat, how come I wouldn't let him kiss me?" Annie asked.

"Sounds like he crossed a line you simply couldn't accept. You set a boundary that time."

"Not well."

"It wasn't very elegant, but it worked."

"Yes, it did, didn't it? But what I really called you for was to help me feel better about the move to New Jersey. Everyone's pressuring me to stay. Shouldn't I set my boundaries and do what I feel is right?"

"*Do* you feel it's right?"

"Of course. It's what I should do."

"'Should' is a very dangerous word. I'm not sure you really believe it is the right decision, deep down inside you."

"How will I know? When will I know? I have to decide by Monday."

"When you learn to trust yourself more, you'll begin to make decisions that are best for you. Until then, we'll work with what you have. Is there any way you can delay the decision? Have they told you that you must make it by Monday?"

"Not really. I feel that they want me to make it soon. I probably have another two weeks."

"Then let's use them." Carol explained the process they'd follow and said she'd e-mail a coaching contract. Because time was of the essence, the women decided to have their next call on Monday.

Annie spent the next few hours filling out expense reports for her trip and reading through the material that Jim had given her. Her mind kept drifting back to the conversation with Carol. Maybe she could change how her life had always been if she listened to her instincts more. To test the theory, she thought about John. Wasn't there something about him that made her cautious?

No.

Drat.

About four o'clock the phone rang again. Annie answered without thinking. "Annie Gerhard. How can I help you?"

"Wow. That's formal."

"Who is this?"

"Sorry, it's John. Is it okay to talk? I mean, are you working or in the middle of something?"

"No, I'm fine. How are you?"

"I wanted to find out how your trip was. Do you think you'll be transferring?"

Annie put a positive spin on the trip to New Jersey, leaving out her aggressive behavior. *No need to scare the man off.*

"David's trial is coming up, isn't it?" he asked.

"Next week."

"You've had a tough week. How about I take you to dinner tonight? Give you a break?"

"John, we've been through this before. I don't think it's wise."

"Annie, it's only dinner. I'm not asking you to run away to Tahiti. You can even bring David."

"He's eating at a friend's house tonight. I was making a batch of spaghetti sauce to use for dinner and during the week. I'd invite you over, but the house is really a mess. I suppose I could freeze it. Do you really think ...?"

"Annie, I'm trying to make your life easier, not more difficult. You don't need to invite me for dinner. I'd really like to see you, though. Let me treat you."

Annie thought back to her conversation with Carol that morning. *What do I want? I haven't the faintest idea.* But all of a sudden a dinner with John sounded like a wonderful idea.

"Okay. I'll go."

"Really? What changed your mind? My charming conversational style?" Annie could hear the laughter in his voice.

"I don't think so," Annie said with a smile on her face. "You're good, but not that good. I realized you're right. It's been a tough week and next week doesn't look any better. A dinner with a gentleman sounds great to me."

"Come by the bookstore at six. We can walk to dinner from there."

"Where are we going?"

"I'm not going to tell you. Wear something nicely casual and you'll be fine. It is Santa Cruz after all."

John was right. It was difficult to dress incorrectly in Santa Cruz, pretty much anything went. When they finished the conversation, she hung up the phone.

What the hell had she done?

Chapter 11

John heard the clicking of heels on the wooden floor and he looked up from the information desk computer. Annie was walking toward him, her eyes on his and a flirtatious smile on her bright red lips. His date for the evening was dressed in green slacks and a light brown sweater that accentuated her curves.

The clerk beside him coughed discreetly. John tore his eyes from Annie and remembered the customer in front of him. He looked back down at the computer screen.

"Yes, we have a copy of *Bird by Bird*," he said to the customer. "It's in the reference section. I'll show you where it is." "That's okay," the customer said. She glanced over her shoulder. "It looks like you have other things on your mind." She walked toward the back of the store with a chuckle.

As soon as she left, he turned to the clerk beside him. "Will you be okay by yourself?"

"Sure," the clerk said waving a hand at Annie. "How about you?"

"Me? I'm going to be just fine."

"Have a nice dinner," the clerk said.

"Uh, huh." John walked to Annie, smelling a sweet whiff of Obsession as he drew closer. "Sorry to make you wait."

"Customers are important. There's a lot to look at here." She gestured toward the shelves of new releases.

"Find anything?"

"Not really. According to these books, the world is, if you don't mind the cliché, _going to hell in a hand basket.' Too depressing for me."

"You like happy endings," he said.

"Yes."

"How do those romance writers get all those happy endings?"

She was silent for a moment. "I think that the heroine figures out what she wants and goes after it. She doesn't let anything stand in her way."

"What do you want, Annie?"

She looked up at him, the expression in her eyes loosening the tightness in his jaw. He wanted to kiss her. Right then—in front of God and everyone.

"I don't know," she whispered.

"Hard to go after something if you don't know what it is."

"How about you? What do you want?"

To kiss you. "A house of my own." *And you in it.*

"Along with the right woman and two-point-five kids," Annie said, looking up at him from under her lashes. The heat in her voice dropped right through him, his jeans tightening with his rising desire. This had to stop. He could feel every eye in the store staring at them. "I put aside some books for you," he said and turned toward the information desk. "Guaranteed happy endings." He grinned back at her, breaking the tension between them.

"Great customer service."

"We aim to please, ma'am." He felt as if he was a schoolboy offering a hand-picked daisy to a girl he had a crush on. He handed her two volumes by Sheryl Woods.

"Perfect!" she said, her eyes lighting up even further with happiness. "Can we put them aside and I'll pick them up after dinner?"

"Sure." He scribbled her name on a slip of paper, rubber-banded it to the books, and put them back under the shelf.

# # #

Annie watched John bend over to slip the books behind the information desk, her hands itching to caress his hard back. Her mind had taken a leave of absence when he asked her what she wanted. At that moment, the only thing she'd wanted to do was kiss him.

But then what? Would he be put off because she'd gone after what she wanted? Or would he immediately try to get her into bed with him?

That wouldn't be too bad, would it? The thought made her smile. She shook her head to clear the image of his naked body. *Down, girl.*

He gestured for her to lead the way to the Pacific Avenue exit. Unlike with Mark, there was no proprietary hand at her back. She was surprised to find she was disappointed.

The weather was warmer than the East Coast had been and the sidewalks hummed with people emerging from the rain-soaked winter. Twinkling lights in the sycamore and cherry street trees provided a stage background for a violinist bowing "Nessun dorma" from *Turandot*. It was good to be home.

They quickly reached Jade Alley and the bistro that bore its name. The two-story façade was covered in floral murals, *trompe l'oeil* windows and a small, gated area that held tables and chairs for warm night dining. California may not have Revolutionary history, but it had style.

"In or out?" John asked. "In, I think." At John's nod, Annie started up the stairs, feeling his gaze on her back as he followed her. She hated having anyone follow her upstairs exposing the most vulnerable part of her anatomy. *I hope my butt looks okay in these slacks.*

She waited for John at the top of the stairs, gazing at the small crowded restaurant. While the tables were the same dark pine as the restaurant Mark had taken her to, the atmosphere wasn't as pretentious. Light streamed in from the windows, reflecting off the mirrored glass behind the bar. The unique smell of roasted garlic, pungent vegetables, and the seared meat of a California grill wafted from the kitchen area at the back of the restaurant.

The maître d' sat them at one of the back tables and presented them with bound menus and a wine list. He was followed by a waiter who took their drink orders—a chardonnay for her and a Pinot noir for him, both locally made. Once the bustle stopped, Annie leaned back and opened her menu, gazing up at the man sitting across from her. He was staring at her. She quickly looked back at the menu, feeling the slow heat of embarrassment creep up her neck.

After the waiter brought their wine, she was forced to abandon the safety of the menu. Unlike Mark, who had kept up a steady monologue, John allowed silence to weave into the threads of conversation. When the small talk ran out, he was quiet. He simply smiled.

"What are you smiling at?" she asked.

"You."

"Why?"

"You're really pretty. Fresh and wholesome, not like those skinny girls in dark clothes with the hardware in their faces who come into the store."

"Yep, Midwest corn-fed. Skinny was never part of my life."

"C'mon Annie, don't put yourself down. I didn't mean it that way. I thought women liked to be told they're attractive."

The last guy who told me I was attractive attacked me.

"Thanks." Should she tell him? It would probably put an end to the evening. He'd think she was the same as that woman in Montana who dumped him. The evening would be ruined.

But that wasn't being honest. Bad news to start a relationship without honesty.

"What is it?" John asked.

"Nothing."

"Hmmm."

She had to be honest. "When I was in New Jersey I went out with a guy. I didn't mean to go out with him. All of a sudden it happened." Was that really true? She couldn't seem to stop talking. "Maybe I did mean to go out with him. I dunno. I'm moving there. I guess I thought, why not."

She looked at him. His face was closed and the smile was gone.

"Anyway, I couldn't wait to get away from him," she continued. What was it her mother always said? *In for a penny, in for a pound.* "Mark, his name was Mark, was obnoxious. And then he tried to kiss me when we were walking back to the hotel."

There. She'd told him. So much for a nice evening out. Maybe she should end it now, before they got dinner. He wasn't going to want to be with her after this and she didn't want to sit through another bad dinner date.

"What did you do?" "I pushed him away." Pushed sounded much more ladylike than the actual shove she'd given Mark.

"Oh."

The silence lengthened, interrupted by the waiter who came to take their orders. Annie asked for the perfect spring meal—asparagus, new potatoes, and lamb chops—although she wasn't sure she'd be able to eat if John continued to glare at her. The waiter left after taking John's order of pepper steak and twice-cooked potatoes. Annie shifted uncomfortably in the lengthening silence.

"That was fast," John finally said.

"What?"

"Getting involved with someone in New Jersey." *I knew it. I shouldn't have said anything.*

"Look. I'm not involved. I never want to see the creep again. It was dinner—not a relationship."

"And I suppose this is just dinner, too," John said.

"Yes." Annie saw the hurt flicker across his face, before the mask settled back over his features. "Oh, God. That didn't come out the way I meant it."

"But you did say it."

"John, I really didn't mean it the way it came out. Perhaps I should leave now before I say anything else stupid. The dinner in New Jersey didn't mean a thing, but I don't see why you should believe me. I thought we could be friends, but I guess not. I don't want to have a miserable dinner. I'm sure it's not too late to cancel the dinner order." She picked up her purse and stood.

"Sit down."

Surprised by his commanding tone, she sat.

"I don't want you to leave," he said. "I overstepped my bounds. Forgive me?"

"Uh, sure."

He looked at his hands. "I guess I was jealous. Not a particularly attractive trait. Jessica used to complain about it all the time. I really do mean the apology."

"Are you still in love with her?" she asked, feeling the lump in her throat.

"In a way, yes. I'm in love with the memory of her and our life together. But my heart is big, Annie. There's room for someone else."

Someone like me? Annie shook the thought from her head.

"What about Fred?" John asked. "Do you still love him?"

"No," she said sharply.

John raised his eyebrows. "That's pretty emphatic. What

haven't you told me? Did he hit you?"

Annie looked down at her wine glass, feeling shame creep into her heart. May as well get it all into the open now. That way, they could start fresh.

Almost all of it. There were some things she wouldn't tell anyone.

"Only once," she whispered. She could see his hand tighten on the stem of his wine glass.

"Is that when you left?"

She shook her head, her memories deepening her shame.

"Fred made promises. He said he'd never hit me again and he didn't. Whenever we started to fight after that, he'd leave, no matter how drunk he was."

"So nothing ever got resolved. What made you finally leave?"

Annie took a deep breath. "He came home drunk one too many times. I was already in bed when he fell in, gave me a boozy kiss, rolled over, and began to snore. I lay there for a while, wondering why I was still there. I finally understood I was waiting for a change that wasn't going to happen. I'd moved on and he'd climbed further into the bottle. While he was asleep, I packed up David, left him a note, and moved to Elizabeth's."

The waiter brought their meals and Annie changed the subject, telling John about the musician she'd seen in Princeton. He must have sensed her need for a break because he picked up her thread, telling her about musicians he'd seen. They discovered that they were both avid collectors of CDs by obscure singer-songwriters. Annie had picked up her collection while traveling, John when performers came to Missoula.

"I really like music with roots and stories behind the music," she said. "Some of the songs have been growing and changing for years. And some of it is pretty close to what the original American settlers heard."

"The diversity is fascinating," he added. "It seems to me that different parts of the country play slightly different folk music. The Rocky Mountain music has a stronger pull from blue-grass while the Boston area musicians tend to be more political, always singing about issues of the day, protesting one thing or another."

"I hadn't looked at it that way, but I suppose you're right."

The easy conversation continued over coffee and a velvety flourless chocolate torte that they shared. Some of the tension that Annie had felt since returning from the East Coast began to leave her; she could feel the balled up muscles between her shoulder blades begin to release.

They were finishing up the last bit of dessert when John asked, "Do you think you'll go?"

"I wish I had an answer. Two days ago, I was sure I was going; now it's not so clear." It seemed natural to talk to John about the confusion in her mind, uncertainty that had been churning since her conversation with Carol.

"I've been working since I was sixteen," she said. "Sometimes I was working three jobs at once. It got me out of the house and didn't allow me a chance to think. I've always used work that way. I'd go until I was exhausted, sleep, and do it again the next day. Once I had David, I could add his activities to my list of things to do." She gave him a half-smile. "Not a good way to live, but it's provided for David and me and I've managed to get him to all his activities—mostly on time. I'm not sure what I'd do if I wasn't busy all the time. And there's the money and health insurance. I need it if David gets sick." She nodded to herself, convinced once more of the wisdom of staying with JCN. "I need to keep my job."

"What about another company?"

Annie shook her head. "Companies in the valley are keeping the young engineer types and letting managers, planners like me, and older, more expensive workers go. They'll keep a few key senior engineers of course, but the rest is management by accountant. It's frustrating. Things roll along smoothly with everyone in place and then the economy dips or the stock price falls and they go into secret meetings to figure out how many people they need to lay off to satisfy Wall Street. People are let go, morale dips, and everyone left behind works like a dog to make up for the talent they've laid off in the name of profit."

She took a sip of her decaf coffee before she continued. "Eventually, everything starts falling apart. So they start hiring former workers as contractors, paying them more than they did when they were on salary. They still save money because they don't need to pay benefits anymore. When some economic guru says the downturn's over, hiring begins. Everything's good until the next time Wall Street earnings fall."

John grinned at her. "Quite a soapbox you've got there."

Annie laughed. "Yep."

"Let's get out of here," he said. "How about a walk around the block?"

She looked at her watch. She had about a half hour before she needed to be home for

David. "Sounds good."

After they left the restaurant, he reached for her hand, his eyes steadily on her face as he asked silent permission. She slipped her hand in his in answer.

Chapter 12

John's thoughts were spinning as he and Annie walked toward the bookstore. The murmurs of other strollers and chirps of returning spring birds provided the background score. Flowering trees gave the air the vague scent of perfume that smelled like something his mother might have worn.

John wrestled with his feelings. He wanted to make love to Annie. He'd known it the moment she'd slipped her hand in his, her skin soft against his roughened palm. Her touch had sent a charge up his arm, infusing his body with white heat. What would her lips taste like? How would it be to trail his mouth down her neck, nibbling his way to her breast?

But now wasn't the time. Would it ever be? His mind turned over the story of her "date" in New Jersey. He'd smoothed the moment over, but it was still churning in his gut. He needed to stop thinking about it.

"How's David's shoplifting charge going?" he asked. "His court date is next week, isn't it?"

"Yes," Annie said. She stepped over the bump in the sidewalk where a tree root was winning the battle against man's need to pave everything over. "The attorney said he'll probably get probation. I asked him about taking him to New Jersey with me, and he said there'd be paperwork, but it shouldn't be a problem."

"That must be a relief."

They were silent as they came around the corner by a large Greek Orthodox church. John could see the glow of streetlights from Pacific Avenue and hear the thrum of a Friday night in downtown Santa Cruz. The pulsing urban beat brought back the urge to kiss her and taste the sweetness of her mouth.

He stopped near an alley, a dim spot the streetlights didn't quite reach, looked down at Annie and saw the same desire he felt in her eyes. Lowering his mouth, he tasted her lips, the sweet acidity of chardonnay still lingering on them.

Annie's mouth softened against his. He pressed his lips more firmly, pulling her closer, feeling the lines of her body against his. She slid her arms around his waist, drawing closer to him, her breasts against his chest. The heat built in his groin and a moan escaped his throat as he explored her lips with the tip of his tongue, requesting entry. Annie parted her lips in surrender, but he was the one captured by her sweet aroma. He was lost in her, the heartbeat of desire throbbing in his ears.

He let himself delve further into her mouth, the night sounds of the California coastal town receding. His concentration was only on the woman in his arms and the feel of her body against his. He could feel his arousal pressed against her as he pulled her close, but for the moment all he wanted to do was sate himself with her mouth. He wanted to explore every inch of her with his tongue, slowly take her when she was ready and not a moment sooner. Annie was a woman who needed tenderness, a gentle awakening to what love could really be, not what her ex had passed out in its name. Nothing like what that bastard in New Jersey had tried to take.

John lifted his mouth from the sweet depths. His movement startled a morning dove from the sidewalk, its frenetic flapping carrying it to the safety of a nearby telephone wire.

He looked intently at the woman in his arms. She could make him whole again—he knew it. "Annie, stay here. Give us a chance. All I want is some time. I haven't felt this way since Jessica died— I never thought I'd feel like this again. I don't think anyone's ever treated you right, certainly not Fred. Let me show you what you've missed."

Her eyes looked up into his with longing, but then they clouded over with uncertainty. What was stopping her? Was there more to the story in New Jersey than she was letting on? He had to know. He stepped back from their embrace. "What really happened with you and that guy in New Jersey?"

"I told you. Nothing happened with the guy in New Jersey." Her words were sharp and defensive. Should he believe her? A whisper of jealously seeped into his mind. He needed the truth. "Why did you go out with him? Couldn't you wait until you actually moved before you went out with someone?" His voice sounded bitter, even to his own ears.

"I told you. He asked and I automatically said yes." She paused, as if she'd heard something in her words she'd never heard before. She shrugged. "He seemed like a nice enough guy and a perfect gentleman, maybe a little self-centered, but he had impeccable manners. That is, right up until the point he pushed me against the wall and tried to kiss me."

"What did you do?"

"Like I said," she was beginning to sound impatient with him, "I pushed him away. Well, actually, I shoved him and ran to my hotel. He followed me in, but the hotel clerk made him leave." She took a deep breath. "It was pretty scary, actually."

He immediately felt ashamed. It had been pretty horrible situation and he was making it worse. He held out his hand. "I'm sorry. Men can be idiots."

She stared at his hand suspiciously. Then her lips twitched with a smile and she took his hand. "True," she said.

He guided her back into his arms, meeting her resistance with caresses. "I'll try not to be an idiot too often," he whispered into her silken hair.

Her reply was muffled because her face was against his shirt.

She leaned into him, as if she couldn't get close enough. The scent of lavender and mint drifted up from her golden mane.

He reached under her chin, tilted her face up, and lowered his lips to hers. She returned the kiss with passion and pressed further against him with desire. His hands roamed her back, caressing her curves. He wanted to slip his hands under the sweater she wore and feel her skin. She moaned and reached her arms around his waist again.

The soft murmur of voices entered his consciousness. Glancing up, he saw movement on the next block. For a moment, he thought it was only the glare of the streetlight against the plate glass window, but then he saw the group of kids walking toward them. Reluctantly, he pulled away.

"People?" she asked.

"Yes. They probably wouldn't recognize us in the dark, but I've got your reputation to think about."

"It's your reputation you should worry about. For a big city, Santa Cruz is a very small town. You don't want every woman thinking you're easy."

John laughed. "I don't want every woman. I want you. Stay here, Annie. Stay and take a chance on us. We can make it work."

For a moment, he thought she'd agree. Her eyes were shiny with hope and desire. "I'll get the job done quickly," she said. "I'll come back once a month until I can come back for good. Can you take a chance on me?"

Her earnest face looked up at him. She was different from Deborah ... but things happened. He didn't want a repeat of the pain he'd had with Deborah when she'd taken up with the professor in Bozeman. He couldn't take that chance. Reluctantly, he shook his head. "I don't think it will work for me. Maybe I'm not grown up enough or maybe there's too much water under that particular bridge. I'm afraid I'd make your life miserable with my jealousy and fear. You don't deserve that."

He watched her face shut down and the hope go out of her eyes. His heart saddened for both of them.

"Shall we go back?" he asked. She nodded and started walking down the street, John striding beside her. This time he didn't reach for her hand.

When they got to the corner by the bookstore, she stopped. "I'll walk to the garage myself."

"I don't mind."

"It's better this way. Thanks for a lovely evening, John." Annie stood on her tiptoes and kissed his cheek. Turning, she walked down the street, head held high, her rocking hips keeping in time with the click of her heels.

He was a complete idiot.

# # #

"Just get me the damn report," John snapped.

"My, aren't we the pleasant one today," Sunshine said. "Must have been a terrific date last night." John glared at her and she scampered out of his office. "Yes, sir. One report coming on up."

John slammed his hand on the desk. He wished he had a pencil to throw; it would have been much more satisfying. Cupping his hands over his eyes, he tried to concentrate.

Dammit! He couldn't get her out of his mind. Why was she so hell-bent on moving? Why couldn't she take the chance?

But then, why should she? They'd only known each other a few weeks. It was nothing to place a lifetime on. But he knew in his gut, just the way he'd known with Jessica. Annie would bring him joy. They'd both had to deal with the curve balls that life could throw and had hopefully gained some wisdom from the experience.

A knock on the doorjamb alerted him to Sunshine's presence before she tossed the file on his desk.

"I'm sorry," John said to her retreating back.

She paused and looked over her shoulder. "Want to talk?"

He shook his head. Growing up male in Montana didn't lead to sharing.

John glanced at the sales report. The extra effort they were putting into e-mail marketing was paying off. Phone sales were up. Good. Maybe his little independent bookstore could stay in business in spite of the Amazon juggernaut.

Looking around the office for something else to do, John came up empty. He'd have to go down to the floor, or take the rest of the day off. He glanced toward the front of the store. Sun streamed through the plate glass window. He stood up and headed out of the office. His horse could use a ride in the Forest of Nisene Marks. So could he.

# # #

Slam! Punch! The sigh of escaping air.

Annie grabbed the dough from the bowl and tossed it on the counter. Damn him! Damn that kiss! Damn that professor in Montana!

"Finally find a good one," she muttered. "And I have to move away. He has to stay here. Of course. That's the way my life always works."

Whack. The bread dough landed halfway off the counter. Pulling it back from the edge, Annie settled into the rhythm of kneading. Push. Fold. Push. Fold.

My life is full of problems. Problems caused by other people.

Okay, maybe stabbing Conrad in the foot wasn't the smartest idea, but she was good at her job and that should be enough. She hated corporate politics. It was like a bunch of boys playing King of the Mountain. She wished she could leave it all behind.

Annie's hands stopped kneading. Could she? Maybe she *could* find some temporary work. Job agencies were always looking for good project managers. If she didn't have to worry about corporate politics, she could leave at the end of the day. It might leave her time to resurrect her singing career.

Another voice from the chorus chimed in. This one sounded suspiciously like her mother. *And lose your security? What would you do? Sing? That's not a vocation—that's an avocation. You can't make money at it. It took you long enough to land a real job. You wouldn't do well living in a car. And what about David?*

David.

Annie sighed and went back to kneading. Time to put that nonsense out of her head. She'd have to slog on through. Her mother's voice was right. She couldn't depend on singing for a livelihood.

She couldn't depend on a man for one, either.

# # #

Monday morning, Annie went to Silicon Valley for an outplacement meeting. As she drove up the mountain, Annie was captivated by the long fingers of ocean fog caressing the valleys. From the summit, the mountaintops looked like islands in a frothy soup. Spring had arrived on the coast—yet, not to her life.

Her foot automatically came off the gas as the taillights braked in front of her. Maybe the morning commute in New Jersey would be easier.

Currents of melody ran under words that flowed into her mind. Annie grabbed for the pad of paper that sat between the seats, and scribbled as the traffic stalled in front of her.

Summer changes, seasons befall
Water hewn mountains, life hewn souls.

When the traffic began flowing again, her muse departed, but the brief spark of creativity had given her soul a lift.

She was late when she got to the building for her required class. Mandatory classes to teach you how to lose your job. Great. Maybe the e-mail about the new job would come from Jim this week. Waiting to hear from other people about her life was getting old.

Hours later, she dug out the pad she'd brought from the car and surreptitiously put it in her lap. No longer able to feign interest in the instructor or the topic, she began to mull over the words she'd written.

One of the strangest aspects of her move to California all those years ago was the difference in seasons. Contrary to popular wisdom, there were seasons in the western state; they were just more subtle than those in Michigan. Small changes marked California seasons. It was the big changes, like nature's earthquakes and forest fires that forced major rebirth in her adopted state.

Idly, she tapped her pen on the pad, checking out the instructor to make sure her vacant expression hadn't been noticed. Two more lines emerged:

Fires roar, redwoods fall
My soul will change again.

Her words stared back at her. When she'd been faced with the reality of taking care of David and Fred's lack of responsibility, she'd upended her life to do what had to be done. After the divorce, she'd felt as if she was stepping off a high wire into the unknown. JCN had been good to her financially. Her bosses had understood when she'd stayed home for David's illness or left early for a soccer game. But now the corporation had turned its back on her. She was a cog in the machine, replaceable. Maybe it was time to try something different.

People in the room stirred and Annie glanced at her watch. Lunch break. Only a few more hours and she could escape to the coast.

But, she told herself, she should really be paying attention to this lecture. If she didn't go to New Jersey, she needed to know her options.

Chapter 13

On Wednesday, the day of David's court appearance, Annie knocked on his door early. He didn't give her any problems about getting up, but he looked pale and red-eyed. When he got to the breakfast table, she saw that he'd made an effort to look neat, avoiding the slouching pants and oversized sweatshirt that had become part of his dress since he started hanging out with Larry and his crowd of losers. One struggle avoided.

They cleared the coastal fog as soon as they drove onto Highway 1 to go north, only to sit in early morning commuter traffic until they reached Santa Cruz. Annie turned the NPR station up loudly to cover the sound of silence in the car. They took the mountain road toward Felton, leaving the clog of cars behind. The crisp blue sky was pierced by the majestic redwoods that strode up the road beside them.

Although they pulled into the juvenile hall parking lot fifteen minutes before they were due to be there, it was already crowded. Annie dropped David off at the door to sign in while she cruised for a parking space.

She couldn't find a space in the tiny lot. Frustrated, she squeezed her car into a spot that could have been legitimate, or could have been a walkway. She no longer cared. If she got a parking ticket, so be it. Her son was inside and he needed her. She started the climb up the short hill between the parking lot and the building.

She was out of breath when she made it to the waiting room. David was sitting over to the far left, staring at the novel in his hand. She walked over and sat down on the metal chair next to him.

"I signed in," he whispered when she got settled. Then he went back to staring at his book.

Annie took out her own book and began to read the same sentence over and over. Nothing made sense. She glanced at David. Since he never turned a page, Annie was sure he wasn't having any better luck reading than she was.

She gave up and scanned the packed room. Whole families were there to stand up for their wayward child. Neatly dressed teens chatted nervously with each other, hands moving in a jerky language of their own. Extended Latino families, from clear-eyed grandmothers to wide-eyed toddlers took up corners of the room. Annie caught the eye of another single mother dressed in a business casual outfit. They smiled wanly at each other before Annie shifted her eyes away.

It was an audience that waited for an opening. Men and women in dark suits entered the lobby, rolling briefcases overstuffed with papers and looking for the person they needed to guide through their walk-on role.

One of the suits called out David's name. David barely raised his hand in response. Annie started to stand, but the man waved her down. He sat down on the other side of David and leaned across him to introduce himself.

"I'm Bill Thorton," he said, looking through the papers in his folder. "I've spoken to you and your son a few times on the phone. It seems pretty simple. David'll probably get probation and community service. Not much to worry about. They'll call us shortly. Just hang tight and it will all be over soon. Any questions?"

Annie had a thousand questions. What was going to happen? How long would they have to be here? Was Bill Thorton any good? It didn't feel like the right time to ask.

Mimicking the behavior of the parents around her, she shook her head at the already standing attorney. Annie and David went back to staring at their books.

After another hour of pretense, David's name was called. Annie threw her purse in the gray tub provided by the security guard and walked through the metal detector. David's pockets were full of change and paperclips. He beeped as he went through the detector and had to remove his belt. Once more and his watch went into the gray tub. The other waiting families watched the small drama out of boredom, a few of the kids wearing a grin that said, "Newbie."

Bill Thorton was waiting on the other side of the metal detector. He escorted them into a small room on the side of the hallway. Maroon-painted cement walls were highly overrated as an architectural flourish.

"Look," the attorney said, "here's the deal. You plead guilty and the DA has agreed to give you six months' probation and two months' community service. I suggest that you take it. They have videotapes of you doing the crime and the store is intent on prosecuting. They've been hit by too many shoplifters lately and they aren't happy."

David's mouth turned down. "What's community service?" he asked.

"Picking up litter around town, usually. It's not hard and it's usually on Saturday mornings."

"Can't do it," David said.

"What do you mean?" the lawyer asked.

"Got soccer. I can't let my team down," David said, his hands clenching.

The lawyer looked David in the eye. "Listen, son," he said. "I know you don't think this is much, but I assure you that it is. You aren't going to do your team much good if you are in juvenile hall.

So I suggest you take the plea, miss a few games and do yourself a favor."

"David," Annie said. "Do what he says."

"That's it. I'm just supposed to do what everyone says. Go to New Jersey. Miss my games. Never think on my own."

"Well," the lawyer pointed out. "Your best thinking got you where you are right now."

David stopped talking. "Okay," he said. "I'll do the community service." Then he turned to his mother, "But I'm not going to New Jersey."

Annie opened her mouth to reply, but the lawyer jumped in. "Good," he said as he slammed his briefcase closed. "Let's go to court."

Thorton led the way down the hallway and put his fingers to his lips to indicate silence before he quietly opened the heavy wooden door to the court. He gestured Annie and David to the seats behind the railing before going through the gate to the left hand side of the courtroom. He added his stack of papers to those already on the long table and sat down next to a well-dressed woman. Annie's mind took in all the details without really absorbing them.

The table to the right was likewise piled with papers where two men thumbed through the stacks. The judge whispered to the clerk while the lawyers scanned papers and spoke into each other's ears. To one side were several kids in orange jumpsuits. Occasionally, a lawyer went and had a short, but urgent conversation with one of them.

Seemingly at random, the judge thumped his gavel, checked his list and called a name.

Another half hour went by before he called David's. Bill Thorton stood and motioned

David through the gate. Annie started to rise, but the lawyer shook his head. Her son was on his own with this. One of the men from the right-hand table stood up as well.

"How do you plead?" the judge asked after reading the charges out loud.

"Uh, guilty," David replied.

"We've reached an agreement with the district attorney for two months' community service and six months' probation, Your Honor," Bill said.

"Is the District Attorney in agreement with this?"

"Yes, Your Honor," said a voice from the other table.

"The court also imposes a three hundred dollar restitution to be paid before the probation is released," the judge added. "Do you understand that you are entitled to a trial and are waiving that right?" the judge asked David.

"I do," David said when his lawyer nudged him.

The judge droned on and on about David's rights and what he was giving up. It was so formal. So real. And three hundred dollars? Another bill for Annie to pay. David didn't have a job and his father wasn't going to help. As for getting David to community service, that would be another one of her responsibilities while she planned for the move to New Jersey with her rebellious child.

Maybe if she'd raised David better, if she hadn't gotten divorced, if her ex wasn't a drunk, this wouldn't have happened. If the stupid corporation hadn't made her transfer to New Jersey, this wouldn't have happened. Her life coach was wrong. There was nothing she could do to change her life. Everyone around her needed to change first. A new voice emerged from her chorus. *Really? Is that true?*

She was taken aback by the thought. Was she enabling David, just as she'd enabled Fred? What was her responsibility in this mess? Was she so busy taking care of everyone else that she wasn't taking care of herself? Or worse yet, not letting them stand on their own two feet?

She looked at her son thoughtfully. It was time for him to take responsibility for his actions. He'd have to figure out a way to pay the three hundred dollars by himself.

# # #

John looked around his rental house kitchen while his morning eggs sizzled on one of the two burners that actually worked. Décor from the 1950s, tired linoleum, and outdated appliances killed the spirit of his inner chef. He hadn't made an omelet in months. The house was a temporary solution he reminded himself, only until he figured out where to set up permanent housekeeping.

He quickly finished up breakfast and dumped his plates in the sink to soak. Add a lack of a dishwasher to his list of woes. He had to find a new place to live.

It certainly wasn't going to be the west side of Santa Cruz, he thought as he left the house. The west side was overrun with college students, nice enough when they came into the store, but too many of them sported the dreadlocks and facial hardware of the counter culture.

John sighed and thought of what Sunshine had said the day before. His manager was right; he was in a mood. Sunshine. People in Montana didn't name their kids Sunshine.

Yep, definitely grumpy, he thought as he drove toward downtown, ignoring the crystal clear day and rampant budding of trees, shrubs, and flowers. He threaded through the back streets toward the parking garage, feeling his mood sink further. *Whatever prompted him to move to this damn town anyway?*

Abruptly, he zoomed past the garage entrance and headed back to Highway 1. Twenty minutes later he pulled into the Soquel ranch where he boarded Starfire. He gave a brief nod to the woman who owned the place as she headed toward her kitchen garden. Sweet nickers called to him from the barn and he smiled when he saw the chestnut quarter horse he'd owned for five years.

Practiced habits of saddling and bridling soothed him. The smell of leather and horse recalled the wooded pines of the Rockies and his spread by the Bitterroot. Maybe moving to California hadn't been the right choice. Had he come because he wanted to own his own bookstore? Or was he running away from painful memories? Starfire rubbed him with her head, as if sensing his need for comfort.

As he rode toward Soquel Creek, John replayed the scene with Annie. He'd wanted to build a relationship with her. Surely there was some job around here for whatever it was she did. She'd tried explaining it to him, but anything to do with computers and the world "over the hill" in Silicon Valley held no interest. As far as he was concerned, the computer and the Internet were useful tools, but the high-tech companies surrounding it created a world of smoke and mirrors. People were forgetting how to have real conversations and solve real problems because they were lost in their "Second Life" on the computer.

Starfire's hooves gently clopped in the riparian loam. The sound reminded him of the hours he'd spent with his wife riding near the river before she'd become ill. He smiled at the memories, good memories now, not bearing the searing pain they had after her death. He'd always miss her, but was ready to move on. Too bad the woman he was ready to move on with was moving to New Jersey.

His heart ached when he thought about the conversation they'd shared. It would be so easy to fall in love with her.

Don't be an idiot, Johnson. You've already fallen.

He pushed Annie out of his mind and rode unthinking, gazing

at the fast-moving creek and rapid unfolding of spring growth, the rhythmic motion of the horse lulling him into a deep peace, the kind that went to the bottom of his soul. Maybe next time he should bring a fishing pole. He missed his favorite fly-fishing hole near Hamilton, but there were enough creeks and rivers nearby to satisfy the craving. Maybe he'd try ocean fishing, although the crash of waves didn't bring him the same peace as the rushing water of a mountain stream.

He went back to contemplating his love life. Maybe he'd tried to rush things too fast with Deborah because he was still grieving for Jessica. Perhaps he'd pushed Deborah too hard and she'd made a commitment she'd never intended to make.

He let the thought play out in his head as he turned Starfire around. Was he making the same mistake with Annie? Was he asking too much of someone he just met? He didn't know her life; didn't know what drove her; didn't have a kid to raise—a kid in trouble.

He'd take a different tactic. He'd be Annie's friend—no demands. She needed his support, not more grief. Maybe she'd see the value of staying in Santa Cruz. How much time did he have? He thought back to their conversations. There were only a few weeks to convince her that taking a chance with him was going to be worth it.

The first thing he did when he got to the office later that morning was pick up the phone to call Annie.

# # #

After all the lawyers and the judge stopped talking, David came back through the courtroom gate with his lawyer and tapped Annie on the shoulder. "Let's go," he said.

She followed Thorton and her son down the hall and into the

waiting room.

"Once they process the paperwork, she'll call you over," Thorton said, pointing to a harried-looking woman in a window-shrouded cubical in the corner of the waiting room.

"There'll be instructions in the papers about community service and paying your fine. You have six months to do it, but it's better to do it soon. And," he continued as he turned to Annie, "I suggest that you don't pay it. Make him earn it."

She nodded.

Turning back to David he said, "Your probation officer will contact you within a week. Keep in touch with him. Good luck."

Thorton stuck out his hand and David stared at it for a moment before shaking it. The lawyer shook Annie's hand, turned on his heel, and went back through the metal detector to the courtroom.

It was over—at least for now.

The trip back to town was silent. Annie dropped David and his backpack off at the high school and drove home. She was exhausted and her head was throbbing.

Automatically, she looked at the answering machine. The light was blinking. She hit the play button.

"I know you had David's court appointment today and was wondering how you were doing," John's voice began. "It's got to be tough and I thought you might need a friend. If you feel up to coming down to the bookstore this today, I'll buy you a cup of coffee. I'd stop by, but I don't want to intrude." There was a pause and then the message continued. "I know you don't want a relationship and I'm okay with that. I thought you could use a friend, though."

She looked suspiciously at the answering machine. It was nice to have someone care, but she wasn't quite sure about the "friend" part. The kiss they'd shared had definitely not been on the friend level.

She made a cup of tea and took it and her cordless phone outside to enjoy the perfect coastal day, a counterpoint to the surrealism of juvenile hall. The sun's hot rays were buffered by the occasional breezes caressing her arms. She stared at the fountain in her garden sanctuary. Around her, irises and lilies bloomed and the climbing rose in the corner was dusted with peach-colored blossoms. The riotous noise of the morning receded from her head, and the fountain's music soothed her mind.

She glanced at her watch. Carol would be calling soon. Annie was looking forward to talking about the day's events and her growing realization that there might be some changes she could make. The phone rang and she picked it up.

"How did it go?" Carol asked.

"It was okay, I guess."

"Really?"

Annie could tell she didn't believe her. Of course, she didn't believe herself, either. "No, not really. It was pretty awful."

"Do you always pretend things are better than they are?"

"That's a good question."

Carol's response was the silence Annie was coming to expect from the coach.

"I suppose I do. I mean, why tell people how awful things are? They don't really want to know, anyway."

"What about people who are close to you—your friends?"

"They're tired of hearing me whine."

"Is that what you call it? Whining?"

"Well, yeah. That's what my dad always said. 'Quit whining, pull up your big girl panties and get on with it.'" Annie imitated her father's scornful voice.

"How did that make you feel?"

Annie reflected on the question. How did it make her feel? "I don't know."

"Can you remember a time when he said that to you?"

Annie thought back to her childhood. "I had a little kitten. She was black with little white feet. I called her Mittens. Dumb name, I know. Anyway ..." Her voice became matter-of-fact. "I didn't keep her in the house. I let her out and she got run over. My dad was really nice about it—he dug a grave for her and everything. Then it was like it had never happened. I couldn't talk about it. I remember I said something about missing Mittens and he yelled at me, told me to quit whining and the rest of it. I was scared. I never talked about Mittens again. Until now." Annie was surprised to find tears running down her cheeks.

"When did that conversation happen?"

"The day after Mittens was killed."

"Oh, Annie." The coach's voice was soft. "When your father told you that, how did it make you feel?"

"Really bad." Annie shrank into her chair. "I was little at the time, but I remember feeling even smaller. I wanted to hide. To become invisible."

"And so you did. You became invisible by never telling anyone how you really feel."

Annie pondered the insight. "I guess you're right." She sat there in silence. Feeling small and vulnerable, bereft of the shield of indifference she always put up. But what good was feeling anything going to do for her? She had a decision to make.

"But what's the point? It's done. I was a little kid. My dad was teaching me that stuff happens in life and I have to get over it."

"Do you really think one day is enough time for a little girl to get over the loss of her pet?"

"Why not?" The question sounded harsh even to her own ears.

"Annie, is that what you'd tell your son?"

"God, no."

"Then why was it okay for your dad to say that to you?"

"I ... I guess it wasn't." Annie felt her defenses lower again.

Carol let the silence roll on for a little while longer. "I'm willing to bet your dad did that to you often—told you to move on when you really weren't ready. You learned to stuff your feelings about things quickly."

Annie wasn't totally convinced. "How else can you function? I'm only doing what I have to do."

"Are you?"

"Yes." Annie slammed her fist on the table, knocking her tea to the ground.

Carol didn't say anything.

Annie waited for her to speak.

And waited.

After she realized that the coach wasn't going to say anything, she asked, "What is it you think I should be doing?"

"What do you want to do?"

"Do you always answer a question with a question?"

"Often."

"I don't have any choice. I have to move to New Jersey."

Carol chuckled. "I agree that you don't *see* any other choice, not that there isn't one. If you could change anything in your life, Annie, what would it be?"

"That's easy. I wouldn't be laid off. I wouldn't have to move to New Jersey."

"So you love your job at JCN?"

"Love? No."

"How do you feel about the job?"

"Truthfully?"

"Of course." Annie could almost see the smile on Carol's face.

172

"Truthfully ..." The silence dragged on. Once again Carol waited. "I hate my job," Annie finally said. "I'm tired of technology. It's like a pressure cooker. Over and over you do the same thing. There's no change, except to learn new technology. It was fun once, but now it's horrible ... it's not what I wanted to do at all! If Fred wasn't a drunk, I could have spent more time at home with David. Maybe I ..."

"Maybe what?" Carol prodded.

"Maybe I could have made it as a singer-songwriter." There. It was out. Carol could laugh now, like her parents and Fred had laughed.

But Carol didn't laugh. She didn't say anything either.

"It's too late," Annie said. "I have responsibilities."

"How can you make it 'not too late'?"

"What do you mean? I told you. I have responsibilities."

"Do you like to sing?'

"Yes!"

"Do you sing?"

"In church."

"Anywhere else?"

A few Christmases ago, she'd had a few glasses of wine at Elizabeth's Christmas Eve party. When the rented karaoke machine was dragged out, the liquid courage had enabled her to step up and perform. Everyone had complimented her on her voice.

"Once in a while," she admitted.

"Good. Here's my challenge to you," Carol said. "I want you to sing at least three times a week. I don't care if you do it in your car or in the shower. Will you do that?"

"What good is that going to do?"

"It'll exercise a muscle you've forgotten how to use—doing something you enjoy for no useful reason at all."

"Doesn't make sense to me."

"It will. Give it time."

Annie considered the idea. She didn't see how it would help, but what could she lose by singing three times a week as long as no one was around to hear her? "Okay, I'll do it."

"Since coaches are never satisfied, I have one more request," Carol said with a laugh.

"What is it?"

"Don't sound so suspicious. I want you to get a journal. It can be a plain notebook, nothing fancy. And, before you ask, you can't keep a computer journal. There's a connection between our heart and our pen that can't be duplicated on a computer. Besides, I want you to write first thing in the morning, before you get up and any other time the mood strikes you. Write a list of things that you want. Use it as a tool to unload the chatter in your mind. Then we'll take a look at it for the nuggets of wisdom."

"I'm not sure how wise I am."

"Probably wiser than you think."

Annie shrugged. What the heck? "Sure," she said.

After scheduling another appointment the following Wednesday, Annie said goodbye. She retrieved her empty teacup from the ground. Do something she wanted? Anything she wanted? She thought about John's message. He still wanted to see her. *And I want to see him.*

Chapter 14

When Annie walked into the bookstore three hours later, Sunshine was at the back desk.

"Oh, good. Maybe his mood will improve," the head manager said. "He's upstairs." She gestured toward the bookstore office perched over the bookshop floor, the windows reflecting the glow of the florescent lights.

"Has he been grumpy?"

"Like a bear."

"Oh." Sunshine and Annie grinned at each other.

Annie glanced up to the second floor office windows and discovered John staring at her, a cautious smile touching his lips. He raised a finger in a "just a moment" gesture and mouthed, "I'll be right down." She wandered toward the magazine racks, her attention drawn to a guitar-laden cover. She picked up the latest issue of *American Songwriter* and was immediately absorbed in an article about the latest innovation in guitar strings.

"Hello," John said from behind her. "I'm glad you came."

She shut the magazine quickly and slotted it back on the rack before she turned around.

"It okay," he said as if seeing her thoughts. "People read the magazines without buying them all the time. I've gotten used to it." "I didn't mean to ..." she began as she looked up at him. She could feel her shoulders relax in his accepting presence.

"It's fine," he said, laughing. He reached around to pick up the magazine she'd been reading, his eyebrows rising as he glanced at the title. "An odd title for someone in the tech industry."

She hesitated. "I used to sing occasionally. At coffeehouses," she admitted.

"That's right. I remember now. I want to hear more about it," he said, taking her arm and guiding her to the little café in the front of the bookstore. He still had the magazine in his hand.

Once they had their coffees, decaf for her, regular for him, he asked about her singing. She told him of her coffeehouse gigs and the invitations for house concerts she was starting to get before she quit. He was such a good listener that she told him about the fantasy studio she dreamed of, a room of her own to create her songs and CDs. "Of course, nowadays, I'd probably simply create MP3s and put them online."

"You are a techie."

"Sometimes it helps to be a little of both." A thought struck her. "Maybe I could even set up a studio and record MP3s for other singers."

"That's a great idea! What made you think about singing again?"

"The concert in New Jersey started me down the path." She considered how much she wanted to tell John. Did she really want him aware of her growing uncertainty about moving? She stirred her coffee and decided to keep the answer as succinct as possible.

"I'm working with a life coach," she began. "I don't know if you know what they are."

She gave him a questioning look.

He gestured at the store behind him. "I read a lot." He grinned. "Wasn't it Rhonda Britton who had that show—*Fearless Living* or something?"

"I think so. Anyway, Carol, my life coach, suggested that I sing three times a week. She seems to think it will help me. I don't see the point, but she's the coach." She shrugged.

John leaned back in his chair. "I've told you about the novel

I'm writing," he said.

Annie nodded.

"Every morning I get up and work on it for an hour—before breakfast. It's my meditation. Even if it never gets published, it's something I need to do. There are days the words simply won't come and I feel like giving up. But even if all I do for an hour is stare at a blank page, I do it."

"Why?" she asked softly.

He took a sip of coffee. "I think it's because it's something that's uniquely mine. I'm creating it. The need to create is a primal urge. Not only did our ancestors kill the wooly mammoth, they painted its picture on cave walls. The poorest people in the world create art, music, dance, and theater. They regard it as their birthright. It's only us westerners who think everything has to be done by specialists for profit."

She stared at him. *Maybe I've been looking at this problem all wrong.*

Her face must have reflected her puzzlement because he asked, "What are you thinking?"

"I'm not sure I can put it into words. But I think it's important for me to do a bit more than singing in the shower three times a week."

"I like that," he said with a smile. "And when you're ready, you can do your comeback performance right here."

She laughed. "I think that's a long time away."

"You'd be surprised. Don't sell yourself short." He looked at her intently, his blue eyes searching her own.

She felt tears well and a lump form in her throat. No one had ever believed in her that way before. She stared back at him and felt moisture on her cheek.

He brushed it away with his thumb. "Tears of happiness, I hope."

She nodded.

They sat in comfortable silence and sipped their coffee.

"What happened with David today?" he finally asked.

She summed up the court hearing. "Thanks for listening," she said when she'd finished. "You do it well. I feel better, like someone is sharing the burden, even though it's none of your worry."

"Things that affect you are my concern. I care about you, Annie. I want to be your friend."

"Thanks, I could use one around now." She glanced at her watch.

"Do you have to go?"

"Yes. I need to get home for David." *And I have a lot of thinking to do.*

She got up and he immediately stood with her. "Thanks for coffee," she said.

He picked up the issue of *American Songwriter* from the chair where he'd laid it. "We never did get to discuss this, but I thought you might like it. It's on the house. And don't forget what I said—your comeback performance is right here. Don't accept any other offers."

"I won't." Impulsively, Annie gave him a quick hug. "You're a great guy, John. Thanks for listening." She took the magazine from him and walked out the coffee shop door.

# # #

John picked up the kitchen phone on the third ring.

"I've got a house for you!" Beth Brighton, his realtor, exclaimed. "Do you have time to see it today? It won't be on the market long."

Typical realtor hyperbole, John thought, glancing at the

calendar by the phone. In the current market, houses could take a year or more to sell. Still, his Saturday was clear. A mental review of his "to do" list in the bookstore told him there was nothing urgent that Sunshine couldn't handle. His office manager might have an odd name, but she knew how to manage a bookstore.

"Sure."

"I'll pick you up at 9:30," she said.

"I'll meet you there." He didn't want to be trapped in a car with a realtor trying to sell a house, even if it was a fancy car with warmed leather seats.

Reluctantly, she gave him an address on Old San Jose Road and they agreed to meet at ten.

Driving his Tacoma pickup up the mountain road, John was seduced by the spring growth. Of course, nothing in California ever really stopped growing, even in winter. He thought ruefully about the overgrown grass at his rental. After decades of blizzards, story-high snowdrifts and ice-packed roads of Montana, the central California climate was a relief. Sooner or later, though, he knew he'd miss the seasons' dramatic changes.

John stopped outside the house that matched the description Beth had given him. He'd arrived early so he could view the surroundings without her interference. It's too big, he thought, staring at the forest green Queen Anne style house that dominated the huge expanse of lawn.

Beige roof finials and crestings laced the eaves of the house, leading to a circular tower that dominated the left corner. The house was warm and inviting in a Norman Rockwell kind of way. However, it still required a lot of upkeep, like most Victorian-style houses.

A few well-situated live oaks hinted at the forest tract behind the house. John glimpsed a well-maintained red barn that would be a perfect place for Starfire. He could feel the desire for the house rise in his chest. At that moment, Beth pulled up behind him in her silver gray Mercedes.

He slammed the door harder than he'd planned when he got out. "I can't afford this," he said.

She linked her arm in his and whispered conspiratorially, "It's a steal. That's why you had to see it today. The old lady who owns it has Alzheimer's. Her sons finally found a place for her in a facility that specializes in caring for those patients. But they have to move her quickly and they need the money to do it. Believe me, this place is priced to sell and sell quickly in any market."

John felt a wave of sadness. To be deprived of all memory at the end of life was cruel.

His memories weren't always the best, but they were part of who he was. Eric, one of the owner's sons, met them at the door and began to show them the house.

The architect had been faithful to a modified Queen Anne style inside as well as out. While there were crown moldings and plaster cornices, the living room fireplace had clean lines instead of the ornate mantelpieces common in houses of the period. The carpenter who'd finished the inside of the house had had skill; the rooms were warm with character.

The house turned out to be smaller than it looked from the outside. Built in the 1800s as a farmhouse, it had been added on to and remodeled into the showplace it became. Eric told him that the rabbit's warren of rooms had been changed to spacious accommodations: a gracious living room, dining room, office and three bedrooms. It was still too big for him, but there was plenty of room for guests. Or for a family, John thought as an image of Annie rose in his mind. He quickly pushed the picture away.

When they entered the kitchen, an old woman looked up from her coffee and smiled, her kind face wreathed in a cloud of white hair. She had on a pink housecoat like his mother used to wear when she cooked. "Dan," she said, rising from her chair. "How nice of you to come home early. Would you like some coffee?"

"Dan was my father. He died years ago," Eric whispered.

John smiled graciously. "Thank you, my dear," he said. "But I think I had enough at the office. I'll see you later. There are things I need to take care of in the other rooms."

"I missed you, Dan."

"You too, my dear." Moved by compassion, John leaned down and kissed her gently on the top of her head.

She stared up at him, panic in her eyes. "Who are you?"

"An old friend," John said, thinking fast. "You probably don't remember me. It's been a long time since we've seen each other."

"Oh. That's okay then."

The old woman sat down again and looked at her coffee. A bewildered look passed over her face. Then she shook her head, sighed and picked up the cup.

Eric motioned for them to leave the kitchen. "Thank you," he said to John when they were outside the house. "That was kind."

"My grandmother had Alzheimer's before she died. It was hard to watch her try to hang on to her memories as they drifted by. Your mother seems sweet."

"She is. But don't be fooled. She ruled the house when we were younger."

"Yeah. My mom, too." The men grinned at each other.

The barn and corral out back won him over. It was beautifully built and maintained. The three stalls had fresh straw beds and the tack room had enough hooks and shelves to keep needed equipment stored neatly. Starfire would be very comfortable.

"Thank you," John said as he and Beth took leave of the son. "And thank your mother, as well."

"Sure," Eric said. "I hope you're interested. The house seems to fit you." He waved at them as they walked down the long driveway to their cars.

"What do you think?" Beth said grabbing his arm again. "It's very big." "Maybe you'll meet someone and raise a family," she said, moving a bit closer to him.

John stepped back. He was aware that many of the divorced women in town had their sights set on him, but he still wasn't used to it.

"Maybe. But it's still more than I need or can afford."

"I saw how you lusted after that barn," she said, drawing out the words. "You need it. Aren't you tired of driving over here to see that horse of yours? Wouldn't you like to just walk out the kitchen door to ride?"

"It's still too much."

"I don't think so." She grabbed his arm and quoted a figure that was well within his reach.

"How can they sell it for that price?"

She shrugged. "Bad market. Bad circumstances. It brings the price down every time. And I think you could go even lower."

John thought of the old woman in the kitchen and shook his head. "No, I couldn't."

"Then you're ready to make an offer?"

He took one more look up the hill to the house. "Let's go back to your office."

As he rode down the hill in his truck, he thought about the commitment he was making to California. He'd questioned his decision to move here a few days earlier. Was he buying the house in hopes that it would influence Annie? Maybe he should bring her up here to give him her opinion. Women always liked to give opinions, didn't they? No, that would be too pushy. Take it slow. He'd have to make this decision on his own.

It was a large house for him alone, though. He'd rattle around in it like he'd done in the Missoula house after his wife had died.

But that was the past, he thought as he pulled into the real estate office parking lot in Costanoa. Beth eagerly met him at the door.

"It's the perfect place for you, John."

"Perhaps," he answered.

An hour later, he'd signed the dozen pieces of paper required to make an offer on the house and written a hefty check. He glanced at his watch—noon already—and stood up to leave. Beth walked him to the empty front office.

"You'll love it, John," she whispered and moved close to him. "All you need is someone to share it with." She reached up and put her arms around him and pulled him close. Startled, he didn't resist. Beth stood on her tiptoes and kissed him on the cheek. "There's more where that came from," she whispered in his ear.

"Beth," someone called as the door opened. "I've got the forms for the chamber raffle. Oh. You're busy."

John pulled himself away and turned to see Elizabeth standing by one of the front desks. Damn! He glared at Beth Brighton, pulled his keys from his pocket, and stormed past Elizabeth to his truck. As he got in the front seat, his cell phone rang. He glanced at the number—local area code, but he didn't recognize it. He almost didn't pick it up. Maybe it was trouble at the store. He clicked the connect button.

"Hello?"

"Hi John," a woman said. "It's Deborah. I need your help."

Chapter 15

Annie shivered as the chill from the metal bleacher of the high school soccer stadium leached through her coat and jeans, sinking its icy fingers into her butt. Why did they have to have soccer games on a Saturday evening when the kids had all day to play? Her relatives from Michigan would laugh at her now—a mere fifty-six degrees and she was wrapped in a wool coat and leather gloves with a pair of fleece-lined Uggs on her feet.

Fred always gave her a hard time about her thin blood, but he'd left a message on her voicemail saying he wasn't able to make it. Again. So here she was, shivering alone.

Fred's been missing a lot of Friday and Saturday nights lately. Is his drinking getting worse?

Her misery lessened as she watched her goalie son deflect another goal with a flying leap. She stomped and cheered with the rest of the parents.

In the last few minutes of the game, the opposing team snuck a winning goal past David. *Damn. He would be a bear the rest of the evening.* When she finally got him in the car, he grunted, asked what was for dinner, and descended into silence. Dinnertime, too, was void of conversation as David shoveled food in his mouth and was done in less than five minutes. After a few attempts at talking, Annie gave up. She watched David slouch back down the stairs.

Around eight-thirty, the phone rang.

"Hello?"

"Oh, hi Annie."

"Hi, Fred. David's home from soccer, but I have to warn you.

The other team won by getting a goal past him at the last minute."

"Annie, I need to talk to you."

"Oh. Okay." She closed the dishwasher and walked into the living room.

There was a pause at the other end of the line. "I'm calling to say that I'm sorry."

"For ..." She drew out the word.

"I ... I ... started going to AA. That's why I haven't been able to make it to the games as often. It's been two weeks since I've had a drink. I know that's not long, but I wanted to let you know."

She didn't know what to say. *Congratulations? Too bad you didn't stop years ago?*

"That's good, Fred," was all she could come up with.

"I've already started to understand some things ... Well, I realized them before, but I didn't have the courage to say them."

She was silent. She knew it was a difficult conversation for him, but she didn't know how to help him. And she wasn't sure she wanted to try. Pockets of bitterness still ran deep in her soul.

"I didn't mean to hurt you, Annie," he finally said. "I did love you, but I didn't know how to show it. You were so smart. I felt so stupid. I used to say that you made me feel stupid, but that wasn't true. I did that to myself. You were a good person, Annie. You *are* a good person."

She stared at the wall in front of her. What did it matter now?

"It's okay, hon," Fred continued. "You don't have to say anything. I just needed to say that. It's part of making amends. It's only a small part of what I need to say to you, but it's a beginning."

"Okay." Those few sentences didn't make up for the years of abuse.

"Are you taking the job on the East Coast?" he finally asked.

"I think so."

"I guess that means I'll have to find a bigger place."

"Why?"

"So David can move in with me," he said matter-of-factly.

"David's coming with me."

"You're taking him away from his friends? And from me? Where he's gone to school all his life? I don't think so."

"You can't support him. You can barely support yourself."

The words stung the silence.

"That was a low blow," Fred said.

"It's the truth."

"Maybe it was, but things are changing. They gave me a raise at work and my car was paid off in January. I can afford a two-bedroom place. With child support from you, we can make things work."

"You expect me to pay you child support? Not on your life. David will be fine coming to New Jersey. He'll adjust."

She knew she was being unreasonable. Her son didn't want to move. Neither did she. But to spend years without David, only seeing him once or twice a month? She couldn't even imagine.

"Yeah, like he's adjusted so far just hearing about the possibility. Why do you think he got in trouble?"

She thought she heard David on the stairs. She'd have to be careful with her answer. Then she heard the footsteps descend again. Good. He didn't need to listen to this conversation.

"David's just acting out. He'll be fine."

"Annie, he won't be fine. Not everyone can stick a mask on their face like you can and pretend everything is fine while their guts are being ripped apart inside."

"No, some of them crawl into a bottle like you do."

"Like I did. No more. But, God, you're bitter. I never realized how much." As the silence between them grew, she heard the slam of the garden gate. It must have been left open. A gust of wind could have slammed it into the fence.

"I'd hoped this would go better," he continued. "I'm sorry, Annie. I'm truly sorry for all the hurt I caused. You didn't deserve it. I loved you, but I didn't know what that meant. I hope you can forgive me someday. I really do."

He sounded sincere. Why did he pick this moment, in all of their life together, to become sober?

"Will you think about forgiving me, Annie?"

"Yes, Fred. I'll think about it." She could promise that much. A lump formed in her throat, a lump made up of all the destroyed dreams she'd had about her marriage. *I need to end this conversation. I can't bear it.* "I've got to finish some things up. Do you want to talk to David? Remember, he's in a bad mood because of the game."

Her ex took time before he replied. "I can handle David," Fred finally said. "Put him on."

"Hang on. I'll get him." She started down the stairs, phone still in her hand, feeling awkward about how the call was ending. "Fred? Thanks for letting me know. It was good of you."

"Anytime, darling," he said, the saying a vestige of the charming drunk he'd been. She shivered. After all these years it was hard to know where the man ended and the bottle began. She supposed it would take time to figure that out again—for both of them.

"David!" she called through her son's closed door. There was no answer. "David!" she called again, knocking hard to be heard over the stereo. When there was still no answer, she pushed open the door and gave a quick look around the room. His bedroom window was wide open and her son was nowhere to be seen.

"No ..." she said. Her stomach clenched.

"No? What is it, Annie?" Fred asked.

"David's gone. He must have heard me talking and taken off

out his window."

# # #

John walked into the local wine bar and spotted Deborah at a table in the back by the fireplace. Although her chestnut hair was still rich with color, her face had become more hardened. The playfulness he'd found attractive in Missoula was gone. He sat down, the long red tablecloth getting tangled in his legs. "Hello, Deborah," he said.

"Hi."

A waitress appeared to take their wine orders and, too quickly for John, left them alone. *What am I doing here? And, more important, what does Deborah want?*

"John, I've missed you," she said.

He didn't reply.

"You're not going to make this easy, are you?" she asked.

"Is your boyfriend here with you?" he asked as the waitress brought their glasses of Merlot.

She shook her head. "I'm not with him anymore."

"Oh? What happened?" he asked, swirling his wine.

A tear trickled down her face. "It was horrible. I thought he really loved me. Really, John." She looked up at him from under thick eyelashes. "I never would have hurt you otherwise."

"Uh-huh."

"You've got to believe me. I thought I was just a rebound for you after Jessica died. I thought you'd never care for me the way I wanted you to. When Pat came along I saw a chance for happiness and I grabbed it."

"So what happened?"

She played with her napkin, unfolding and refolding it. He let the silence drag out as he gazed into the fire over her shoulder.

"He went back to his wife."

"He was married? Didn't you know that?" He flipped his gaze back to Deborah. Sometimes he didn't understand the perfidy of his own gender. Or women, for that matter. Deborah had made a commitment to him and rather than be honest and talk to him about changing her mind, she'd gone to bed with someone behind his back. Seems like her "boyfriend" had had the same moral standards.

"They were separated. He said that they were getting divorced. He told me that he'd never met anyone like me; that I supported his dreams and his wife only nagged at him. He said with me by his side he could get out of the state university system and into a real school like Harvard or Stanford."

"He lied," John said bluntly.

She nodded, the single tear turned into a flood.

John felt his resolve soften. What she'd done to him was wrong, but she'd paid heavily for it. He put his hand over hers and looked straight into her eyes.

"I'm sorry for what's happened to you, Deb. I truly am. I know how it feels."

"Oh, John. I know. Can you possibly forgive me?"

He hesitated. Forgiving wasn't forgetting. You could forgive a snake for being what it was, but not forget to look where you put your sleeping bag at night.

"Yes," he said. "I can forgive you."

She dried her eyes with her napkin and put her hand over his. "Is there a chance for us?" she asked.

"No." His answer was rapid and final.

"You're sure?"

"I'm sure."

She studied him. "There's someone else, isn't there?"

John nodded. *At least, I hope there will be.*

189

# # #

Annie put the phone down. Elizabeth and Bobby would be there soon. They'd been together at a restaurant when they got her call. Fred was staying at his place in case David showed up there. She glanced at her watch. It was getting close to nine and it had been dark for an hour. Where could David be? If this was how he was reacting to the plan to move, how would he act when they actually got there? If he ran away after the move, she wouldn't be able to call on her friends to help. She'd be truly alone.

Like you deserve to be, the demon voice in her head began. Annie tried to shut it out.

I'm doing the best I can. Why can't everyone understand that? Why can't I get a break?

She sank into a chair. *Oh, God, I've made such a mess of this. I keep trying to do the right thing and all it does is get worse. What's that saying? Insanity is doing the same things over and over and expecting different results? I must be insane.*

But I don't know any other way to be.

Carol's words came back to her. Just because she couldn't see any other way to be, didn't mean there wasn't any.

Annie put her chin in her hands, her elbows propped on her knees and stared at the floor. She'd think about that later. Right now she needed to figure out where David was.

Bobby and Elizabeth arrived a few minutes later, but Annie barely noticed them—she was too busy sitting on the couch, examining nothing, worrying about David.

Elizabeth's arms went around her and Annie began to cry.

Bobby must have made tea, because all of a sudden there was a cup of steaming tea on the coffee table in front of Annie.

After a few minutes, Annie dried her tears and looked at her friend. "I'm sorry to be such a bother. I couldn't keep going alone anymore. All I could do was imagine the worst. What if someone hurts my baby?"

"Hush, Annie. You're not a bother. You're human. Sometimes you forget that. It was only a matter of time before you got to the end of your rope. I don't think the worst has happened to David. He's mad. Teenagers do stupid things when they get mad. Remember all the problems I had with Sarah at that age?"

"But there's no note and it doesn't look like he packed any clothes," Annie said.

"Then he's at a friend's house."

"What if he's in trouble again? What if he's hanging out with Larry and that gang of creeps?"

"He's going to come home eventually—when he gets hungry. And," Elizabeth added, "if he is with Larry and his friends, we'll know that soon, too. David's not a good criminal—too easily caught."

"I don't want him caught. I can't bear the thought of them putting handcuffs on him again." She shivered.

"Let's not borrow trouble," Elizabeth said. "David's got your genes—steady, loyal and responsible. Let's think the best and start making phone calls. Do you have a list of his friends?"

"All except Larry. David never would give me his number."

"Well, maybe one of the other kids knows it."

Bobby walked into the room, cell phone in hand. "I called the hospital and police station to eliminate those two places. He's not there."

"Thanks," Annie said, trying to smile.

The trio split the list that Annie gave them and began calling. Fifteen minutes later they'd called everyone on the list with no results. No one knew Larry's number, either.

Bobby went into the kitchen to start up the teakettle again.

The phone rang and Annie scrambled to answer it.

The news was good. "He's at Fred's!" she called out to Bobby and Elizabeth. "Thank God," she said into the phone. "I'll be right over to get him."

After a few minutes of conversation with Fred, Annie hung up the phone. Her voice toneless, she said, "David doesn't want to come home. He's staying with Fred tonight, sleeping on the floor." Sighing, she slumped on the couch and put her chin in her hands. "I wish I knew what to do. All my life I kept putting one foot in front of the other no matter how hard it was. I was the rock while everyone around me was falling apart. Maybe it was stupid, I don't know. But right now I don't know which direction to go."

"Have you talked to the life coach?" Elizabeth asked.

Annie nodded.

"Is it helping at all?"

"We've had a few conversations. I think that's why I'm in such a muddle. I'm questioning everything I thought I knew."

"That's not a bad thing."

"It is when you need to make a decision. I feel totally incapable of deciding anything right now. Sometimes I think it's clear—I need to move. Other times, I think it may be possible to stay here. You know, find a new job. I wish a note would come down from God giving me instructions."

Elizabeth laughed. "I don't think it works that way."

"Probably not." Annie looked up at Elizabeth. "I think I really want to stay. My friends are here. And ... I really like John. There's a possibility there."

"Um ... Great!" Elizabeth said, clearly working overtime to sound cheerful. "It's what I've been asking you to do all along."

Annie wasn't fooled. Her eyes narrowed as she looked at her friend. "What aren't you telling me?"

Elizabeth looked at Bobby who'd come back into the room

with more tea. He shrugged, shook his head and sat down in the rocking chair.

"Give," Annie said.

"Uh, well, I stopped by Beth Brighton's office the other day to drop off the chamber raffle tickets, and, uh ..." Elizabeth trailed off.

"If I know what it is, I can deal with it," Annie said.

"She was kissing him."

Annie snorted, unaffected by this news. "Beth Brighton has a thing for any guy who's not attached. Ever since she divorced husband number two, she's been after number three. She even went after Fred, for God's sake!"

Bobby let out a guffaw and Annie joined him in laughter, releasing the tension in the room—but only slightly. Elizabeth didn't join in the laughter. Annie stopped mid-chuckle.

"There's something else," she said. "Isn't there?"

Elizabeth nodded. "On our way here we walked by the wine bar in Costanoa. John was in there with a woman I didn't recognize. They looked like they were having a very intense conversation." She paused. "And they were holding hands."

"Oh, no," said Annie in a small voice. She burst into tears again.

Chapter 16

When the phone rang the next morning, John knew it was going to be Deborah. She'd become one determined female. He'd told her there was no chance for them, but she refused to give up hope. Kind of like what he was doing with Annie, he thought, smiling ruefully.

If he wanted a chance with Annie, he knew he had to get Deborah out of his life.

"Hi," Deborah said when he picked up.

"Hi, Deb. Look, you've got to stop calling. I feel sorry for you, but there's nothing I can do for you. You made your choice and I had to live with it. I've moved on. You'll need to do the same. Like I told you last night, I don't want you to call."

"But if you only understood, you'd give us another chance."

"I do understand. I'm sorry for you. But I don't have any feelings for you anymore."

"I have feelings for you, John." Her voice became low and seductive.

He shook his head. "I hate to do this, Deborah, but I'm going to hang up now. Please don't call again."

Feeling like a complete heel, he hung up the phone on the protesting woman. He grabbed his hat and walked out the back to the truck, once again noting the unkempt lawn and peeling paint, more glaring in the bright morning sun. The new house should close soon, Beth assured him. He couldn't wait. A home would be perfect, especially if he could find the right woman and fill the home with family and friends.

Who was he kidding? He'd already found the right woman.

What he needed to do was entice her to stay. As he drove toward Soquel, he pondered their last conversation. She'd lit up when she discussed her music. He understood why she hadn't pursued it as a career. Like him, she took her responsibilities seriously. But it seemed like she was taking them too far, locked in a job she didn't like that was forcing her to move when she didn't want to do it. What made her so chary of taking even a low-risk chance and looking for another job?

It had to be more than Fred. She seemed well past him. He'd need to invite her for coffee again soon and see if he could learn more. Maybe uncovering her fear would be the key to getting her to stay.

Sunday morning gave him time for a longer ride on Starfire, so John hitched the trailer to his pickup and loaded in his mare. Riding through ancient redwoods gave him plenty of time to explore and think. Like riding through the Rockies, he felt closer to God under those trees than in almost any church he'd been in.

He'd been back to the little church in Costanoa a few times, finally convincing most of the women that he wasn't looking for a new wife. He liked the pastor and some of the programs that the church was involved in that made the world, and the neighborhood, a better place to be. Joining in would allow him to help the community he was beginning to call home.

John had unloaded Starfire and was checking the saddle strap when a woman called out. "What a great horse!" He looked up to see Elizabeth jogging toward him. Good. Maybe he could get some news about Annie.

She stopped jogging and walked up slowly to the chestnut mare, holding her hand out as if she were allowing a dog to sniff it. Starfire obliged, her soft muzzle caressing Elizabeth's hand, tickling her hand with horse whiskers. Finally, the mare snorted her approval and Elizabeth moved in to rub the horse's glossy nose.

"She's beautiful," she said. "I've been horse-crazy since my teens. You're lucky to have her."

"Yes, ma'am," John said, trying to figure out how to introduce the subject of Annie as Elizabeth oohed and aahed over the horse. He finally bit the bullet. "How's Annie doing?"

Elizabeth gave him a sharp glance. "Okay."

"Anything new on the job front?"

"No," Elizabeth said sharply.

"Did I do something wrong?"

Her eyes flashed. "I don't want to see my friend hurt. She's been hurt enough already. So why don't you stay away from her?" She turned and started to walk away.

"Wait, Elizabeth. What are you talking about? I'm not going to hurt her." Then it hit him. "You're talking about the kiss you saw. Beth threw herself at me. I didn't initiate it. You saw me get out of there as fast as I could. My manager, Sunshine, says Beth's after every single man within a hundred miles. That wasn't my fault."

"That's not all I'm talking about. I saw you last night—holding hands with that woman."

Deborah. Was there no end to the trouble that woman was going to cause him? "She's an old friend in trouble. It didn't mean anything."

"It didn't look like an old friend. Apparently everyone else is to blame for your actions. You're just like Fred. I don't know how Annie manages to attract men like you, but apparently she's not over the losing streak yet. Stay away from her!"

Elizabeth turned away again and ran toward the entrance of the park. Santa Cruz County was turning out to be like a very small town—no secrets anywhere. John shook his head and swung his leg over Starfire, turning the mare up the trail and urging her into

196

a quick trot. He needed time away from trouble-causing females.

# # #

Annie attended David's early morning soccer game the next day, her feelings close to the surface. David mumbled hello before heading off to join his team.

Fred shrugged. "He hasn't said much. I've let him be for now. Hopefully, he'll open up to you." He looked over at her. "I really think you should reconsider this move, Annie."

She started to speak, but he raised his hands in surrender. "I'm not going to say any more right now. But I want you to think about what it's doing to David."

She felt like that's all she was ever thinking about. When was the answer going to come clear to her?

"Why'd you run away?" she asked her son after they were both in the car and pulling away from the soccer field.

David shuffled his feet on the floor mat. "I heard you telling Dad you were taking me to New Jersey. I keep trying to tell you I don't want to go there. You don't believe me. I thought if I left, you'd miss me and change your mind. Then I thought if I stayed with Dad you'd see we could make it work since you're all bent on leaving."

Teenage logic at its best. "I hear what you're saying," Annie said. "I'm trying to do the right thing—make sure we have enough and that there's money for college. Keeping my job seems to be the only way to do that. But I don't want you miserable either. And I definitely don't want you acting out anymore—understood?"

"I get it. Does that mean we're staying in California?"

"No, it means I'm going to think some more about other options."

"What's that supposed to mean?"

"It means I promise to see if I can come up with another idea and you promise to stop acting out. Okay?"

"Okay."

Annie could hear the relief in his voice. "Promise?"

"Promise."

The phone was ringing when Annie walked into the house with David. "Hello?" Annie said.

"Hi, Annie. It's John."

"Oh. Hello."

"I thought I'd take you to coffee if you aren't too busy," he said.

"I'm sorry John, but I'm really busy."

"Let me bring you coffee then."

"No, I don't think so."

"Look," John said, "I ran into Elizabeth this morning and she told me she'd seen some things—things that could be misinterpreted. I guess she told you, too."

"It's no concern to me. I'm moving to New Jersey, remember?" *He doesn't need to know any differently.*

"It's important to me. I'd like to come over and explain."

"No explanations necessary. I've got to go. See you next time I stop by the bookstore." Annie hung up the phone quietly, feeling a loss she couldn't quite explain. Maybe this is what Carol meant by denying her feelings. What was she feeling about John? Could she be in love?

I don't have time for love. I have a teenager to take care of.

Annie slammed the door on her emotions and went into the office to surf the web, looking for new bread recipes. Getting her hands in some yeasty, sticky dough would improve her mood.

"Mom?" A freshly washed David stood at her office door. "Can I go over to Kerry's? We've got a chemistry test on Monday and she said she'd help me study."

"Who's Kerry?"

"Ah, Mom, you know who Kerry is. We've gone to school, like, together, like, forever."

"Kerry Sunderson?"

"Yeah."

Annie searched her memory—finally the image surfaced—a round-faced child with café-au-lait skin and brown corkscrew curls. "I remember now. She used to be at all your birthday parties. Where's she been the last ten years?"

"Around. We just haven't talked much. So can I go?"

Annie felt her eyes widen slightly. David and Kerry hadn't talked much ... until now. Was her son actually developing an interest in girls? What kind of girl had Kerry turned into?

"Um ... sure ... just make sure I have their phone number."

David rolled his eyes. "I'm not five."

"No, but you've sure been acting like it—running away, shoplifting."

"M-o-m, I promised I wouldn't do it anymore."

"I would be more comfortable having a phone number. What if something happened to me or your dad?"

"See, that's why I need a cell phone. Then you could always find me."

"How about you make restitution first, and then we can talk about a cell phone."

"Yeah. I'll get the number." He thundered down the stairs and was up a moment later, one hand holding a backpack, the other thrusting a grubby note at her. "See you."

"Home by ten!" Annie yelled at his departing back. She smiled to herself and turned back to the computer. In spite of everything, her son might turn out okay.

The doorbell rang a few hours later. Yelling that she was coming, Annie ran to the door and yanked it open. John.

They stared at each other.

"May I come in?" he finally said, removing his hat. "We need to talk."

She stood there for a moment, debating whether to let him in or not. Finally, she stood aside and gestured for him to walk up the stairs. "I can make some tea or coffee."

"Whichever is easiest."

"No problem either way."

"Then I'd love a cup of coffee. Thanks." John followed her into the kitchen. Annie glanced around the room, glad she'd cleaned up after her earlier bread-making. The yeasty smell of fresh-baked bread still lingered.

"Is that fresh bread I smell?" he asked.

She nodded.

"Smells good," he said. "Make it yourself?"

"Yes. It relaxes me. Would you like a slice?"

"No, thanks. Maybe some other time."

They were silent until the coffee finished percolating. She tried to think of something to say, but couldn't come up with any topic she wanted to risk discussing with him.

She handed him a cup of coffee, grabbed one of her own and led the way to the living room and sat on one edge of the couch. "Don't worry about the furniture," she said as he waved the mug around, looking for someplace to put it. "With a teenage son, I ordered extra furniture protection; it won't stain."

He sat his cup and cowboy hat on the coffee table. "Annie."

"John, it doesn't really matter who you see or don't see. We don't have a relationship or the hope of having one. I've thought it over and it's smart for you to move on. I'm fine with it." *Good job, said the chorus member in charge of protecting her heart.*

"Where I come from," John said, "'fine' is a code-word for 'everything's in the crapper.'"

Annie's eyes opened wide before she started to laugh. She laughed loudly, hysterically, uncontrollably. Her body began to release the stress of the last few weeks in ever-increasing waves, waves that turned her laughter to sobs. For the second time in an as many days, tears streamed down her cheeks.

John gathered her in his arms and kissed the top of her head. "It's okay. Let it out," he said. She stiffened. Men in her life usually ran away when she started crying; they didn't put their arms around her. What did he want?

Could he want what he was giving her? Simple comfort?

She was tired of asking questions that had no answers. It was time to let go and the softness of his flannel shirt seemed like the perfect place to shed her tears and fears. She relaxed into his chest and let herself cry.

He held her and caressed her back.

The sobs eventually ran out. "I'm sorry," she choked into his chest.

"Hush," he said. "There'll be time for talk later. Relax."

There was really no choice. She let her eyes close and her exhausted body slump into his. Seduced by the comfort of his body, she drifted into a light doze of exhaustion.

When she woke, she was disoriented by the closeness of a lean male body. Her neck was cramped from the angle she'd been sleeping and she was startled to see her hand draped on his thigh. She snatched back her hand, pushed herself upright and stared at John. "How long was I asleep?"

He checked his watch. "About a half an hour. You needed it."

"And you just sat there?"

"Uh-huh." His blue eyes inspected her. "I got used to it when Jessica was ill. She'd get angry at what was happening, cry hard like you did and then fall asleep in my arms for a time. It was a comfort to us both."

"Thank you. No one's ever done that for me before."

"Then no one's ever really loved you before."

The words hung in the air.

She stood up abruptly. He rose as well. They stared at each other intently.

John put his hands on her upper arms and pulled her closer. His kiss was cautious at first, feathery touches that left her wanting more. She closed her eyes, and felt her lips grow soft under his. What was she doing? He still hadn't explained the woman in the wine bar.

Her breath hitched.

Shut up, she told her chorus.

John's lips became more demanding, his tongue caressing her lips. She parted her lips to receive his probing tongue. He tasted like strong coffee and crisp fall nights. She felt his hands moving across her back, pulling her closer to him and reached her arms around him, smoothing the flannel shirt as she caressed the lean muscles underneath.

His arms pulled her closer, his hands more urgent. Annie felt his hunger and her own heart opened in response. The hard shell that protected it began to crack. She became supple, yielding to his demands.

The kiss became deeper and Annie opened her eyes a little, turned on even more by the sight of evening stubble across a lean cheek. She moaned, leaning into him.

What the hell was she doing?

Her body stiffened again.

John pulled back, lifting his lips from hers, but still holding her in his arms. "I'm sorry. I shouldn't have done that."

"Oh, yes, you should have. It was amazing."

"Then why ..."

"I didn't mean to. All of a sudden I realized that I was

behaving badly. I mean, all I can give you is a one-night stand and all I want is more."

"Why can't you have it?"

Good question. "I don't know, but I think I should figure it out before we do any more of ... of ... that." She fluttered her hand in his direction.

"Oh, I don't know. How about you stop thinking and find out what happens." He closed in on her mouth again.

The muscles in his arms flexed as he drew her closer. The bulge in his jeans pressed against her, as a gush of heat and liquid rushed between her legs. *What would he be like naked?* She wanted to strip off his clothes and rub her hands all over his skin. She caressed his back. Desire trumped any thoughts of reticence and she moved her hands lower, where his shirt was tightly tucked into his jeans. She wanted to feel his butt, pull him closer to her, feel that bulge between her legs.

The cell phone hanging on John's belt rang.

"Damn," John said, "I'll ignore it. It'll stop in a minute."

"Maybe it's important. Who is it?" In her experience, unexpected calls always meant trouble.

He sighed, unclipped the cell phone from his belt, flipped it open and glanced at the number, keeping one hand on her arm. He shook his head, punched a button and flipped it closed. "Where was I?"

Suddenly, she remembered Elizabeth's story of seeing John with another woman. She stepped back from the embrace and picked up her coffee cup. It was cool. "Anything important?"

"Deborah—remember, I told you about her—I dated her after Jessica died."

"Oh." Annie sat in the armchair. "Are you back together?"

"No." He sat on the edge of the couch nearest the chair.

"Deborah must have been the woman in the wine bar," Annie

said.

"I meant to tell you about that, but I kind of got distracted."
He grinned.

She wasn't going to let this go. "Is she here for business?"

He shook his head. "I wish. It turns out the man Deborah fell
for in Bozeman was married. He went back to his wife. Deborah
came down here in hopes of starting up again. I told her 'no.'"

"Then why were you holding her hand?"

John took a deep breath. "I know what it feels like to be
betrayed. She meant something to me once, not as much as she
should have, but something. She looked so sad. I wanted to
comfort her. That's when Elizabeth must have walked by. It's all
that happened. Trust me." He took her hand.

Trust him. Isn't that what they all said? Then when they had
you, the problems came out. *I wonder what he's really like?*

She pulled her hand away and stood up. "I'm sorry, John, I
can't. This is happening too fast. There's too much going on. I'm
not ready."

John stood and pulled her around to face him. "My time with
Deborah is over, Annie. I've found what I'm looking for. Give me
a chance to show you. Don't throw it away because you're afraid.
I'll never hurt you purposefully, Annie. I'll treasure you and keep
you safe."

"You can't guarantee that."

"No, I can't control the world around us. I can't change the
fact that you lost your job, or that David's in trouble with the law
or that Fred was a jerk. But I can control myself. I can be your
partner no matter what happens and I'll never let you down." He
looked into her eyes. "Give us a chance, Annie."

Could she trust him? Would he still like her when he really
got to know her? Or would he believe she wasn't good enough, like
every man in her life before him? Right up until his death, her dad

had told her no one would ever marry her. She'd proved him wrong by marrying Fred. But Fred had turned out to be a drunk. When Fred was drunk, he got nasty. Once he'd told her the same thing her father had—she didn't know how to make a man feel like a man.

"I think you'd better go," she said.

Distress settled on John's face; his eyes and mouth drooped. "You're wrong, Annie. I don't know how to prove it to you, but I'll figure it out. I'm not giving up."

"Just go, John," she whispered. She picked his hat up from the table where he'd left it and handed it to him.

He held her shoulders gently and kissed her cheek. "I'll be back." He walked down the steps and out the front door. Annie slumped down on the couch. *Am I being a total fool? What if Carol's right and I am good enough, lovable enough? What if I just make lousy choices in men? Maybe there's a man out there who can love me the way I am.*

Maybe that man is John.

Annie leapt up from the couch and began to roam the living room, picking up papers, glasses, and coffee cups. She straightened pillows and magazines. Her tidying travels carried her to the kitchen. Once the cups and glasses were in the dishwasher, there was nothing else to do. She'd have to find something else to distract her from questioning her entire life.

Wandering into the bedroom, she spotted the journal she'd picked up at Carol's request. A raised painting of the face of a beautiful woman, long tresses woven with flowers and birds, adorned the cover of the still-blank pages. She'd picked it because the picture made her think of possibilities—an attitude she could use.

She stared at the blank page for a while and then began with words that Carol had suggested. "I want ..."

I want a hot chocolate.
I want a million dollars.
I want peace on earth.
I want to stay in California.
I want to love ... John.

The journal fell into Annie's lap with the last sentence she wrote. There it was—the truth. She wanted to love John. No, the truth was she was already falling in love with him.

Annie sighed and put the journal on the bed. *What was the use of wanting things so badly with no way of getting them?*

She picked up the book and hurled it across the bed. The pen went flying after it, carried to the far wall. Grabbing a pillow, she curled around it and once again broke into loud sobs. Would she ever stop crying? Images of her life tumbled through her mind. Her father on the good days ... and the not good days. Looking him over when he walked in the door, checking to see if he was hitching up his pants in a particular way—her indication that he'd had too much to drink and she'd better remember to lock her bedroom door.

The memory of that horrible night when she'd found her father. She pushed that memory back into the dark corner of her mind where it lived.

Falling in love with Fred, escaping Michigan for California ... their first few happy years together. Her joy at pregnancy, her fear as Fred began to drink more. The absolute horror when she realized she was checking his sobriety when he walked in the door, just as she had with her father. But she couldn't lock Fred out of their bedroom.

Annie cried and cried, her pillow soaking up her tears and muffling her sobs. Finally, she lay in a fetal position around the pillow and fell asleep again, exhausted. She roused herself when David came home a few minutes before curfew.

"Did you have a nice night?" she called as she went to lock the front door, something her son could never remember to do. "Yeah. Kerry makes the periodic table look simple. It still seems dumb to need to know it, but I think I'm ready for the test."

"That's good," she said as she went into the hall to give him a hug goodnight.

"What's the matter, Mom?" he said.

"Nothing. Why?"

"You look terrible. Like you've been crying or something."

"Thanks. Must be allergies."

"You sure?"

"Yeah. I'm okay. Thanks for asking." Annie held her son close, warmed by his concern. Elizabeth was right. She'd done a good job.

Chapter 17

The next morning, Annie groaned when she saw her reddened eyes in the mirror. Cold water and make-up concealed the worst of the damage, but the bags under her eyes were a dead give-away to anyone who cared enough to look. Fortunately, no one at work cared at all.

Driving over the hill took all of her remaining patience. She'd left a little later than usual and had been stuck in the worst of the traffic as a result. It was stop and go from the summit of the range to the town of Los Gatos where the road widened out. Traffic like that took all of her concentration—a fender-bender was all too easy. After she pulled into the office parking lot, she decided she was grateful. No time to think meant no time to wonder if she was doing the right thing.

She slipped into her office and booted up her computer. Quickly she scanned her e-mail. Damn. Nothing from Jim in New Jersey. She'd gotten an e-mail from him the week before saying he still didn't have the approval from Conrad. The director was on a business trip in Europe and not responsive. She had wondered briefly if Jim was telling the truth, but had squashed the thought like the gnat it was.

Time was running out. She needed to know if the job was hers. She dashed a note off to Jim, telling him she was still interested, and reminding him that she needed to know before her termination became official. What else could she do?

Perhaps she needed to let the universe know her intention to accept the job. That might speed the process up.

Oh, God, I'm talking to the universe. I've been living in Santa

Cruz too long.

Still ...

She grabbed a crumpled piece of paper from her purse. Her list was somewhat worse for wear. She carefully checked off the things she'd completed.

1. √ Tell David
2. √ Tell Fred
3. √ Find out details from Randy NJ Director Jim Borzetti
4. √ Connect with new boss in New Jersey
5. Start transfer process
6. Call realtor
7. Contact corporate housing for help to find an apartment in New Jersey
8. Hold a garage sale
9. Pack
10. Move
11. √ Pay Parking Ticket
12. √ Call Public Defender
13. Clean garage
14. Convince Fred that David's place is with me
15. Convince David that he'd be better off in NJ

Nearly half were checked off. Of course, they were no longer in any kind of order, but she should be satisfied. Why wasn't she? Maybe if she called a realtor, she'd feel like she was moving things along as best she could. Pushing aside her doubts about the wisdom of a move to New Jersey, she looked up real estate firms in Santa Cruz on the Internet. Recognizing a name, she called the office and left a message for her acquaintance. The woman agent called her back at noon.

"This isn't the best time to sell," she said.

"I don't have a choice."

"Will the company help? Is there someone I should be working with?"

"I don't know. I'll check into it." Another item went on the list as they made an appointment for the realtor to view the property.

By three in the afternoon she'd run out of things to do in the office. Many of the employees who were scheduled for lay-off didn't even bother to come in any more. She figured she'd get to that point eventually if the job from New Jersey didn't come through, but she wanted to wait as long as possible. Staying home would mean admitting defeat, and she wasn't ready to do that yet.

Besides, staying home gave her too much time to think.

Still, it would be nice to go home early—maybe stop in Costanoa and get a cheese pizza as she and David used to do in the old days. She didn't have to pick up her son from soccer practice until seven, so there was plenty of time. She sent an e-mail to her boss, letting Randy know she was leaving, threw her briefcase together, and headed out the door.

An hour later, box in hand, she walked out of the pizza store. She headed toward "her" bench behind the concrete stone wall. Two slices of cheese pizza and a bench with an ocean view. It didn't get much better than that.

As she passed Crystal Visions, the local mystic shop, the smell of patchouli oil snagged her attention. A sign in the crystal-filled window stated, "The psychic is in." She shook her head and continued her purposeful stride to the ocean.

When she got to the bench, she sat and opened the pizza box, savoring the sweet aroma of oregano and crushed tomatoes. The gooey cheese almost slid off her slice, but she nabbed it with her forefinger, willing to suffer the sting of heat for the succulent combination.

She and David had always had cheese pizza when they came down here for their weekly jaunts before her son became a teenager and declared his dissatisfaction with all things Mom-organized. She'd kept a supply of plastic pails to build fragile sandcastles and a shovel so David could attempt to dig to Asia when the mood struck him.

Sighing, Annie took a bite of pizza. Letting the warm flavors fill her mouth, she thought about the sign she'd seen at the Crystal Visions. She wondered what a psychic reading would be like.

Her slices of pizza finished, she walked toward her car, aware there was still plenty of time before she had to pick up David. She passed the bookstore, catching a glimpse of her reflection in the plate glass window. Sea air had made her hair curl haphazardly around her face. She looked crazy enough to be someone who went to a psychic. Why not?

The tinkle of small chimes announced her arrival. She made her way back through the candle-cluttered shop to the cashier and paid for her session.

Instead of the henna-haired woman with flowing robes that she'd pictured, the psychic was a trim, middle-aged brunette with glasses who was dressed in neutral tailored slacks and blouse. Annie seated herself at the small round table and waited to be told what to do.

"Your first time with a psychic?" the woman asked.

Annie nodded.

"And you don't really believe, do you?"

"Not really."

"That's fine. My name is Patricia. I believe I have a gift, but you don't have to. You can use whatever I tell you however you want. Ready to begin?"

"Yes."

"Let me hold your hands. Close your eyes and try to relax."

Annie did as she was told. She felt a tingling in her hands, but figured it was nerves.

"You're very troubled," the woman began.

No brainer there. Her face probably looked haggard.

"And you're taking good steps to work through it. A woman is in your life. She's very capable. You'll do well to trust her."

Annie almost opened her eyes. How the hell did she know about Carol? She heard the squeaks as the psychic shifted in her chair.

"There's another woman coming into your life. Someone who is close to you by blood. But you've never met her. She has something important to tell you."

Well, at least it's not a tall dark stranger.

The psychic went on to talk about family and false lessons learned, but not much of it made sense to Annie. The fifteen minutes passed quickly and the woman told her to open her eyes. "How are you feeling?"

"A little disoriented." Annie blinked her eyes several times to remove the fog that seemed to surround her.

"One more thing before you go," the woman said. "I think you need to do two things to help you make the choices you need to make. The first is to find someone who does bodywork—your pain is buried deep in your tissues; you need assistance to release it. The second is to write out your life story."

"Okay," Annie said, ready to agree to anything to end the session. She looked at her watch, trying to recapture reality and looked up to find the psychic looking intently at her. *It's like she can see my soul. No, that's not possible. I don't really believe in this.*

"I hope you get something to ease your pain," the woman said, smiling gently. "I enjoyed meeting you. You have a lot to offer the world."

"Thanks." Annie rushed from the store, anxious to escape the unfamiliar territory of tarot cards and multi-limbed Hindu *Vishnus*.

After she picked up David, she slipped into jeans and tee-shirt and checked her personal e-mail. A note from Facebook caught her eye. Vaguely, she remembered setting up an account on the site, but didn't spend much time there. Too many of her friends were hooked on games like Farmville and she wasn't interested in their latest imaginary purchase.

The note contained a friend request from Beverly Gerhard. *Weird.* Annie clicked through to view the request. The Facebook photo showed an older woman with slender features and a faint resemblance to her father. The only information given was that she lived in Georgia. Maybe she was a second cousin once removed—whatever that meant. She didn't appear to be a stalker, but people lie on the Internet all the time. What the heck—time to live dangerously!

Annie clicked the Accept button to access the rest of the information. She learned that Beverly had once been a modern dancer in New York, retiring to teach at the University of Georgia in Athens. She appeared to have lots of friends, but no other Gerhard relatives. Who was she? Another thought struck her. Could this be the relative the psychic had mentioned?

A shiver ran from Annie's head to her toes.

It was after eleven p.m. in Georgia. She probably wouldn't hear anything until the morning. Shrugging her shoulders, she put it out of her mind and checked through the rest of her e-mail.

# # #

At the appointed time Tuesday morning, Annie picked up the phone and called Carol. "I still haven't heard from Jim about the job in New Jersey," she told the coach. "I may not have to make this decision after all. I don't know what I'll do then. This is my only choice."

"Really?" Carol asked softly.

"What other choices do you think I have?"

"What could you do?"

"Get fired."

"And then what?"

"Go on unemployment until it runs out?"

"And then what?" Carol asked again.

"Go on welfare. Sell my house. Move in with my mother. Strike that last one," Annie said. "I'm *not* moving in with my mother."

"But it is a choice."

"Not from where I'm standing."

Carol chuckled. "What else?"

"I could look for a job. I could take a job singing torch songs at a local joint." Now she laughed at the mental picture of draping her body over a grand piano and teasing the pianist with a pink boa.

"And ..."

"And I'd sing so hard I'd lose my voice and I'd take the pink boa and become a stripper, but they'd catch on that the body is too old so I'd have to get a shopping cart and become a bag lady." Annie put her coffee cup down, suffused with laughter at the image of herself in a raggedy raincoat adorned with a pink boa.

Carol waited until Annie's laughter died down before she said, "The bag lady image is one most women carry in their heads. It rarely comes true, but most women spend their lives doing things they don't want to do because of the idea. How much money do you need to live?"

Annie told her. She knew the figure down to the penny.

"Will unemployment cover it?"

"No. And what about sending David to college?" Annie asked.

"What about it?"

"I can't afford that if I don't have a job."

"How old is he?"

"Fifteen."

"I think you have some time. Does he have a job?"

Annie admitted that David didn't. They brainstormed ways for David to help contribute to his college fund. Now that Fred was sober, Annie thought, maybe he could contribute, too.

"Get David involved. Give him more control over his own life. He's growing up, Mom. You've done a great job being mama-bear up to now, but you need to teach him to find his own berries. I want to go back to one of the ideas you had earlier—singing for a living."

"You can't be serious. I don't thinking singing for a living is realistic. I'd never make the money I need to make."

"So ..."

"So it's a ridiculous idea."

"Have you enjoyed singing over the last few weeks?"

Annie thought about singing in the shower and in the car. "It was strange, but I did have fun while I was doing it. I even looked for my old guitar. It's in pretty good shape— needs new strings, but other than that, it's playable."

"When are you getting new strings?"

"What's the point?"

"Your resistance is interesting. What do you think will happen if you get strings for your guitar?"

"I don't know." By now, Annie knew that Carol wasn't going to accept that for an answer, so she began to think. Why hadn't she gotten strings? "I guess, it would make it real."

"Tell me more."

"I'd find out how rusty I've gotten over the last fifteen years. I'd definitely have to build up new calluses." Annie sighed, recalling the pain in her fingertips before the calluses had built up the first time. "I think," she paused again as her voice choked. "I think, I'd find out how much I missed it—how much I missed me." Tears stung her eyes. "I feel like a fool. I took a left turn and wound up selling out, just like my parents."

"No, you didn't. Life is a balance between doing what you need to do to have food and shelter and attending to your spiritual and creative lives. It's when we get too involved in one or the other that problems can occur. You were too busy gathering nuts and berries to take time for a good wallow in a mud bath. Perhaps it's time to find a different bush, where the berries are easier to gather and you have time to play."

Carol's soft words soothed her. Maybe it wasn't too late for her.

"But what do I do? I really need this job. Do I move to New Jersey? I'm sure they have guitar strings in New Jersey."

"I'm sure they do. And it's a possibility. But you have to look at the whole picture. What else would you give up if you moved? You know that you'd lose the job and the security if you stay, but what do you lose if you go?"

"My friends, my house, maybe my son," she said, thinking about Fred's subtle threat to go to court to prevent her from taking David out of state.

"Is it worth it?" Carol asked.

"Doesn't sound like it, does it? Still, I may not have to make the decision. It's taking a long time for Jim to offer the job. Maybe the director remembers I stepped on his foot and won't let Jim hire me." "I think you need to make the decision on your own, regardless of what Jim does. That way, you keep the power in your own hands. I have another assignment for you. I want you to create a list—at least fifty ways that you could earn money other than move to New Jersey. I don't care how bizarre they are, in fact the more crazy they are, the better. I want you to get your creative juices flowing."

"All right," Annie said doubtfully.

"One more thing."

"What?"

"Get the guitar strings."

Annie grinned. "Sounds like a great idea."

She hung up the phone, but it immediately rang again. The realtor.

She wasn't encouraging. When she found out how much Annie owed on her mortgage, she said, "You're underwater. You can't get that much for your house."

"So what am I supposed to do?"

"See if your company will cough up the difference. They used to, but with this economy ..."

"I suppose I could rent it out. How much could I get?"

The realtor told her.

"But that wouldn't even cover my mortgage, never mind taxes or insurance."

"Check with your company," the woman said. "It's your best bet."

Annie was finishing up for the day when the phone rang. "Mrs. Renquist?" a raspy voice asked.

"Gerhard."

"Are you David Renquist's mother?" the voice asked impatiently.

"What's wrong? Who are you?'

"This is Kathy Plum. I'm an administrator in the emergency room."

"What's wrong? Is David okay? Is he hurt? I'll be right there!"

"Mrs. Renquist!" The woman's commanding voice stopped Annie as she was about to hang up the phone.

"What? I said I'd be right there."

"I heard you. But I need you to calm down." The woman's voice softened. "We don't need you getting into an accident. I know you're worried, but it's not too bad. Your son was hit in the head during soccer. He's a little bloody, but he'll be okay. We need your permission to treat him."

"Where's his father?" Fred was supposed to watch David play and bring him home.

"He's here, but since you're the legal guardian, we need your permission."

"You've got it. I'll be right down."

"Wait ..."

Annie couldn't wait any longer. *I'm calm enough!* She flung down the phone and flew out the door, not bothering to lock it. Her hands shook as she started the Prius and drove to Monterey Bay General. She ran the long distance from the parking lot to arrive breathless at the front desk.

"My son, David Renquist," she said to the plump woman in the first cubicle.

The woman looked at the computer screen and slowly tapped a few keys. "Let's see, Renquist."

Annie wanted to scream. What was taking this woman so long? Didn't she understand the concept of "emergency room"?

"Ah ... there it is. They're treating him now." She reached for a stack of papers in the black plastic trays to her right. "We need you to fill out these forms. We'll also need a copy of your insurance card."

"I want to see my son."

"They're treating him. You can see him in a few minutes. Please sign here." The woman tapped her pen on a line on the form she'd placed in front of Annie.

Annie groaned, dug out her insurance card, and handed it to the woman. While the woman went to get the card copied, she scanned the insurance form and signed it. After several minutes, the woman returned with her card. She grabbed it and asked, "Where is he?"

The clerk gestured to the swinging doors at the end of the waiting room. "Ask the nurse at the station which cubicle he's in."

She didn't wait to hear any further instructions, but pushed through the swinging doors. Hearing Fred's voice rumbling from behind a curtained alcove on the left, she pawed at the fabric until she found the opening between the panels. She gasped when she saw her son. His bright green goalie shirt was streaked with blood.

"What happened?"

"He was accidently kicked in the head when he dove for the ball," Fred said. "He passed out for a moment and they want to check him out. He's got a mild concussion."

"So much blood." She slid around to the side of the bed and stroked her son's arm.

"Head wound," Fred said.

David's eyes fluttered open. "Hi, Mom. I made the save." He grinned at her.

"I'm sure you did, honey. Rest."

Her son closed his eyes. A short Latina nurse poked her head through the curtain slit. "I need to clean him up so you can take him home. Doctor will be with you in a moment to tell you how to take care of him. You can wait out here." She drew the curtain aside and gestured for Fred and Annie to leave. Once outside the curtained room, Annie and Fred looked at each other, searching for the small talk that used to come easily. After a few moments, Fred asked, "What are you going to do about your job?"

"I haven't heard anything. I don't know if they'll offer me the other position."

"You can move to New Jersey if you want," he said, crossing his arms over his chest. "But you aren't taking my son anywhere."

"Fred, we'll discuss this later."

"We're discussing nothing later. That's always been your way, telling me what to do. But now it's going to stop. You aren't ruling my life any more. And you aren't ruling David's. He's staying with me."

"You can't take care of him," Annie said. "You can barely take care of yourself!"

"That's not true ..."

"Stop arguing!" David's voice came from behind the curtain.

"Hush," the nurse said. "Don't get excited. It's not good for you." She poked her head out and glared at them. "Don't you know better?" she hissed. "This is a hospital!"

Annie felt her face flush red and she stared down at the floor.

An Asian doctor walked up to them, clipboard in hand. He gave them a curious glance. "Which one of you will be taking care of him?"

"I will," Annie said. The doctor cut his eyes to Fred, who nodded.

The doctor launched into his instructions. "Sign here." He handed her the clipboard, tearing out a yellow copy of instructions for her when she returned it.

David walked out from behind the curtain, face clean above the bloodied shirt, cleats in his hand. He glanced at them and turned on his heel to go out through the doors, his parents trailing behind.

"I'm sorry," Fred said after they put their son in the passenger seat. "It wasn't the time or place to discuss it. But Annie, we do need to talk about this. You can't keep going on making decisions for everyone else in your life, even if you think you're right."

"I am right," she said with a small grin, hoping to defuse the situation.

"Not all the time." Fred held her eyes. This was a new Fred, sober, stable and tenacious. She was going to have to deal with it.

"Okay. Let me get through the next few days and then we'll sit down and talk about it."

"Sounds like a plan." Fred stuck his head in the driver-side door. "Behave," he said to his son.

"Yeah, Dad."

After they got home, David took a shower while Annie made herself some St. John's Wort tea. While she waited for the water to boil, she thought about Carol's assignment to brainstorm job opportunities. She got out some paper and sat down at the kitchen table to begin her list. Fifteen minutes later, her tea was cold and the paper was still blank.

Chapter 18

Mercifully, the phone rang.

"Hi," her friend said.

"Elizabeth!" Annie exclaimed.

"You sound like we haven't seen each other in years. What's up?"

Annie quickly filled her in on David's accident and her argument with Fred. Elizabeth murmured her sympathy. "Any news on the job front? And how about John—have you heard from him? I ran into him yesterday at Nisene Marks."

"Yes, he told me."

"So you have seen him."

"You could say that. Actually, I did more than see him," Annie said. "I cried on his shoulder. And ..."

"What?"

"I let him kiss me again."

"Oh, Annie, you didn't. After he two-timed you with that other woman?" Elizabeth asked.

"It wasn't like that at all. She's his old girlfriend, fiancé, really, and she came into town unexpectedly."

"Is that what he told you? It looked like a little more than that to me."

"I think John likes to touch. Some people are more like that than others. Probably has to do with raising animals or something." She sounded over-eager.

"Honey, you've got it bad. Your excuse-making has gone into overdrive."

"Well, maybe, but I kept my head. I sent him away before it

went too far."

"God, Annie, why'd you do that?"

"I thought you'd be happy. First you say I'm getting too close, then you say I shouldn't have sent him away. Which is it?"

Elizabeth chuckled. "A little of both, I suspect. I want you to be happy and never get hurt again. I suppose that really isn't possible. There is something solid and trustworthy about John. I think he has to clean up some loose ends, but there're possibilities."

"Not for me."

Elizabeth sighed. "I give up. But you still haven't told me about the job. Have you heard anything?"

"No."

"Disappointed?"

"I think so."

"Sounds like you're not quite as determined to go as you were."

"I suppose not. I don't know. It's so confusing. I used to know exactly what I needed to do. Now, I don't know what I want. Or, I do know what I want, but can't seem to get it. At least I think I know what I want. Oh, Elizabeth, I'm all mixed up."

"Is the coach helping at all?"

"I think she's the reason I'm all muddled. Maybe it's one of those things that has to get worse before it gets better." Annie hesitated. "I did something today I've never done before. I went to a psychic."

"Why?"

"I'm so confused—I'm looking for anyone who will give me a clear answer!"

Elizabeth laughed. "So what did she ... or he ... have to say?"

Annie told her of the psychic's predictions that someone would come into her life who would help her. "She wants me to write my life story and get a body worker, whatever that is. You know what's weird, though?" Annie asked. "As soon as I got home I got this strange message from Facebook. A woman with the last name of Gerhard was trying to connect."

"Do you know who she is?"

"No, but I made the connection anyway. Maybe tomorrow I can find out more about her. She looks like my dad ... only, I don't know."

"What?"

"This woman, Beverly, looks happy."

"What's so odd about that?"

"I don't ever remember seeing my father happy. He would be happy-drunk or happy-manic. Sometimes I had the feeling he was faking 'happy,' but I never saw him with the peace that was in this woman's face."

"Maybe she's peaceful because she's doing what she wants instead of what she should," Elizabeth said softly.

"Ouch."

"I didn't mean it that way. It's what I want for you—peace from the inside out. The idea that your dad was often faking 'happy'? Sometimes I think you do that, too."

Annie pondered the statement. "You may have a point. I feel like I should be happy. My kid's okay—most of the time. I have a nice home and money enough. And I have good friends." She smiled. "But ..."

The word lingered in the silence.

"... I feel like there's something more—something I'm missing."

"Maybe you should do what the psychic said," Elizabeth suggested.

"I feel like I've been writing out my life story forever," Annie said with a groan. "Every shrink I've ever been to, Al-Anon, they all want me to write my story. I know it by heart. And where would I find a body worker? What is it anyway—a glorified massage therapist?"

"I don't know about the life story. I've never done one," Elizabeth confessed. "I do know a body worker though. I went to her after Joe died."

"You never told me that!"

"It never came up. Besides, that's before we met. It really helped. I can't tell you why."

"What was it like?"

"It was as if she massaged out all the hurt in my muscles. She'd give me a massage and ask me questions along the way. Sometimes I'd start crying when she worked on a particular part of my body. She stuck with it and I cried until I was done. Every time I went, I felt a little more of the grief and despair go away."

"How long did you see her?"

"Six weeks. I'll give you her name, if you want."

"Sure." Annie glanced at the blank paper on the kitchen table. "What are you doing tomorrow night?"

"Why?" Elizabeth sounded wary.

"You can help me with my next assignment from the coach."

"What's that?" Elizabeth asked warily.

"Thinking of ways for me to earn money without moving to New Jersey."

"That sounds like fun!"

"Only to you. I'm an absolute disaster at the assignment."

"That's because you haven't thought of the really bizarre things there are out there to do. You could write fortune cookie fortunes. Or deliver singing telegrams."

"Wait until tomorrow. Then you can think of as many weird jobs as you want!" When Annie hung up the phone, her heart was lighter.

She stayed home the following day to keep an eye on her son. The doctor had advised her to keep him home a day to ensure that the concussion wasn't worse than it appeared. She idly went through her work e-mail. It was finally dwindling as the project closed down. A few more reports and it would be done. No new work was coming in and there was no message from Jim about the job in New Jersey. The laid-off limbo.

Bored, she logged onto Facebook to check out the woman who had contacted her— Beverly Gerhard. If her father were still alive, Beverly would be about his age. Annie searched the Internet for more information. Apparently, the woman had been a well-known modern dancer, working with Alvin Ailey's American Dance Theater as a performer and then a teacher. Photos showed a woman performing an astounding leap, legs muscle-carved, her pale skin standing out against the predominantly black ensemble.

She had to be a relative. But how? Annie glanced at the phone. Would her mother know? Sighing, she dialed her mother's number. It had been close to a month since she'd spoken to her and it was about time, much as she dreaded the conversation.

"Hi, Mom," she said when her mother picked up. "How are you doing?"

"I thought I'd never hear from you again. It's been so long."

"Only a few weeks."

"Good daughters call their mothers weekly. You know I've been so lonely since ... since ... your dad died."

"Mom, he's been gone close to twenty years. I think it's time to move on."

"You know I can't do that. He was my life."

Annie sighed inwardly. They had the same discussion every time she called. Her mother lived in a fantasy world where the man who had beaten her regularly was Prince Charming. No matter what tactics Annie had tried, her mother had stuck with her beliefs. The woman who had kept her safe growing up was gone, destroyed by too many years of her father's abuse. Annie had eventually learned to quit trying to bring her back.

"Mom, do you know who Beverly Gerhard is?"

"That tramp. Has she been bothering you? I swear, there's no privacy these days— everyone poking their noses into someone else's business. When I was growing up, everyone knew what went on in a family was private. Now everyone's trying to run someone else's life. I—"

"Mom!" Annie raised her voice to interrupt her mother's diatribe. "Who is she?"

"Your father's sister. She disobeyed your grandfather. Got herself knocked up and wouldn't marry the guy your grandfather picked out for her. Said she had things to do, packed up her suitcase, and left town." Her mother's voice dropped to a whisper. "We heard she had an *abortion*. The tramp wouldn't even keep her baby."

Stunned, Annie couldn't say a word. An aunt—she had an aunt she'd never even known about, an aunt who'd made a career as a modern dancer in a famous dance troop.

Her mother launched back into her favorite speech about the deterioration of the world, caused by women's libbers, liberals, and hordes of illegal immigrants. Annie let her ramble as she mulled over the news that she had an aunt and possibly a cousin. When her mother ran down, she made excuses about needing to take David somewhere, promised she'd call again in a few weeks and hung up the phone. She hadn't told her mother about the impending layoff. If her mother cared at all, which was unlikely, she would blame Annie for losing her job.

Annie was clearing up after dinner when Elizabeth pushed the door open and called, "I'm here and I'm ready!" She tossed a heap of magazines and books on the kitchen table.

"What's that?" Annie asked.

"Brain stimulation! There are lots of things to do out there! New careers are being created every day and we don't know half of them. How's David?" Elizabeth sloughed off her light jacket and sat down.

"He's on the road to recovery—should be able to go to school tomorrow. He also seems to be on the phone with Kerry all the time. It can't take that long to get schoolwork."

"Told you he'd be dating soon."

"Oh stop ... I'm not ready for this."

"Ready or not, here it comes."

Annie smiled. "I guess so." She looked at the pile of magazines in front of her as she dried her hands. "Now what?"

"Do you have paper?"

"Right here." Annie grabbed a dingy gray notebook from the counter.

"That's not very inspiring. I knew you'd pick something like that to plan your future. So I brought you something." Elizabeth pulled out a bright pink notebook with writing across the front from her voluminous purse.

Annie scanned the front. "Today is the first day of the rest of your life," it announced. "Count on you to find something like that. But remember, all we're doing is writing a list. I'm not committing to anything."

"You will."

For the next hour the women pored through magazines and wrote down every occupation they could find. When Annie wanted to eliminate something as being too outrageous, Elizabeth forced her to write it down. "We're brainstorming," she explained. "There's no vetoing in brainstorming."

"But I can't be a flight attendant," Annie protested. "I'm too old, too short, and overweight."

"The rules changed. Didn't you notice? Now you need to be able to strong-arm passengers who don't want to obey the rules. It's not fun anymore. That's why they let anyone do it. Write it down."

By the time they wound down, Annie had a list that covered three pages. While many were clearly ridiculous—she suspected becoming a stunt person was a little far-fetched— some had possibilities.

"Thanks," she told her friend. Elizabeth straightened out the magazines and scraps to be recycled. "What's this?" she asked as she picked up a flyer from the counter.

Annie glanced over. "Shakespeare Santa Cruz. I try to take David to at least one performance in the glen every year, remember?"

"Got to give the kids culture. Didn't you work there one summer?"

"It was my second year at Santa Cruz. I worked in the recording studio for the festival creating the music for the scenes and dances. They did *Midsummer* that year. Music is so important for that play. I loved to sit up in the back, especially for the night performances. Sometimes the fog would drift into the upper branches of those old redwoods. You could almost see the ghosts of old actors darting through the trees."

"Sounds creepy."

"No, it was marvelous." Annie hugged herself in memory. "It was a magical time, a time when anything was possible. I could even see myself doing some song writing for the festival in the future." Her arms dropped. "But then I got pregnant and everything changed. Don't get me wrong. I love David. But it closed some roads for me professionally."

"Until now," Elizabeth said.

Annie grabbed the list and added, *Theater music composer*.

"There," she said.

"Good, I'm off, then." Elizabeth hugged Annie. "Oh, I almost forgot." She pulled a crumpled piece of paper from her jacket pocket. "The body worker."

Annie took the paper. She wasn't sure it would do any good, but at least she'd feel better after a massage.

She went to the office the next day, although she wasn't sure why. She spent most of the day staring at her empty e-mail inbox and wondering if she'd ever hear from John again. Maybe he finally believed her and would stay away. Her mouth drooped at the thought.

There she was being contradictory again. She wanted him to call, but when he showed up, she sent him away.

Still no message from Jim in New Jersey. What was it with people these days? Didn't they know how to communicate? She sighed. She was running out of things to do at the office and no one stopped by to talk with her. It was as if she had layoff leprosy. By Thursday, she called the body worker and made an appointment. It was something to do.

Friday she gave up the pretense and stayed home. Maybe the job in New Jersey would never materialize. She'd better start thinking about Plan B. She took out the list that she and Elizabeth had pulled together. Not much on it looked realistic.

She checked Facebook to see if she'd heard from Beverly. She had one unread message.

"Thank you for being open enough to connect with me," the note began. "I doubt your parents ever talked about me. I'm your father's sister, your aunt. Your family wouldn't let me see you ... I'll tell you why when we meet. If I came to California, would you be willing to see me?"

Annie stared at the screen. The woman would drop everything and come to California? Wasn't that a little sudden?

What was she really like? She could be like her father, mean and belittling. Or was she the callous person her mother seemed to think she was? Truth and her mother weren't the closest of companions. Still, was she ready to meet this stranger? Annie closed out Facebook without answering the message and left for her appointment with the body worker.

The body worker's office was carved out of one of the old Victorians on the hill near the university. Yellow walls with sunny prints surrounded a variety of plants. New age music wafted from discretely placed speakers.

Annie quickly filled out the paperwork that Sukesha, the practitioner, gave her. When she was finished, Sukesha sat down next to her and read it over.

"Do you have any places that are sore now?" she asked.

Annie pointed to her upper back. "I do a lot of computer work. I'm always tense there."

"Ah, yes. Anywhere else?"

Annie shook her head.

"As we work together," Sukesha continued, "we'll discover other areas that are holding old hurts for you. My sense is that you're very disconnected from your body. My aim is to reconnect you, allow you to experience the pain in a safe place and help you let it go. You may find that you cry. That's okay."

What had she gotten herself into? Body work sounded like a lot of mumbo jumbo. But, she was here and she may as well have the first treatment. She could decide later whether she wanted to come back or not.

Annie disrobed in the adjacent massage room and lay down in clean white sheets that smelled of lemon. Sukesha draped a downy comforter over her. "Warm enough?"

Annie nodded. At first, nothing that Sukesha did seemed different from the other massages that Annie had received. As the masseuse worked on her upper shoulders, though, Annie felt uncomfortable. It was a restless feeling, a need to get away from the probing fingers. Sukesha was seeing too much with her hands. Annie's breath caught.

"It's okay," Sukesha said. "Go with the feeling. Let it out."

Panic started to rise. What if she couldn't get away?

"You're safe," Sukesha murmured. "No one will hurt you here."

Annie gasped as a strong wave of darkness swept through her body. And then it was gone. There was nothing. The gentle ting of wind chimes blended into the soft sound of harps in the background music. Light streamed into her soul. She settled into the soft fabric and dozed.

When she awoke, she was alone. She slowly got up and dressed, feeling dazed. Sukesha waited for her in the anteroom.

"How do you feel?" she asked.

"Drained and confused. What did you do to me?"

Sukesha smiled. "You were ready. You must be doing some work with someone else. A therapist, perhaps?"

"A coach. I didn't think we'd done much yet. We only started a few weeks ago."

"It appears to be effective. I tune in to the energy fields in your body. What feels tense to you can look like a dark orange-red to me. That's the energy that needs to be released before you can feel better again. There are many areas of your body that need release."

"But what actually happened? I felt ... I don't know ... like a dark angel flew out of my body."

"That's a pretty good description. You let go of some deep seated anger and tension."

"Why was it there?"

"I can't tell you that. You'd have to remember it yourself.

That's why it's good to work with a coach or therapist while you do this work as well."

Annie paid Sukesha and made an appointment for the following week. On the way home, she puzzled over the experience. She wasn't sure what had happened, but she felt lighter and the muscles in her upper back were less sore. Talking to Carol on Monday would be interesting. When she got home, she checked her messages.

Only one. From John.

Chapter 19

By Friday evening, John still hadn't heard from Annie. Maybe she'd been at work all day. He stared at the phone. *Ring, dammit!*

You know, Johnson, your finger's not broken. You can punch in the numbers yourself.

Sighing, he dialed Annie's number. He knew Annie was trying to protect him from being hurt. But he was a grown man and he was willing to take the risk to fight for a chance at love. He knew what life could be with two partners who loved and cared for each other. Maybe she didn't. He'd just have to show her.

"We need to talk," he said after Annie answered.

"John, I ..."

"I know, you're moving. I still want to see you for coffee. I have an idea. Can you come to the bookshop tomorrow?"

"Can't you tell me what you need over the phone?"

"No, I can't. I can meet you anywhere. It doesn't need to be at the bookstore." He felt her hesitation. "It can be a public place," he said. "That way you don't have to worry about being kissed."

She laughed. "I'm not afraid of you. In fact, why don't you come here?"

"Okay." It couldn't be that easy.

"David will be around to chaperone us," she added.

"Oh." It wasn't that easy.

She laughed again. "I thought you were going to be good."

"You seemed to enjoy being kissed."

"I do. I enjoyed it too much, but John—"

"There's no such thing as too much."

"I think there is for me."

234

He let it go. She was like a mare that had been abused by a callous owner and he needed to be cautious. "I want to talk with you, tell you my idea. I promise there's no more than that." *For now.*

"Then why don't you come over tomorrow? David needs to rest and I'm feeling cooped up. Company will be good."

"What happened to David?"

She told him about the soccer incident. He hung up the phone, glad she'd agreed to see him.

He mulled over what she'd told him. Annie wasn't having an easy time—first her job, then David getting into trouble, and now this. She needed a good friend, not someone trying to get her into bed.

He smiled to himself. He'd have to show her that he could be a good friend *and* a good lover all rolled into one. He hoped he could pull it off.

# # #

The shining sun lit up her living room while Annie tidied the house the next afternoon.

Although she couldn't see the ocean, the swishing sound of waves floated in through the open window, soothing her spirit. The sweet smell of jasmine snuck in to entwine with the bitter aroma of coffee.

She'd decided to simply enjoy John's company over coffee. There wasn't much she could do today about the rest of it. The thought stopped her short. She couldn't remember the last time she'd enjoyed the moment without wallowing in her worries. Maybe the coaching and the body work were helping after all.

She looked around the living room and kitchen, changed the arrangement of her Delft candlesticks one more time and declared the space perfect. She swept back into her bedroom with a light heart. I'm in denial, she thought as she picked out the rose blouse to wear. But sometimes denial is a nice place to be.

I'll pretend that everything will turn out perfectly.

Maybe it will, said a new voice from her chorus. David was on the phone with someone when she came in to tell him about John's visit. "Who's that," she whispered, pointing to the phone.

"Kerry. Have fun with your coffee. I'm fine." He waved her out his bedroom door with a grin.

A half hour later she and John were in the kitchen, sharing coffee and the sugar cookies he'd brought from the Pacific Cookie Company. He'd entertained her with the latest of his store manager's antics when he turned to another subject.

"Are you still thinking of moving?"

"Do we really need to discuss this now? I thought we were having a pleasant time without discussing anything serious."

"Moving doesn't solve anything."

"You moved. Did it help you?"

"Yes, it did. The difference is that I dealt with my problems before I left Missoula. I was coming to a new life, not running away from anything. Or anyone."

"Except for Deborah."

"I had dealt with Deborah. Deborah hadn't dealt with Deborah."

"Is she still around?"

He shook his head. "I convinced her there's no future for us. She headed back home on Saturday."

"I haven't heard back from the guy in New Jersey," Annie confessed. "So I don't know if I'm going anywhere. It's a lousy time to sell my house and David certainly doesn't want to move. My problem is if I don't have a job, I'm going to lose everything anyway."

"Come work for me. One of my long-time employees has decided to retire and move to Hawaii. I need a replacement."

She smiled sadly. "Thanks, but that's not going to cover my salary."

He looked down at the table. "I thought it could be a stop-gap until you found something—give you a little income. It'd also give you some time to work on your music."

She thought guiltily of the unplayed guitar in the garage. She'd never gotten around to purchasing replacement strings. John's offer would supplement her severance package and unemployment and keep her afloat longer—maybe long enough to find a job to keep everything going. It would still be a struggle. Keeping her full-time job would be a better strategy. "If the job in New Jersey comes through, I still think it would be best to take it. But thank you for the offer. I'll keep it in mind."

"How long before your job is terminated?"

"Less than two weeks."

She rose. "More coffee?"

She watched him study the tabletop. He was a good man, and, if she was honest, the sexiest man she'd ever gone out with. Were they going out? The thought surprised her.

She studied his strong hands wrapped around the coffee cup, and shivered with pleasure. He must have sensed her stare because he looked up. When he saw her looking at him, he grinned. Her resolve disappeared.

He stood, rounded the table and placed his hands on her arms. "Then I don't have long to change your mind." He lowered his head and took her lips with his. She gave a muffled protest, but it was half-hearted. Soon she was responding, providing passion for passion. How much longer would she be satisfied with kisses?

A thud on the stairs below him made her pull back. Damn!

David came into the kitchen. An ugly scab had formed on his forehead.

"What happened to you?" John asked.

"Soccer."

"Looks nasty."

"Yeah. Are you that guy from the bookstore? The one Mom's been seeing?"

"Yep."

"Any luck convincing her to stay here?"

"I'm working on it."

David grunted. A moment later he was standing in front of the open refrigerator. He pulled out the milk, poured himself a glass and leaned back on the counter, looking at his mother.

She stared back at him, not believing her son's boldness.

David shook his head. "Good luck," he said to John and went back downstairs.

"Nice kid."

"I can't believe he was ... that he ..."

"Said what he felt?"

She nodded.

"Kids surprise you sometimes. Maybe you need to listen to him."

"John!"

A slow smile crept across his face. "Just saying. I'm an outsider. You don't have to listen to me."

"Thanks for your opinion." She stressed the last word.

"Okay, got it. Butt out." He leaned over and brushed her lips with hers. "Keep next Friday night open. I'll think of something fun for us to do." He trotted down the stairs, whistling as he went out the door.

# # #

Curious about Beverly, Annie logged into Facebook the next morning and sent a message to her aunt to set up a time to talk on the phone. A minute after she clicked "Send," a window popped up.

"Got your message," Beverly's chat began. "But I think what I have to say needs to be said in person."

"Why?" Annie typed back.

"Because things get lost over the phone. This is too important."

"Can't you give me a hint?"

"I'm sorry to tease you, but I want to see you. I can be there next week. You don't have to put me up. I've got a friend in San Jose who I haven't seen in years that I'd like to visit, too."

"I really hate to see you fly across the country when we can easily talk on the phone."

"Sweetheart, I've never even met you—or your son. I'd love to spend time with you. Even if it's only a little."

Annie stared at the screen. What did she really know about this woman? She took a deep breath and typed, "Okay."

"How about this Tuesday?" Beverly replied. "I'll fly out Monday night. We can have lunch."

"That's only two days from now."

"I told you—it's important to me."

Annie stared blankly at the screen. *What have I gotten myself into?*

Monday morning Annie had her regular call with Carol. She told Carol about David's soccer accident, but didn't tell her about John's job offer or Beverly's impending visit, although she wasn't quite sure why.

"Read me your list of job possibilities," Carol said.

Annie looked at the wrinkled notebook paper. "Well, it starts off with consulting, and substitute teaching."

"And ..."

"Office work."

"Annie, read me the list. There's no judgment here. In fact, wilder is better."

Annie took a deep breath. "Surfing instructor, bartender, flight attendant, secretary, research assistant, babysitter, gardener. No, scratch that ... I kill everything I plant."

"No judgment. With the proper training you can do anything you want. Keep going."

"Okay. Dancer, exotic dancer, stunt woman, movie extra, cabaret singer, flag person on a road crew ..." Annie read rapidly through the rest of her list.

"Good! How does it feel?"

"Ridiculous. I can't do any of those things."

"Why not?"

"Well, I suppose I could be a nurse, teacher, or secretary." Her father's prescribed list of female-appropriate jobs echoed in her head. "Or, I could find another husband and learn to be a better wife."

"Wow ... all of that. That sounds like old male thinking. When are you going to let it go?"

"What do you mean?"

"I'm sure that was drummed into your head by your dad. How long has he been gone?"

"About twenty years."

"Don't you think twenty years is enough time to stop listening to your dad, especially since he's dead?"

"I suppose."

"Then why don't you?"

"I don't know."

"I suspect you do know, but it's buried in something that

happened that you're not ready to tell me."

Annie was silent. She could play that game as well as Carol.

"So you were fifteen when your father died," Carol said.

"Yes."

"What did he die from?" The coach asked quietly.

"He shot himself."

"I'm sorry. That's really hard. Who found him?"

"I did."

"Oh, honey. You were too young to face that."

"I'm not sure anyone's old enough to face that." There'd been so much blood. Her dad had gone into the bathroom, sat on the toilet seat and blown his brains out. She'd found him when she'd come home from school. She'd dropped the books and stood there, unable to move.

She'd run around the house looking for her mother before she remembered it was grocery shopping day. She stood in the bathroom door and screamed at him to get up, even though she knew it was impossible. A neighbor must have heard her, because she suddenly appeared next to Annie and drew her away from the bathroom before calling the police.

She hadn't found the note her father had left her until later that night. It had been in her underwear drawer.

"I can see why you hold onto his beliefs so strongly." Carol interrupted her memories. "People feel guilty when someone close to them commits suicide, particularly kids. They wonder if they could have done something to prevent it. It sounds like you've spent your life in atonement trying to be the daughter your father wanted."

Annie cringed. No matter what she did, she'd never be the daughter her father wanted. She couldn't.

"Maybe."

Carol let the silence linger. Finally, she asked, "What aren't you saying?"

"What do you mean?"

"I feel like there's something you're not telling me."

"No ... nothing." *Liar, liar pants on fire.*

"Maybe something you aren't ready to admit."

"There's nothing. Really. Wasn't finding my father dead enough?"

"It was plenty."

Silence.

"I had my first body work session," Annie announced.

"Annie, I know there's something more ... maybe something that you've never told anyone. And I also know that you're still not ready to talk about it. But I urge you to do it soon, if not with me then with someone else. When you bring whatever happened out into the light, you'll begin to heal. Will you think about that?"

She hesitated, hating to admit she was hiding something. But maybe the coach was right. "Okay." "Good. Tell me about the body work session."

They finished up the call ten minutes later.

She spent much of the day drifting around the house, avoiding the dredged-up memories. There was no e-mail from Jim. Time was running out. Her layoff would be effective at the end of April—a week and a half away. Maybe the decision had been taken out of her hands.

A long walk on the beach shook the dregs of horror from her mind. As she walked, she began to think about what would happen if she didn't get the job offer. She'd pinned everything on it and never truly considered the possibility of not getting it. Didn't they think she could do the job? Or maybe there were consequences for her "accidental" injury of the hand-roving corporate director. She shivered, remembering his meaty paws on her skin.

She shoved the thought from her mind. It was time to get practical. She returned to the house, determined to start looking for a new job, even a temporary one.

The phone rang while she was finishing up dinner.

"Annie?" a strange woman's voice asked.

"Yes."

"This is your Aunt Beverly. Hello, dear."

"Oh, hello. Where are you?" She'd totally forgotten the woman's arrival.

"In San Jose. Our flight came in about ten minutes ago and I couldn't wait to call you, to hear your voice. I'm so excited to see you tomorrow!"

"Yes, me too."

"Where do you want to meet?"

They arranged to have lunch at Michael's on Main. She tossed and turned that night, wondering what her aunt had to say. An hour before lunch she started getting ready, taking extra care with her makeup to hide the circles under her eyes, but she still arrived at the restaurant fifteen minutes early.

Beverly Gerhard arrived at Michael's right on time. "Thank heaven for GPS!" she exclaimed. Thin, with a gray pixie haircut, Beverly moved with a grace that must have come from decades of dancing.

"It's so nice to finally meet you," she said, enveloping Annie with a hug. She stood back with her hands on Annie's shoulders. "You are beautiful, like I knew you'd be. You're the spitting image of your great-aunt Ruth. "

"I never knew her."

"She couldn't stand her brother, your grandfather, so she didn't come around much. I think she died when you were about five."

There was so much she didn't know, Annie realized. They

seldom went to her father's parents' house—her father and grandfather didn't get along—and her grandparents died when she was ten. She didn't know anything at all about aunts, great-aunts, or cousins.

Her mother was an only child whose parents had died before she was born.

"I can't wait to learn more about my family," she said as they walked inside.

"It smells wonderful," Beverly said. "Oh, how beautiful!" The hostess seated them at a window overlooking the kitchen garden. Huge oaks necklaced with strings of lights hung over the unseen river.

"It's even prettier at night," Annie said.

"What's good to eat here?" Beverly asked.

"Almost anything. You have to have an order of crispy sweet potato fries though—it's the specialty."

"Let's split them. And I'll have a Corralitos Cobb Salad," she said to the waiter. "It sounds delicious. I love to try new things."

"Make that two," Annie said.

Suddenly, Annie ran out of things to say. Who was this woman? Was she the demon her mother had called her or someone else?

"What have you heard about me?" Beverly asked.

"I didn't even know you existed."

"Well, someone must have told you something because you're looking at me like I have horns and a tail."

"Oh! I'm sorry. I didn't mean ... it's just ... well ... Mom didn't have anything nice to say."

"I imagine," Beverly said drily.

"It's none of my business. What do you do now? How did you become a dancer?"

"I think it probably is your business. I'm sorry I stayed away so long. But they were all against me—my parents, your dad, even your mother. I was buried by their righteousness. I had to leave to survive."

"Mom said you were pregnant."

"I bet she said I had an abortion, too."

"Yes."

Beverly shook her head and leaned back so the waiter could serve their drinks. Idly, she ran her finger down the condensation on the glass. "I think I need to begin at the beginning." She looked up at Annie. "Some of this may be hard to hear, but it's important. Can you handle tough stuff?"

I've been handling it all my life. She nodded.

"Mark, your father, was about five when I was born. I was an 'accident.' My dad told me my mother slipped up and he was burdened with me. I didn't even have the decency to be born a boy."

The words were clipped and unemotional, as if the memories were too painful to relive.

"I could feel my father watching me as I grew. It was like he was waiting for something. Everyone was always tense, watching him, waiting. Then everything would explode. He'd yell and scream about the stupidest things—his shirts weren't hung up correctly, or my mother had used the car without his permission. He'd hit her. Mark hid me in his room." She looked at Annie. "Your father was a good man once."

"He didn't stay that way." Annie's stomach churned.

"Physical abuse is passed down, unfortunately. It takes a strong person to break the cycle and your father wasn't brave enough. I learned more about abuse after I ran away. It was part of the healing process for me."

She leaned forward. "There's a cycle. After the craziness subsides, the honeymoon begins. In our family, there were dinners, flowers, and pretty jewelry for my mother. We'd go to movies as a family. Eventually, the tension would begin again. We were living on top of a bomb and we all knew, even though we never talked about it, that the bomb would eventually go off. Sometimes I think my mom hung the shirts up wrong just to trigger it and get it over with."

"Why didn't your mother leave? Why didn't *my* mother leave?"

"Abusers are very clever. They manipulate their victims into thinking that they're powerless. My mother was convinced she'd starve without my father. She believed he'd take us away from her and she'd never see us again. Like most victims, my mother believed she deserved the treatment. If only she'd been a better wife, lover, cook, whatever, she wouldn't be hit."

Annie heard the words echo in her own mind. If only I'd been a better wife, daughter, mother ... "I think I understand that," she said slowly.

Beverly paused. "Yes, I think you do. And I'm sorry for that."

"Why should you be sorry?"

Her aunt sighed and took a long sip of iced tea. She tented her long fingers, her rings gleaming in the sun streaming through the window. She looked outside, as if trying to gather strength from the natural beauty outside the window.

"It's a shame to bring such horror into this peaceful place," Beverly said. She looked at Annie with her deep hazel eyes. "Remember I said that I felt like my dad was watching me, waiting for something?"

Annie nodded.

"The first time I got my period, my parents made a big deal of it. It was odd, because they'd never made a big deal of anything else in my life. When I was finished for the first time, they had a special supper—I think Mark stayed at a friend's house to avoid it. My father said, 'You're a woman, now, Beverly.'"

Annie felt like a stone dropped in her gut.

Chapter 20

"My mom gave me a gift after dinner," Beverly continued. "A very pretty white nightgown. She had a strange expression on her face when she told me to go put it on and come out to show them." Beverly's voice tightened. "I could hear them arguing while I changed. It stopped when he slapped her. When I saw how the gown made me look, I really didn't want to go out."

Beverly took a long drink. "It was sheer. I left my bra and panties on, but I still felt exposed. I didn't want anyone to see me like this, much less my father. I heard him bellowing for me to come out. My mother came to the door, her cheek red and tears in her eyes. She took me by the hand and led me out."

"I think you know what came next," she said to Annie. "My mother went to her bedroom and my father took me back to mine. He ... he raped me." Beverly's voice choked.

Annie's mouth went dry. "How old were you?"

"Thirteen."

It was the same age that Annie had been when she first got her period.

The two women sat in silence.

"You'd think I should be over it by now. It's been forty years," Beverly finally said. "But I don't think you ever get over a betrayal that deep." She drained her glass. The waiter, who'd been keeping an eye on them from a far doorway, immediately came to refill it.

"He came to my bedroom a few times a month after that. It continued through my high school years. He threatened to kill my mother if I told anyone. I believed him and never told."

"How did you survive?"

A small smile came to Beverly's face. "When I was little, my mom had taken me to dance lessons. I loved ballet and jazz. She only paid for lessons for a couple of years and then said they were a waste of time. I stopped going, but I never forgot the feeling. I was in my own little world of music and movement.

"When I was in high school, a new dance teacher came to town—someone who'd retired from a dance troop in Los Angeles. I saved from my lunch money, stole from my mother's purse and my dad's wallet. I figured they owed me. I talked my way into a scholarship and got my lessons. Claire, the teacher's name was Claire, said I had talent and took me on as an assistant. She gave me private lessons and encouraged me to go to New York when I graduated."

"Did you ever tell Claire about ...?"

Beverly shook her head. "Not until I had to. Saying it aloud would make it real. When it was only in my mind, I could pretend it wasn't really happening."

The waiter came to serve their meals. With unspoken agreement, the women changed topics. Beverly told Annie about her friend in San Jose. Annie gave Beverly an abbreviated picture of her life—college, marriage to Fred, and David's birth. As the meal wound down, Annie realized she still had unanswered questions. How had her aunt escaped? How did she become a dancer in New York?

The waiter cleared their plates and they ordered coffee. "It's too bad you can't stay and meet David," Annie said.

"Perhaps next time. Unfortunately, this is a busy time of year for dance instructors— spring recitals eat up a lot of time. And, since this is my first full year in Athens, I need to make it work."

"What made you move to Georgia?"

"To answer that, I need to finish telling you my story. That's why I took this trip. After my husband died, I felt a strong urge to reconnect with you. I guess I felt guilty for abandoning you all those years ago. I want to tell you my story in hopes that you'll forgive me."

Annie felt Beverly's gaze bore into her. It would be difficult to hide secrets from her aunt. And she wasn't ready to talk about herself. "I don't think there's anything to forgive you for. But I do want to hear your story. What happened next? How did you get away to New York?" *And what about the baby?*

"I learned to lie there doing imaginary *jetés* in my head until it was over." Beverly's breath caught. "The only time it didn't work was the day I saw Mark watching. My dad had left the door slightly ajar. He was on top of me, grunting, when I heard the door squeak. I looked up and there was Mark, outside the bedroom, staring at me. I mouthed the words, 'Help me.' He didn't move. Then I saw him smile. He just stood there and watched, smiling."

Beverly used the napkin to blot a tear that had slipped from her eye. She grasped Annie's hand. "That's why I felt it was important to come here and why I feel bad about staying away all those years. I worried that Mark would turn out to be like my dad." She seemed to hesitate for a moment. "Did your father abuse you?"

"No."

Beverly cocked her head and said, "I think we both know that's not entirely true. I can see it in your eyes. I know this is tough. You've probably never admitted what happened to anyone, no matter how many therapists you've gone to. I felt ashamed for years. Like it was my fault somehow."

She took a deep breath. "But I learned that you need to say the words aloud to heal. You hardly know me, but maybe there's someone you trust to tell the truth. Is there?"

Annie steeled herself. "Nothing happened."

Beverly leaned back, her face sagging a little, the dancing

sprite gone from her eyes. "I hope you change your mind someday." She hesitated a moment. "In fact, if you need to tell my story so you can tell your own, you have my permission."

"Oh, okay." Annie didn't know if she'd tell the story to anyone. *Maybe Elizabeth. Maybe not.* "You still haven't told me how you got to New York."

Beverly drank deeply from her coffee cup and stared out the window. Annie didn't think she was seeing the riverside garden.

"I came up pregnant. I couldn't stand the thought of having my father's bastard, but I couldn't abort it either. I finally told Claire, my dance teacher. She helped me set up the appointment, pretended to be my parent, and signed the consent form, but when the time came, I couldn't go through with it. No matter what someone else had done to me, I couldn't take it out on the child.

"The night after I graduated, I ran away. Claire gave me bus fare and the name of a contact in New York who helped me get a place, find a job, and start taking classes again. But the stress and activity must have been too much. One day after coming home from class, I started bleeding. I miscarried the baby."

Beverly's eyes moistened. Idly, she wiped away the tear that trickled down her face. "The guy at the emergency room was a new doctor. He botched the D&C. I was never able to have another child."

It was Annie's turn to reach across and hold her aunt's hand. "I'm so sorry."

They sat quietly for a moment.

"Enough," Beverly said, waving at the waiter for a check. Annie looked around. The room had emptied while they were talking, but like many of the small restaurants in the county, the staff had let them be.

They gathered their things and left the building.

"There was a happy ending," Beverly said as they reached her rental car. "I got to dance with Alvin Alley, one of the best troupes in the country. I met Jerry there. We fell in love and lived in New York until he died a few years ago from cancer. Athens was his hometown. We'd spent many summers there with his family—Jerry had three sisters and a dozen nieces and nephews. They adopted me as one of their own. It felt natural to move there when I retired."

She glanced at her watch. "I have to go, my flight leaves at four." She took both of Annie's hands in hers. "I felt it was important to see you and I'm glad I came. I hope my story can make a difference in your life. Tell someone what happened, Annie. It's important. The truth has the power to change your whole life."

Beverly hugged her and stepped into her car. Annie waved as her aunt drove out of the parking lot.

She'd never felt so alone.

She numbly moved to the Prius. Put one foot in front of the other. That's what she had to do. Keep everything in control, plan every action, don't rely on anyone and it would all be okay—she wouldn't be hurt. Annie felt her face soften and tears fill her eyes, but she couldn't let go, not here in the parking lot.

Maybe Beverly was right; it was time to face the truth. She'd lost her control over most of her life anyway—David, her job, even Fred wasn't the same. Maybe it was time to face the fact that she never really had control in the first place. It was all an illusion.

Annie sighed. She hadn't really lied to Beverly. Her father hadn't raped her. But that didn't mean he hadn't tried.

# # #

After dinner, Annie sat in the living room and stared at the phone in her hand. She hadn't heard from Elizabeth in days, which was strange. But she wasn't sure she was ready to tell her friend about Beverly's revelations. Friendship won out.

Elizabeth sounded distant when she answered.

"What's wrong? You sound awful."

"Do I? Must be allergies."

"C'mon Elizabeth, we've been friends too long."

In the end, they agreed to meet for dinner the following night while Fred was attending David's soccer practice.

Annie hung up the phone and sat quietly, mulling over Beverly's story and thinking about her own. She'd never told the whole truth of her childhood or her father's suicide to anyone, even her mother. Good therapists always knew she was hiding something, but she stopped going when they got too close.

What difference could talking about it make? The memories made her feel ashamed and inadequate. If she told others the story, they'd know the truth—that her father had killed himself because of her. Maybe if she only told part of the story, they'd accept that and move on. She didn't have to tell them the worst.

# # #

When Annie arrived at Elizabeth's, her friend led her to the dining nook where brightly colored plates, linens, and fine crystal punctuated the dark wood. A crisp spring salad with baby greens and cherry tomatoes commanded the center of the table while an uncorked bottle of Thomas Fogarty Pinot noir waited for the meal to begin.

"This is lovely!" Annie exclaimed. "You must have spent hours. What's the occasion?"

"I'm Italian," Elizabeth said with a laugh. "Italians don't need an occasion for food."

She and Annie sat down and started eating, chatting about

the events of their days like an old married couple avoiding a testy discussion. Finally, Elizabeth seemed to have had enough of the pretense. She poured herself a second glass of wine and announced, "I think Bobby and I are going to break up."

Annie was floored. "What? Why?"

"I really don't want to marry him and that's all he wants."

"I've never understood why you don't want to marry him."

"The truth is that I like living alone. I can make a mess if I want to and leave it for days. I can eat out of the freezer and leave the dishes in the sink. I don't have to pick up someone else's socks!"

"Right," Annie said and looked pointedly at the extravagant meal. "Somehow I find it hard to picture you living like a slob and eating out of the freezer."

Elizabeth laughed. "Okay. I'd cook and clean anyway." She thought for a moment. "I think it's ... I don't know ... Bobby's a lot like Joe. He's got big energy. I feel lost around him sometimes. I'm afraid if he was here all the time I'd forget who I was.

"I feel like everyone's always tried to mold me into the vision of what they thought I should be," she continued. "First my parents, then Joe, and now Bobby. Did I tell you Bobby's running for district supervisor?"

Annie shook her head. She knew that Bobby had retired early from his lucrative financial planning job a few years earlier but hadn't realized that he was interested in politics.

"Well, he is. If we get married, he'll want me by his side, campaigning as he climbs from office to office. I'll have to give up my shop and wear Chanel suits and white pearls. And gloves ... do campaign wives still wear gloves and pillbox hats?"

Annie laughed.

"I guess I am getting carried away," Elizabeth said.

"Uh-huh."

"But you do get the picture, don't you? I like being a separate person. I'm still discovering who I am."

"And you don't think you can do that being married?"

Elizabeth shook her head. "My mother catered to my dad's needs. I see my sisters and my brother's wives doing the same thing. When I was married to Joe, I took care of the kids and house. When I had free time, I spent it with him."

"I don't think it has to be that way. I know lots of independent women at work who have husbands, kids, and career and still find time to take a spa vacation with their girlfriends."

"Sounds exhausting."

"They seem to manage." Annie hesitated. "I have to ask something. Are you in love with Bobby?"

"Of course I am. At least I think so. After five years together I ought to be." Elizabeth looked across at her friend. "Shouldn't I?"

"I'm not sure 'should' and 'love' go together very well."

"Do you suppose I won't marry him because I simply don't love him? Have I been using him all these years? Maybe I should talk to someone." Annie stood and fetched her purse. Pulling a small square out of her bag, she handed it to Elizabeth. "I have just the person."

Elizabeth glanced at the card. "Carol Eos, Life Coach." She chuckled. "How's that going for you?"

"It's going well, I think. There's so much going on—the coaching, the body work, John, and now Beverly. I feel like the pieces of my life are churning in a kaleidoscope, but I haven't turned it the right way to make a picture."

"I'm not sure I'd want go through all that confusion." Elizabeth put Carol's card on the sideboard. "Was your aunt helpful? What was she like?"

"Very different from my dad. She's tall and willowy—exactly what you think of when you think of a dancer. She feels so alive, and, I don't know, _light,' I guess. My dad always felt dark and angry."

"From everything you've told me, he was."

"It gets worse." Annie took a deep breath. Elizabeth listened in obvious horror as she told her Beverly's tale of sexual abuse.

"And your dad stood there and watched your grandfather rape her?" Elizabeth looked utterly disgusted. "Did he—did he ever try anything with you?" Elizabeth watched her friend carefully.

Annie shook her head. "No, nothing ever happened." But even she could hear the false note in her voice as she said it.

# # #

John flipped through the *Good Times* as he stood by the cash register. There had to be something interesting to do on a Friday night. He wanted to make the night special for Annie. He heard footsteps and set the paper down to wait on a customer, but looked up to see Sunshine.

"I thought you might be interested in this." She handed him a printed e-mail with the subject line: *Ellis Paul, April 19th*. "One of the times Annie was in here we got to talking about folk music. We like the same people. Rumor has it you're taking her out tomorrow."

"What's this?" John asked, gesturing with the paper.

"It's a house concert. Well, they used to be house concerts. Now they're winery concerts." She must have seen John's total look of confusion. "You've never been to a house concert?"

He shook his head.

She sighed. "You really did live in the sticks. Singer-songwriters, like Ellis Paul, perform in houses across the country. The homeowner has a large room and a mailing list of people interested in hearing them. My friend, Jasper, has been doing them for years. I've seen some great people—Cozy Sheridan, Vance Gilbert, Dave Mallett ..."

"Who are they?"

"Musicians. Like the ones Annie likes to listen to."

"Oh."

"Anyway," Sunshine continued. "Jasper also owns a winery by Swift Street. He switched the house concerts down there since it's more convenient than his house in the mountains."

"Thanks for educating me, Sunshine. I feel less like a country hick now." John smiled fondly at Sunshine. She was a good employee, and, in some ways, a good friend.

"I'm trying to take care of you here. If you really want to impress Annie, this would do it!"

John raised his eyebrows and waited for her to continue.

"See, I signed up for my mom and me to go, but she wound up having emergency surgery and I need to take care of her. The concert's sold out, but you could use my tickets. You could take Annie." Sunshine emphasized the last word and smiled as if she'd given him a huge present. Which she had.

"I hope your mother will be okay. Do you think she'd like him?"

"My mother? It's routine surgery and there shouldn't be complications. And, yes, she likes Ellis Paul—but it's Annie I was talking about. Ellis Paul is borderline famous. I can't believe they can still snag him for a house concert. You'd make points—megapoints."

"Thanks, Sunshine. You're a life saver."

"Remember that the next time you're handing out bonuses," she said. "Tell Jasper you're taking my seats. Enjoy!"

John couldn't wait for the lunchtime employee to come back to take over the register. He wanted call Annie right away.

# # #

Annie paced the living room as she waited for two o'clock, the time of her appointed call with Carol. She'd managed to avoid the story with Elizabeth, but she had a feeling it wouldn't be as easy with the coach.

The conversation started off casually enough with comments on the weather of the respective coasts. But Carol never spent too much time in idle talk. "Are you ready to dig deeper?" she asked.

"What do you mean?"

"From what you've told me, you've spent much of your life trying to appease the men in your life, keeping them calm so you'd stay safe. That's understandable given your father's suicide and Fred's alcoholism. But I can't help thinking there's something more, something you're afraid to tell anyone. Am I right?"

"I met my aunt this week."

"And ..."

Annie told her Beverly's story, hoping the horror of the tale would deflect any further questions about her own life.

"Your aunt certainly had a rough time of it. Did she say why she told you that story?"

"She wanted to explain why she'd never met me before."

"Anything else?" The coach probed further.

"Not really."

"Nice try, Annie, but if this is going to work for you, if you're really going to change your life, you need to admit the truth."

"Funny," Annie said. "Aunt Bev said something similar."

The silence lingered. There really wasn't going to be any way out of this.

"Right after I had my first period, my parents had their worst fight ever," Annie began. "I locked myself in my room, but I could

258

hear shouting and the sound of breaking glass. My father kept yelling, 'It's my right! It's the only thing girls are good for! She's got to be taught her place.' Eventually he left the house ... I could hear the door slam. I waited a while and then came out of the room."

Annie had always kept the horror at bay by sticking to the facts. She took a deep breath. "Mom was in the kitchen. Her eye was swollen and her lip was bleeding."

As Carol kept quiet, Annie began to shudder. The shudders turned into sobs.

"It was so horrible. It was my fault she looked like that. She ... she was protecting me."

Carol waited until her sobs diminished. "Tell me the rest," she said.

"Mom said I had to be careful," Annie whispered. "She could barely talk. She said never be alone with my father. Always keep my door locked. I remember her looking at me ... she was very fierce ... she said, 'If he tries anything, you tell me.' I promised her. She told me to go back to my room. I did. We never talked about it again."

"What did your dad do?"

"He came home later that night and tried my door. He banged on it for a while, demanding to be let in. I ... I was afraid he might push it down, but he went away. I locked my door every night. And I listened to my mother. I never went anywhere with him alone. If he was home and my mom wasn't, I went to a friend's house."

Annie paused. "He tried every night for a long time. Then it was only once in a while—I think he was trying to catch me unaware." Her breath caught. "Eventually, he gave up and left me alone." *Until he died.*

Annie heard Carol's intake of air over the phone. "So you

escaped the rape that your aunt experienced. But you didn't really escape. You know that, don't you?"

"I suppose."

"How do you feel?"

"I don't know. Exhausted, I think. Drained."

"Is there something else you think you should have done?"

"I should have given in. Then he would have stopped hurting my mother. I was a coward. I should have let him do what he wanted and gotten it over with. Maybe if I'd done that, my mother would be more normal now."

"No, Annie. You did the right thing. Your mother wanted to protect you. Unfortunately, she wasn't strong enough to leave, but she did the best she could. She's probably buried the truth, not wanting to face it. Your father was the one who was wrong—not you or your mother. Can you believe that?"

"I've tried all my life to believe that."

"What stops you?"

"I don't know."

"That's what we need to figure out. When's your next body work appointment?"

"Tomorrow afternoon."

"Good. I want you to ask your healer to work on the root chakra. It's at the base of your spine—she'll know what it is. While she does that, I want you to think about what you've told me."

"What good will that do?" Annie asked.

"We carry our memories in our cells. The root chakra is all about survival—your right to exist. Your memories are locked in your body, including the story that you've told yourself—that the abuse was your fault. Somehow you need to release that lie. We'll have to try every method we have to help you let it go. When you do, I think your choices will become clearer. Are you still journaling?"

Annie groaned. "Yes. I suppose I need to continue that, too."

"Yes, dear." Carol chuckled.

They finished up the conversation and scheduled the next appointment.

She'd barely hung up when the phone rang again.

"How are you?" John asked when she answered.

Chapter 21

"I'm okay," Annie said. Her heart surged.

"That's good," John said. "Remember I said to save Friday night for me?"

"Yes."

"I lucked into a couple of tickets for something I hope you'll enjoy. I didn't recognize the name, but maybe you will—Ellis Paul?"

"Really? You've never heard of Ellis Paul? And you have tickets?"

"I looked him up online—he doesn't appear to get to Montana much, so I've never heard of him. And, yes, I have tickets for a concert in a winery by ..." Annie could hear papers rustling. "Swift Street. Will you come with me?"

"Oh, yes. Thank you! This is fantastic!"

"I'll pick you up around six and we can get a quick bite to eat at the Cellar Door Café. Does that sound good?"

"I'll be ready."

"Got to go," he said. "See you tomorrow."

She hung up the phone and wandered to the kitchen to make tea, a silly grin on her face. She felt like a schoolgirl going out on her first date. She had it bad.

The sharp aroma of lemon tea wafted around her as she went back to her home office. Beverly had been right. Telling the story about her father to Carol had made it better, not worse. Annie felt hopeful for the first time in a while. Maybe some of her childhood dreams *were* possible. If she could find a job where she didn't have to invest so much of herself, maybe she could save some of her time and energy for her music.

With a sense of purpose, she began to look at the job banks online. While full-time jobs could be found in places like Cleveland, Ohio, they were scarce around San Jose. And the salary range of the Ohio jobs would never let her keep her house in Costanoa and she'd still have to move. Perhaps a consultant job was the best choice for now.

She found a few jobs that she might be a match for— temporarily managing projects at smaller firms. The pay was close to what she'd been making at JCN, but there weren't any benefits. She'd cross that bridge when she came to it. Maybe it was time to ask Fred to cover David's insurance.

She pulled up her resume and began to work on it, stopping only to have dinner with her son.

That night, she dreamt of her father pounding on her door, yelling to be let in. She forced herself awake, threw off her covers and went to the kitchen to brew some tea. Grabbing a pen and pad, she began to make notes about restarting her music career. The ideas came easily—songs to rememorize, venues to check out. Maybe she should build a website.

An hour later, she returned to bed and fell into a dreamless sleep. The next morning she sent off her resume to the two jobs she'd identified. A quick check of her work e-mail revealed only one new note—from her boss, Randy.

"I need you to come in on Monday. I've heard from Jim and there're a few things we need to discuss about the job in New Jersey."

Drat! The job was still a possibility. She needed to make a decision soon.

Annie sent a quick reply telling Randy that she'd be there Monday morning.

Before she left for her body work appointment, Annie

recycled the box from the printer cartridges she'd ordered, cutting the tape that held it together with her jackknife before tossing the box in the blue recycling can. She thrust the knife in her jeans pocket, locked the door, and took off.

Sukesha was waiting for her when she arrived. Soothing music began to still the chatter in her brain.

"How are you today?" Sukesha asked.

"It's good to be here—a lot going on."

"Yes?"

Annie hesitated. "Things are changing. I'm not sure how exactly, or what's going to happen, but it feels different."

"Yes." Sukesha was a woman of few words.

"My coach asked if you could work on my root chakra. I'm not sure what she expects, but I figured I'd ask. Is it something you do?"

"Yes."

Sukesha led Annie back into the massage room. As she disrobed, Annie felt vulnerable, like she was a newborn experiencing life for the first time, not sure what was out there for her. She lay down on the massage table and covered up before Sukesha entered. Although she couldn't see her, Annie heard the soft swish of the woman's feet on the rattan mat.

"It's good that you're here," Sukesha said as she splayed her hands on Annie's back. "The work we'll do today is deep work. Let it be whatever it wants to be." She placed a tissue box on the floor where Annie could reach them as she lay face down on the table.

That's not a good sign.

"You're safe," Sukesha murmured. She pulled back the covers and began to massage the sides of Annie's spine.

Annie let herself drift with the soft pressure of the woman's hands. Sukesha was soothing—in fact the whole environment—pale yellow walls, melodic new age music and the soft scent of lavender—lulled her to that sweet place between awareness and sleep. Eyes closed, she could feel the energy move lower in her body, awakening the core of her sexuality.

With that energy, memories crept into her mind, recent ones first. She stirred thinking about the kiss she'd shared with John the last time they met. What would tonight bring? Was she ready to move beyond a kiss? Absorbing the energy of the massage without awareness of the person giving it, Annie forgot Sukesha was in the room. There'd been a long dry spell before John. The few men she'd dated didn't turn her on. She skipped over the misery that marked the end of her marriage with Fred, but recalled the tenderness and passion of the beginning.

He'd been tender with her, courting her with flowers, candles and romantic music. She was aware of his desire for her, his hands roving over her body, lighting her on fire.

She stirred on the table as memories of the early years of her relationship flooded her body. Energy swirled around her, feelings of joy and sorrow blending like the colors of light through a prism. Annie was unaware of the soft tears and her body's deepening relaxation under Sukesha's fingers.

All of a sudden, *he* was there in her mind. Her father's eyes following her around, making her feel unclean. She'd shower two or three times a day, trying to rub off dirt she couldn't even see. He'd remind her to keep her legs closed like a lady should, at the same time he stared at her growing breasts. She shuddered as she remembered her doorknob turning when he checked to see if she'd forgotten to lock him out.

Her tears turned to sobs. Sukesha continued to massage her, whispering, "It's okay. Let it go. Release it."

Annie cried until there was nothing left. Sukesha's massage turned to comforting touches. The body worker covered her with warm blankets and stroked her hair, until Annie's breathing returned to normal.

"Are you all right to be alone to get dressed?" Sukesha asked.

Unsure of her voice, Annie nodded. After the woman left the room, Annie lay there for a long while, tuning in to the sound of her own breathing. She was exhausted, but for the first time in her life, the anxiety that had always been with her was gone. It was as if someone had turned off a low frequency motor that she didn't even know was annoying her.

She sat up, keeping the blanket wrapped around her. The feeling of freedom persisted as she sat there, gathering the strength to get up.

Once dressed, she sat with Sukesha in the anteroom. "That was a powerful release," the woman said. "You'll need to take good care of yourself. Drink lots of water and walk outside. The beach would be good." She smiled. "We're lucky to live in such a beautiful place."

She placed her hands on Annie's and looked deeply into her eyes. "You'll be all right, Annie Gerhard."

Annie took the beach road home from Santa Cruz. Idly, she looked at the lazy boats in the harbor and the cars edging the beachfront. Seagulls soared and dove, doing loops that rivaled the best stunt pilot. She envied them their freedom.

Once home, she didn't bother going inside after parking the car. A walk on the beach sounded good to her. She walked the few short blocks to the stairway from the cliff to the beach. She drifted, more than walked down the steps, noticing flowers she'd never seen before poking their luminescent faces from the foliage.

She kicked off her shoes at the edge of the boardwalk. Cool damp sand pebbles quickly covered her feet.

Avoiding the remains of beach fires and shards of plastic toys, she picked her way to the shoreline. She stood on the packed sand and waited. Water crashed around her, wetting her jeans to the knees. Yelling with the shock, she laughed at her own reaction.

She'd never felt so alive.

A squawk alerted her to a seagull up the beach. She walked over to it. Strong wings beat for liftoff, but the bird stayed rooted to the sand, frantically cawing in fear, trapped in fishing line.

She studied the bird for a few minutes, trying to ignore its thrashing and calls. If only she had something to cut the fishing line. Her bulky sweatshirt would protect her. If she put the seagull under her arm ... Annie searched through her pockets for something sharp and smiled when her fingers touched the jackknife from her recycling. She made her move.

It wasn't as easy as she'd imagined. The bird didn't want to get tucked under her arm and used his beak mercilessly to let her know it. But Annie persevered, finally kneeling and straddling the gull to get to its feet. The bird continued its attack on her rear. Good thing she had extra padding there.

"Dammit! Cut that out! I'm only trying to help you!" she yelled. The sooner she cut the line, the better. Fortunately, the knife was sharp and the line had only wrapped around the left foot a few times.

"There!" she said, launching herself off the gull when it was freed. The bird looked at her and squawked its indignation before flapping its wings and soaring off over the bay.

She was covered with sand and gull bites. Her feet and legs were wet and cold. But as she watched the bird take flight, she knew part of her soul was flying with it.

Laughing, she picked herself up and brushed the sand from her clothes. She trudged back up to the boardwalk, washed her feet, and stuffed them into her socks and shoes. It was going to be a beautiful day.

When she'd arrived home from her walk on the beach, Annie went straight to the garage and retrieved her guitar. She wasn't going to be able to support herself and David on the income of a singer-songwriter—at least not yet—but there was no reason she couldn't start playing again. Looking at her watch, she was startled to realize how late it was. John would be here in less than an hour to pick her up.

She flew around her bedroom. When she was done, she looked at herself in the mirror, trying to imagine herself through John's eyes. *Will he like me?*

Her hair was unruly; there was no fix for that. She'd chosen an olive-green sweater to go with the jeans and sneakers John had recommended. Eye makeup highlighted the green of her eyes. Silver and jade earrings dangled from her ears. Okay. Not bad.

But will he want me? The question rose unbidden from her mind.

Annie shook her head. She wasn't sure she was ready for that, even if he did.

The doorbell rang promptly at five. Annie took a deep breath and opened the door.

"You look wonderful," John said kissing Annie lightly on the mouth.

The kiss was too brief; she wanted more.

"Here," John said as he handed her a small box. "I thought you might like these. I didn't want to come empty-handed."

"They're perfect, John. I love Donnelly's chocolates. Let me get my jacket." She ran upstairs, dropped the box on a table, and grabbed her coat. "I'm ready."

He let her precede him down the front steps. "The truck's not the sleekest date-night vehicle, but it's what I have," he said.

"It'll be fine, John." She smiled, filled with happiness.

They chatted amicably as they made their way to the cluster of wineries on the outskirts of Santa Cruz. John found a parking place on the street and they walked past the converted warehouse space to the Bonny Doon winery and café in the back. Tall open doors led into a cavernous room where replicated redwood wine tanks dominated the decor. A hostess escorted them past the tanks to the sleek café in the back.

"Quite different from the last restaurant we went to," John said.

"Yes, but I've never been here before and I like new experiences."

"Me, too." He grinned at her and she grinned back.

Once their order was placed—roasted chicken for him, small crab cakes and a green bean and peach salad for her—it seemed natural to hold hands across the table. John rubbed her hand with the inside of his thumb. Annie shivered.

"Everything okay?" he asked.

"Everything's wonderful," she said, giving him a warm grin. *I was only wondering what it would be like to have your hands all over my naked body.*

"Have you heard Ellis Paul before?" John asked.

Annie told him of the time she'd seen the singer on a business trip to Boston. He'd been performing in a basement café in Cambridge. She described the concert, humming a few lines from some of Paul's songs. He watched her with a slight smile, his eyes never leaving her face. Annie enjoyed the rapt attention. *It's the greatest gift anyone can give—complete listening.*

He entertained her by recounting some of the acts that he'd seen in Missoula, including the legendary Bob Dylan. By the time they finished their meal, they were primed to hear the concert.

They walked to the winery and gave Sunshine's name to the person at the door, a tall thin man with a ponytail.

"Good thing she reserved the space for you. It's a sold-out concert," Jason, the winery owner, said. "Would you like to be on our mailing list for future concerts?"

"Sure," John said, giving Jason his e-mail address.

"Me, too," Annie said.

After they claimed their seats with their jackets, they returned for a glass of wine from the tasting bar. She looked around while John paid for their drinks. Shiny metal tanks lined one side of the rows of chairs while stacked oak barrels buttressed the other. Tiny and industrial though it was, she absorbed the romance of the wine business—the sweet smell of fermenting grapes, the exotic names stamped on the barrel ends and the low murmur of voices from people having a good time.

They sat on the metal folding chairs. He wrapped his arm around her shoulders, glancing down at her as he did so. She snuggled next to him, enjoying his masculine smell.

As good as Ellis Paul was, she was distracted throughout the concert. Her mind raced ahead to the end of the night. Should she invite John in? Was she ready for what might happen?

"Remember what I told you," John said as they walked to the car hand in hand.

"What was that?" Had she missed something important?

"When you're ready to do your first concert, you can perform it at Ocean Reads."

"It'll be a while," she said, exhaling with relief. "But I promise your bookstore will be my comeback session."

"Good," he said and leaned down to kiss her. Annie turned to him, hungry to feel his lips on hers. She leaned into his body and his arms encircled her. As they kissed, she felt his desire mount. He must have felt it, too, because he abruptly broke off the kiss.

"The street is probably not the best place for this," he said with a smile. Putting his arm around her shoulders, he led her to the car. Every nerve in her body tingled.

They chatted about the concert on the way to her house, not mentioning the kiss in the street. He drove with one hand, the other tightly grasping hers. When they reached her drive, he said,

"Hang on, I'll help you down."

He opened her door and she began to step out of the truck, but he put his hands on her waist and helped her out. She took in a quick breath as the warmth of his touch sent waves through her. He pulled her close and she raised her face to receive his kiss. His lips teased hers before he took possession of her mouth. She slipped her hands under his jacket and splayed them against his taut muscles, pulling him closer. She felt him grow hard against her leg.

"Not here," he said and put his hand in the small of her back to propel her up the stairs. She fumbled with her key but finally got the door open.

"David's at a friends," she said at the same time he asked, "Where's David?"

"I feel like I'm sneaking into my parents' house when they're not home." She giggled.

"I know what you mean."

She took his hand and led him to the living room. He pulled her against him, one hand threading through her hair, pressing her mouth closer to his. The other hand caressed her back and then slipped under her sweater. He pulled back for a moment and looked at her questioningly.

She nodded. *Yes ... oh yes.*

He untangled his hand from her hair and slid his palm to her bottom, pulling her close against him. She felt the heat build between her legs, moisture beginning to pool as her own desire mounted. He felt as good as she'd imagined—hard planes and sharp angles— totally male.

She felt his hand tentatively cover her breast. They both groaned with the contact and he increased the pressure. His thumb rubbed her nipple, teasing it up, driving more ache to her groin. Their kisses deepened even further and she slid her hands

271

to his butt, pulling him close.

Gently, he lifted his lips from her mouth. His eyes were shining. "You're so pretty, Annie. I want you, but if you're not ready, we need to stop now, before things go any further. I don't want to be someone you'll regret in the morning."

She stared up at him. It was a big step, especially for someone she'd known only a short while. But he'd always treated her with respect and even now he was asking permission. She had the power to say yes or no, to do what she wanted. Wasn't that what this whole journey she'd been on was about—to discover what she wanted and act on it?

"I'll be happy to see you in the morning," she said and led the way to the bedroom.

Once there, he turned her to face him. "I want to see you," he said. "All of you."

Embarrassment overtook her. "No, you don't. I'm not twenty anymore."

He laughed. "Neither am I. But you're beautiful, Annie, and I want to make you believe it. May I?" He grasped the bottom of her sweater.

She nodded.

He kissed her after each article of clothing was removed. After he'd taken her bra off, he put his hands under her breasts, hefting their weight and rubbing his thumbs against the nipples. She arched back.

"Your shirt, too," she said. "I want to feel you against my skin."

He complied. She ran her fingers over his chest, stroking the fine silky hair that was sprinkled across his skin, and teasing his nipples. She lingered over a scar near his shoulder.

He shrugged. "Penalty of ranch work."

She kissed the scar and traced the puckered skin with her

tongue. He gave a small moan and cupped her breast with his hand. She rubbed her hips against his, the rough texture of his jeans intensifying her desire. When had she become so wanton?

She gasped when he scooped her up and placed her on the bed. "And that's the benefit of ranch work," he chuckled. He leaned over her, and she lost herself in the depth of his blue eyes. "I want to make love to you, Annie," he said. "May I?"

"Yes," she whispered.

Chapter 22

An hour later, John lay with his arm wrapped around Annie, her head on his shoulder. Moonlight streamed through the unshaded bedroom window, allowing the ghostly shadows of furniture to take shape. He heard her give a contented sigh and smiled. He was startled when a few moments later he felt a drop of moisture. He rubbed her arm with his hand. "What's the matter?" She rolled closer and buried her face in his chest. "I don't know." He could barely make out her muffled reply. Her tears increased and she made tiny sobs into his chest. He pulled her closer, stroked her hair with his hand, and waited it out.

"I don't know what came over me," she said. "Making love to you was so good."

He stayed silent. Sometimes Jessica had cried after they made love. He didn't understand it at first, but began to realize that his wife's tears were a release of all the tension in her life, particularly after the cancer diagnosis. He'd learned that the best way to handle it was to be quiet, hold her, and let her process on her own.

He felt Annie shudder. "Maybe that's why I'm crying." She lifted her tear-stained face to him. "That was the best sex I ever had in my life." The tears started again. "Drat!"

She struggled from his arms and reached for a tissue. She dried her eyes, sat up, pulled the sheet over her bare breasts and tucked it behind her.

He could feel her staring at him and flipped to his side, propping his head up on his hand.

"You don't know me well enough," she said. "If you did, you

wouldn't have wanted me." She hiccupped a sob.

He couldn't stay silent any longer. Sitting up, he grasped her hands in his. "What are you talking about? You're wonderful. We've both had things happen in life we wish hadn't happened. I've seen you with your son and I've seen you trying to do the right thing for everyone around you. I know you well enough."

She shook her head. "You don't know everything."

"Then tell me."

She looked at him wide-eyed, took a deep breath, and started her story.

John felt his anger grow as she described her father's abuse and attempts to rape her. If the man wasn't already dead, he'd have hunted him down and killed the bastard himself. How could anyone do that to an innocent woman and child? Sometimes he hated his own gender.

"Oh, honey," he said when she'd finished. "That's not your fault. Your dad was a nasty piece of work." He reached out to take her in his arms.

She put up her hands to stop him. "There's more," she said.

He watched as she stood up and walked to her dresser. Although he was curious about her action, he appreciated the sight of her body in the moonlight. All her curves were in the right places and he felt a stirring in his groin as he watched her.

When she came back to bed, she had an envelope in her hand. She handed it to him. Her name was scrawled on the front. "He left it in my underwear drawer before he shot himself. Open it," she said. "Open it and you'll know why I don't deserve someone like you."

He did as she asked and pulled out a yellowed square of paper. "If you'd been a better daughter," it said, "I wouldn't have had to kill myself. You'll never be good enough for any man."

His rage exploded. "Bastard!" he shouted as he crumpled the

paper in his hand.

She reached out her hand as if to stop him and then halted. Slowly, she climbed back into bed and sat, her back against the headboard, sheets pulled up to her chin. She stared straight ahead as if mesmerized.

"I was only a little girl. All my life I've remembered him splattered across the bathroom. The words on that note are seared in my brain. But I was just a little girl. And my mother was brave enough and strong enough to protect me, even though she couldn't do it for herself."

She drew her knees up to her chest. "I thought marrying Fred would make my dad's voice go away. It did for a while, but I couldn't keep Fred happy, either." She shook her head. "No, that's not right. He was unhappy on his own. We're each responsible for our own happiness, aren't we?"

She looked up at him, her eyes wet with tears, streaks running down her face.

He nodded and gestured to the crumpled up piece of paper. "That note is the last cruel act of a very sick man. You're right. You were a little girl and Fred had his own problems. Maybe now that he's sober, he'll make amends for what happened in the past. You couldn't have kept him from drinking. Believe, Annie." He leant in and kissed her lips briefly. "Believe that you are good. Your heart and soul are brave and true. You've endured more than most women would be able to and survived."

He leaned away from her and studied her. Her eyes were still on his face.

"Is that everything?" he asked.

She nodded.

"So, I know everything about you and you know what?"

"What?"

"I'm willing to take the risk. You are a beautiful woman, in and out. I want to know you better and help you believe what you already know—you didn't cause your father's or Fred's problems. I want to love you because I know you're capable of loving me the way I want to be loved."

He kissed her gently and helped her slide back down into the bed. They held each other for a while before they coaxed each other to arousal. When they were finished, they both drifted off to sleep.

# # #

"Mind if I use the shower?" a male voice whispered in her ear.

Annie's eyes flew open and immediately shut after being hit by the glare of morning sunlight. A wave of warmth sliced through her as the memories of the previous night lit up her brain.

"Not at all," she murmured with a smile. "I keep spare razors and shaving gel for David in there if you need them."

The next time she opened her eyes, the sunlight was blocked by John's face as he lowered his head to kiss her. "Morning," he said.

"Mmm," she hummed against his lips.

"I'd like to stay," he said, "but we're short-handed at the bookstore this morning. Sunshine had to take care of her mom."

"What time is it?"

"About nine."

"Wow. I never sleep this late."

"We had an active night."

"Mmm." Annie circled her arms around his neck for another kiss. "I'll go make some coffee." Reluctantly, she let him go.

"I'll be in as soon as I get dressed," he said.

She slipped on her chenille robe and warm slippers and went to the kitchen, humming as she made the coffee and set out the mugs. *Should I feed him? What do I have?* She started opening cupboard doors. Nothing. She opened the refrigerator and stared for a while. Milk for cereal and that was about it. Neither she nor David were big breakfast people.

"Hi." John, freshly shaven, seemed to take up a lot of room in her small kitchen. "Can I do anything?"

"I'm afraid all I have to give you is coffee. I could run out and get something."

He shook his head. "Coffee's fine. If I get hungry later, I own a café."

"Oh. That's right." She felt awkward all of a sudden.

He came over and wrapped his arms around her. "Thank you," he said, "for being you."

Annie smiled up at him. "Yeah" was all she could manage to say. Her eyes were filling again, this time from happiness.

"When can we do this again?" he asked.

"Sleep together?"

He laughed. "Well, yes, but I want to see you again, too. I mean to court you, Annie Gerhard. I'm going to make myself so irresistible that when I ask you to marry me you won't have any choice but to say, 'yes.'"

Marry him? Wasn't he rushing things? But then she realized he wasn't. He was letting her know that he was serious; that it wasn't a one-night stand.

"It's a package deal, you know," she said.

"Don't worry. I'll include David in the courting. He'll probably be easier than you are." He kissed her, a long, lingering kiss that tasted of spearmint.

"Coffee?" she asked after he released her.

"Sure." He lowered his lanky body into a kitchen chair. Annie could feel his eyes as he followed her around the room. She poured the coffee and sat down across from him.

"What are your plans for the day?" he asked.

"I have to pick up David at the county dump at noon. He's doing his service up there. He took a bus this morning, but I promised I'd get him and feed him. He's always hungry these days."

"Teenage boys are. How's he handling the punishment?"

She shrugged. "Okay, I guess. It's been a little difficult around here lately. He's doing everything he can to let me know he doesn't want to move to New Jersey. And, now that Fred's sober, I've got two of them against me."

"Are you still planning on leaving? I'll have to tighten up my courting plan." He grinned.

"Honestly? I don't know. I saw a few jobs online a few days ago and applied for them." She stared at his rugged face. "I don't want to leave either, so I need to find a way to make it work."

He nodded. "I respect that. Much as I'd like to sweep you off your feet and take care of all your problems, I don't think you'd be comfortable with that."

She shook her head. "Not yet. Maybe someday."

"I'll work on that, too. Speaking of work ..." He stood up and put his mug in the sink. "I have to work late tonight. Can I see you tomorrow?"

"Why don't you come for dinner?" Annie impulsively asked. "Nothing fancy—roast chicken."

"Nothing fancy works for me. I'll bring the wine." He kissed her lightly on the cheek and left.

There was one more thing she wanted to do before retrieving her son.

"Hi, Mom," she said when her mother picked up the phone.

"Well, this is unexpected. You don't call too often. Is that Beverly bothering you?"

Her mother would never change. "I called to say _thank you.'

279

Thank you for protecting me."

Her mother was quiet for a moment. "You're welcome."

Chapter 23

David was excited when Annie picked him up at the dump on Dimeo Lane a few miles north of Santa Cruz. "I've only got one more week!" he said. "Then I can go back to soccer."

Annie glanced over at him. "And you're never going to get in trouble again?"

"Not if I can help it," he said. "This was *so* dumb."

"Uh-huh."

"I'm sorry, Mom. I didn't mean to cause trouble. I wasn't thinking."

She tousled his hair. "It won't be your last mistake, but that's all it was, a mistake. As long as you learn from it and don't keep repeating it, it'll be fine."

"I won't do this ever again, Mom."

"Thanks."

They drove through farmland for a few minutes before he spoke again. "Does that mean we can stop for pizza?" She laughed. "I guess so." That would give her an opportunity to tell him about John.

Once they had their slices and were settled at a booth at Pizza My Heart, she tried to figure out the best way to introduce the subject. For once, David seemed happy. He'd found some "cool" machines at the dump—machinery used to sort recyclables and dispose of toxic waste.

"It's kinda like that stuff that Sarah's learning about," he said. "Maybe I should do that, too, when I go to college."

He tore off another bite. "So are you going to take that job with the bookstore? That'd be crazy. Maybe we could get discounts or something."

Ah, the perfect opening. "Well, there's something we need to talk about."

"It's okay. I know we'd have less money. But I'd help out—get a job or something."

"Remember the guy who came to the house to offer the job at the bookstore?"

"Uh-huh," he mumbled around another bite of pizza.

"Well, we went out on a couple of dates together."

"I know." He went silent for a few minutes.

She concentrated on her pizza. One of the things she'd learned from her coach was that silence was a very effective way of communicating.

"I guess that's okay," he finally said. "He's not moving in, is he?" "No." John had said he was going to court David and she was going to rely on him to do it.

"I suppose that's okay, then. What's Dad going to say?"

"I don't know. But we're not going to get back together. You know that."

"Yeah." He was silent again.

"Do you think we could still get discounts from the bookstore guy?" He flashed her the grin that had won everyone over when he was younger.

"We'll see. You can ask him yourself. He's coming to dinner tomorrow night."

"Okay." Her son went back to shoveling pizza in his mouth.

Annie looked at him. He was growing up. Soon he'd be on his own. She hoped she'd raised him right—that he'd be happy and do well with his life. But it was pretty much out of her control now.

It was time for her to move on.

# # #

By four-thirty Sunday afternoon, Annie had trussed the chicken, de-stemmed and washed the spinach, and peeled and quartered the potatoes. It wasn't a meal Weight Watchers would approve of, but she wasn't feeding dieting middle-aged women. She was feeding a growing teenage boy and a tall, lanky cowboy.

Her cowboy. All right, he was masquerading as a bookseller, but he looked like he belonged on a horse riding the plains chasing cows. Or maybe taming a bucking bronc.

I'm getting carried away.

She giggled.

When the doorbell rang an hour later, she raced down the stairs to open it. She paused a moment to take a breath before she opened the door.

"These are for you." John thrust a bouquet of spring blossoms into her hands. He gestured to the cloth shopping bag he'd hung over his shoulder. "I stopped at Staff of Life on my way here." He stepped inside, leaned down, and kissed her.

A door opening from the downstairs hall made her step back from his embrace. "David," she whispered.

"Hi," John said to David as her son emerged from the hall.

"Oh, hi." David straddled the two steps between the hall and the landing and put out his hand. "How are you?"

"Good. Looking forward to some good home cooking." John smiled at Annie.

David looked at his mother. "Tell me you're doing something normal for dinner." He turned to John. "Sometimes when we have guests she decides to experiment. It doesn't always turn out too well."

She poked her son in the ribs. "Is roasted chicken, stuffing, spinach, and mashed potatoes normal enough for you?"

"W-e-ll, maybe not the spinach ..."

"David!" She laughed. She loved her son when he was like this—playful and teasing.

"I thought it was normal except for the potatoes," John added. "Isn't there a law somewhere that you can't have potatoes with stuffing?"

"You guys," she said with a grin. "Okay ... I'll eat it all myself!"

David leaped past her and raced up the stairs. "Not a chance!"

Annie laughed with pure joy and John joined in. Then he brushed her lips with his.

"Got to get this in when no one's watching."

Dinner continued with light-hearted banter and conversation. David and John were easy with each other and her meal, complemented by John's local Pinot noir, was a success.

"Come on, David," John said after dinner. "Show me where things go in this kitchen so we can clean up. Then I can find out where your mom hid the ice cream I brought."

Annie started to get up.

"Sit," John commanded. "You cooked, we'll clean. Of course, it may take you days before you find everything when we're through," he added as he went into the kitchen.

Annie picked up her wine glass, went to the living room and gazed out the window. It was staying lighter later every evening. They only had a few more months of nice days before the coastal fog settled in for the summer. Suddenly a cloud passed over her mood. She had to go into work tomorrow to find out what Randy wanted. What was she going to tell him?

# # #

Annie drove over the hill to San Jose the next morning with mixed feelings. She'd been doing this commute for ten years. It was tiring, but it was routine. Routine had been her lifeline—an antidote to the chaos of living with Fred and single motherhood. Was she ready to take a risk again?

As she made her way to her office, she absently waved to co-workers. She'd come in a little early for her meeting with Randy so she could finish packing up her things. She'd taken most of her personal belongings home weeks ago. She found herself staring out the window at the almond trees and green hills. Soon, summer valley heat would turn the fields brown, leaving the live oaks dotting the hills as the only visible evidence of life.

Glancing at her watch, Annie shook herself from her reverie and tossed the last few binders into the cardboard box. Then she picked up her notepad and walked to Randy's office.

"Shut the door," Randy told her when she walked in. He didn't give her time to sit before he started in. "What did you do in New Jersey? It was your one chance to keep a job. You were a perfect fit."

"They aren't making an offer?" she asked.

"They haven't made up their mind. They want to see you again. Next week. You're to be personally interviewed by a director—Conrad somebody." He leaned over his stack of paper. "You'd better get there next week and make it right. You're running out of time. There's nothing else—the economy sucks and you know it."

"I'll take the layoff."

"What?"

"You heard me," Annie repeated. "I'll take the layoff. I don't want to move to New Jersey. The job's impossible, Conrad's behavior is borderline sexual harassment, and my life is in California. I'll find something else."

"You're an idiot."

"You always thought so."

"Your funeral. Pack up your things and let me know when

you're done. We'll finish the paperwork and you can leave."

"I'm already packed."

The next hour was one of the most humiliating in Annie's life. She was stripped of her company ID, computer, and codes. She signed paper after paper. Finally, Randy took her to the corporate gate as she balanced her last boxes of personal items in her arms.

"Good luck," was all Randy said as the metal gate slammed closed behind her.

Annie drove out of the compound on autopilot, her thoughts going a mile a minute.

She'd spent over a decade at this place. It had been good to her. But she was never more certain in her life that she was doing the right thing. She was making a change for herself—not for David, or John or Fred, or her parents. Just for her.

Cranking up the music, Annie sang along to Peter, Paul, and Mary. Tears ran down her face as she shouted the words to familiar songs like "No Easy Walk to Freedom."

# # #

When Annie reached the fishhook, she turned north on Highway 1. At a music store near the university, she found what she wanted. Her small purchase fit easily into her purse.

I suppose I should be miserable. I just threw away my security.

Annie laughed. Her feelings were as far from miserable as they could get. Spring was in full force in the city of Santa Cruz and in her heart. Even the run-down houses along Mission Street had flowers bursting from struggling gardens while the handful of boldly painted old Victorians splashed their floral displays. She began to sing a half-remembered song from a favorite Broadway show.

She sang her way down to the bookshop, making up words when she couldn't remember the originals. By the time she got to the parking garage, she was at the end of the song, singing at the top of her lungs.

A smile on her face, she waltzed into the store. She spotted John almost exactly where she'd seen him the first time. Once again, he was struggling with a load of books, his shirt stretched taut against his back. But now she knew exactly what those bare muscles felt like under her hands.

He looked up as she got closer and a smile matching her own spread across his face. He dumped the books on the nearest table and came to her.

"You look so happy," he said, and gave her a light kiss on her mouth.

"I guess you're not going to keep our relationship a secret."

"Hell, no," he said and kissed her again.

"I quit my job."

He put his hands on her shoulders and stared down at her. "For real? No going to New Jersey? No job?"

"Nope. I'm staying right here where I belong."

"That's wonderful!" He drew her to him in a bear hug. "I still have an opening at the bookstore," he murmured to the top of her head.

Laughing, she pushed him gently away and took his hands. "I may take you up on it, but I want to wait until I hear from the consulting firms. Let me see if I can find something in my field first."

"Got time for coffee?"

"I have all the time in the world."

"Unfortunately, I've only got fifteen minutes," John said as he escorted her back to the café. "I have to warn you—the boss in this place is a slave-driver."

Twenty minutes later Annie was driving south. She shook her head in wonder. She'd never felt better in her life. It was as if a straight highway had opened up in front of her. If there were obstacles, she felt confident she could overcome them. It was exhilarating!

"Hi," she called as she bounced into Elizabeth's store. "I quit my job!" she yelled.

Her friend emerged from the back of the store, a toothpick in one hand, a pair of tweezers in the other. "Shhh!" she stage whispered. "I almost dropped hot wax on Sheila Abernathy's nose!"

She gave Annie an awkward hug and looked at her questioningly. "You quit your job? Without having another one?"

"Yep!"

"How's it feel?"

"Great!" It was Annie's turn to look at her friend. "Where were you this weekend? I tried to call you, but you never answered. I wanted to tell you about my date with John."

"How was it?"

"Fabulous."

"I can't wait to hear more, but ..." Elizabeth gestured to the back room. "I've got to go. Call me later? Better yet, come see me."

They hugged and Elizabeth scurried back behind the curtain.

Annie pulled into her driveway a few minutes earlier. Her euphoria wouldn't last too long, she realized. Soon the reality of bills would crash down on her. But for now, she wanted to be on top of the world for however long it lasted.

She brought her office boxes into the garage. She couldn't imagine where to put the company awards that had once seemed so important to her. As for her technical books, they could stay here until she needed them for the next job.

Once her cup of tea was made, Annie took the package out of

her purse and grabbed the guitar she'd dragged out of the garage weeks before. She restrung her old Martin and tried out a few chords.

After supper that night, she told David her decision to quit. "I'm not sure how long it will take me to get a job or consulting assignment, so things will be a little tight around here for a while. You'll need to make your cleats do until fall."

"I don't care," he said, throwing his arms around her. "Anything, as long as we don't have to leave!" He hummed tunelessly as he cleared the table. "I ... um ... was talking to Dad about it and he suggested I apply for a job at a restaurant or something. They're always looking for busboys, especially with the summer coming. I rode my bike to that restaurant you and Elizabeth like and filled out an application. They said they'd see, but they probably wouldn't call until after my birthday in May."

Annie gave her son a hug. "Thanks, kid," she said as tears welled in her eyes and a lump formed in her throat. It was true. She didn't have to do it alone.

# # #

"What are you having?" Elizabeth asked as they settled into their chairs at the Costanoa Grill.

"Oh, since I've thrown all caution to the wind by quitting my job, I'm going to have the Alfredo with prawns."

"Sounds yum. Wanna split?"

"Sure!"

They placed the order, along with a request for two Fogarty chardonnays and side salads.

"Let's start with the important things," Elizabeth said. "How was your date Friday night? Tell me everything!"

"I'm not going to tell you everything ..."

"That means something happened. Did you ..."

"It doesn't mean anything. I don't have to tell you every detail. And, no, it doesn't mean we ..." Annie waved her right hand.

Elizabeth studied her. "You never were a very good liar, you know."

Annie sighed. "We had a really fun time at the concert. Ellis Paul is a great entertainer. He inspired me so much that I got strings and restrung the guitar."

"I can't wait to sit at your first concert."

"It'll be a while. I've got to get some calluses first. My fingers are killing me."

"And then what?"

"Then I'll start learning to play again. Maybe try writing a song or two."

"Ugh! You're impossible. I mean then what happened *after the concert*?"

"Oh. All right. You're right. He kissed me ... and we ... made love."

"I can see it was good," Elizabeth said dryly.

Annie jerked herself back to reality. "Um ... yeah ... it was good." She could feel a huge smile cross her face. "Like I'm sure it's good with you and Bobby."

Elizabeth's expression saddened.

"What's up?" Annie asked.

Elizabeth picked up her chardonnay, took a sip, and placed the glass on her cocktail napkin, carefully aligning the glass's bottom with the indentation on the napkin. She looked up at Annie, her large brown eyes damp.

"We broke up."

"What?"

"He wants to be married, Annie, and I don't. He's running for district supervisor and we ... I felt he'd be better off alone than with an unmarried girlfriend he sleeps with on weekends."

"Elizabeth, nobody cares about that in Santa Cruz. Sounds like an excuse to me."

"Maybe it is. I don't know. I couldn't go on with it the way it was anymore. It seemed dishonest." Elizabeth picked up her wine again and swirled it, staring into the depths of the small eddy in the glass.

The friends sat quietly for a time. Annie thought about the upheaval in their lives as she sipped her wine. It was going to be a year of change for both of them.

The arrival of food broke the somber silence. By unspoken agreement, they changed topics and talked about Elizabeth's business, the coming tourist season, and the best solutions to global warming.

# # #

After getting David off to school, Annie checked into her home e-mail before continuing the job search, as she'd done every morning since she quit her job.

"Yes!" she shouted as she scanned an e-mail from Arthur and Martin, one of the consulting firms she'd applied to. She sped back a response, telling them that she'd be happy to come in for an interview the following Tuesday. She danced around her office, her heart lifted with possibilities. It wasn't a job, but it was one step closer.

She spotted a second e-mail in the queue. Beverly. She and her aunt had kept up with almost daily Facebook messages over the past few weeks. Beverly was planning a longer trip to Costanoa over the summer so she could meet her great-nephew and spend more time with them.

"I've got an interview!" Annie sent the message off.

Her aunt must have been online because a chat window came up. "I knew you would. You've been doing so great. Things will turn around, you'll see. And you'll be happier than you've ever been in your life."

"You know, I think you might be right."

"And how's that beau of yours?"

"We talk every day. He's coming to David's soccer game on Friday night."

"Will Fred be there?"

"Yes. But John can handle it."

"I'm sure he can. It's Fred I'm thinking about."

"Good point." Annie laughed out loud. "Got to run. Coaching call in a few minutes. Need to make some tea first."

"Bye, sweetie."

"Bye, Bev."

Carol called promptly at ten. Annie was bubbling with enthusiasm.

"It sounds like things have really turned around," Carol said when she finished catching her up to date.

"I can't believe it. I mean, everything was against me. I was being laid off, my kid was in trouble, and it looked like my only option was to move across the country. And nothing about that has really changed."

"Except you."

"Except me." Annie had to smile to herself. It was exactly what Carol had predicted weeks ago. Carol let the silence lengthen.

"You know," Annie continued. "I never really thought this would work. How could singing three times a week change my life? But I realize that it was simply a catalyst for other changes. Once I opened myself up to let the music back in my life, I became less rigid. It was as if I could see in color after living in a black and white movie all my life. I still don't totally understand it, but I'm grateful. Thank you."

"You're welcome."

"Are we done?" Annie asked.

"I think we are."

# # #

The sunny warm days continued through Friday. Annie packed up David, his gear, and plenty of food supplies, and drove down to the high school football and soccer stadium. He had to be at the field an hour before the game, so she brought a book to read until John showed up.

Annie's heart lifted when she saw John climbing the stadium steps to her perch. Her smile was reflected in his face, and she knew they could only see each other. She stood when he reached her and leaned into his embrace.

"I've missed you," he said, settling his lips on hers for a lingering kiss.

"Me, too," she replied when he finally released her.

He looked around. "You've got enough food here to feed a small army."

"David *is* a small army after a soccer game." Annie felt someone's gaze on her. She looked down the stairs and saw Fred staring up at them. He didn't look happy.

"There's Fred," she said to John, nodding at her ex-husband as he stood at the bottom of the stairs. "I need to talk to him. I'll be right back."

"Annie." John put his hand on her arm. "Take all the time you need. I know you'll be back." He lightly kissed her on the cheek.

She trotted down the stairs to where Fred waited.

"Hi," she said.

"Who's that?" Fred gestured up the stairs.

"His name's John. He owns Ocean Reads."

"He's obviously more than that to you."

"Yes," Annie said. "He is."

Fred looked at her, his face drooping. "I guess I had a fantasy."

"What was that?" Annie asked gently.

"That if I got sober, you'd come back to me."

"Oh, Fred," Annie said, giving him a hug. "I'm sorry. But it's been over for a long time. We can't go back."

"I feel like a total fool."

"It took two of us. We each had issues we needed to work out. We couldn't work them out together. But we produced a beautiful son."

The corners of Fred's mouth lifted. "So we did." He gestured at John again. "So is it serious?"

"It might be."

"Well, good for you. You deserve some happiness. David said you quit JCN. How's the job search going?"

"I've got an interview next week."

"That's great! David's really happy that you're staying. All the chaos was tough on him."

The teams began running out on the field.

"It's starting," Fred said. "I'm going to sit here. See you later."

"Later."

Annie climbed back up the stairs and sat next to John. She looked at Fred, alone on the bottom steps, bent over, his head on his hands.

"How'd it go?" John asked.

"As well as it could. I feel so sorry for him."

"I know you do. And while he made your life miserable for a

while, you loved him."

"Yes."

"Annie, I have to ask," John took her hand. "Do you still love him?"

She shook her head. "No, I haven't loved him for a very long time."

John put his arm around her and pulled her close to him. "That means there's space in your heart for me."

"That's what it means," she said and tilted her face up for his kiss.

The End

Did you enjoy this story? Please leave a review on your favorite online bookstore.

Why are reviews important to this writer?
- I really want to know what you think. What did you like? Where did I miss the mark?
- Other readers are more willing to take a chance on a new author when there are reviews.
- A good number of reviews help a book get better rankings on Amazon, as well as opportunities to promote the book. More people discover authors you already like.

This author thanks you very much!

*Turn the page for an excerpt from **California Wine**, available now.*

Chapter 1 of *California Wine*

Oh, my.

Elizabeth's eyes locked with a pair of the most intense blue eyes she'd ever seen. They belonged to a man with thick black hair to his shoulders, a strong aquiline nose, and high cheekbones. His smile was warm; his straight white teeth a sharp contrast to his light olive skin.

Why did Italy produce such heart-breakingly handsome men?

She looked down at the restaurant table and then looked up again. He was still staring, the smile even broader.

Maybe her daughter Sarah was right. Elizabeth should dine out more often, especially if the scenery was going to be like this.

The waitress brought her a salad and Elizabeth looked at it morosely. Was it possible to eat salad and not get some stuck in her teeth when a gorgeous man was staring at her? Or worse, drop a huge leaf of oily lettuce on her blouse, calling his attention to her less than abundant breasts?

But the salad looked so good ... tiny red cherry tomatoes interspersed with baby carrots and radishes on a bed of mixed greens. She sighed and stabbed the nearest tomato with her fork.

The red orb escaped her plate and went bouncing off the table to land on the floor, rolled to the center of an open space, and sat there for only a minute before being squished by a waitress' black shoe.

"Such a tragic end for a little tomato." A rich masculine voice spoke near her ear.

She looked up into the blue eyes of the man standing next to her.

"Perhaps if you had not stabbed at it so viciously, it might have survived," he continued. She had to grin at his mock seriousness.

"May I join you?" he asked his hand on the chair.

She considered him. She'd intended to eat her supper alone, go upstairs to her room, run a hot bath, and relax with a good book.

He waited for her answer.

Suddenly, her plan seemed a lonely way to spend one of her last days in Italy. "Sure."

He sat down next to her and a frisson of heat zapped her body. For the first time since her mother had died, life stirred in her heart. She put down her fork.

"My name is Marcos," he said, holding out his hand.

"Elizabeth." She shook. His palm was smooth and cool, and the long fingers fit the rest of his lean body. His touch electrified her skin.

"American? Yes?"

She nodded.

He grinned, looking as if he'd guessed a game-show answer correctly. "Are you here on business? Pleasure? Traveling all by yourself or is your husband with you?"

She took a sip of wine. Her best friend Annie had told her not to reveal too much personal information about herself when she was traveling. What could she safely tell her new acquaintance, a man she knew nothing about, other than he exuded masculinity?

He must have seen the suspicion in her eyes because he waved his hand and gestured. The proprietress of the hotel came over to their table.

"Is there something wrong?" she asked, a frown creasing her forehead. "Marcos, are you being a bother?"

"Nothing like that. I was only trying to assist the lady with her vegetables. They seem to be escaping." Marcos pointed to the stain on the floor.

The woman snapped her fingers at the nearest waitress and pointed. Then she turned back to Elizabeth. "I am so sorry. Would you like me to bring you another tomato?" "Another tomato? No, no, I'm fine." Elizabeth stifled a laugh. "It's nothing, really."

She glanced at Marcos, who was holding his hand over his mouth. His eyes were sparkling with laughter.

"And him," the woman poked a long fingernail into Marcos' shoulder. "Is my cousin annoying you?"

"Uh ..." Now was Elizabeth's chance to get rid of him if she wanted.

Marcos' eyes pleaded for a reprieve.

An impish spark rose in her soul. Why not have an adventure in the safe confines of the hotel dining room? Her trip was almost over anyway. Surely no harm could come from a little fun. Could it?

"No. He's fine," Elizabeth said.

"*Bueno.*" The hotel owner turned on her heel and left, muttering under her breath.

"Cousin?" Elizabeth asked. "She doesn't seem at all like you. She's very ..."

"Serious?" He shrugged. "The women in my family tend to be fire-breathing dragons."

A waitress walking past the table glanced in his direction and blushed. He fired off rapid Italian to her with a smile that would make any woman's heart melt.

The waitress' blush deepened. She nodded and hurried off to the coffee bar.

My, he was a flirt. She'd better tread carefully.

"So now that we have solved the great problem of the little

tomato, we can get acquainted," he said to Elizabeth. "I assume you are traveling alone, or you would not be here by yourself, attacking small, defenseless vegetables."

She smiled in spite of her determination to keep him at a distance. "I'm here with my daughter."

Marcos looked around the room. "And where is she?"

"With a friend from college. They went dancing."

"Dancing. It is good. Do you like to dance?"

The young waitress placed the coffee on the table and stared at Marcos with adoring eyes.

Elizabeth ate a forkful of salad while he chatted with the server in Italian. She did like to dance, but she didn't want to leave the door open for any kind of invitation ... even if he was attractive.

"Yes, I do," she said once the waitress left.

That's not what she meant to say.

He smiled at her. "Then we should do it!"

She shook her head. "No, we shouldn't."

"Ahh," he said. "You don't know me. Perhaps I can change that. Will you come to dinner some night so we can learn more about each other?"

She smiled and shook her head.

"We could go to a place quite near here. We'll tell my cousin, the *dragon feroce*, where we are going. We can even walk there from the hotel so you don't have to get into a car with a strange man. What do you say?"

"We're leaving Italy in three days." It was as good an excuse as any.

"Then I will have to work fast. Say you will come."

"But my daughter ..."

"I'm sure she can have dinner one night without you as you are already without her."

Elizabeth took a sip of wine. A date with a charming Italian was tempting, especially since she'd spent the last twenty years of her life avoiding anything remotely risky.

Still, she hadn't had a date since she broke up with Bobby three months ago. What could be safer than a date with someone she'd never see again? A simple dinner with no strings attached. Everything in control.

She glanced at Marcos. He certainly didn't look like a mass murderer.

He smiled as if he knew what she was thinking, picked up his coffee, and sipped, his eyes never leaving hers.

Bad idea. He was way too tempting. And the last time a man had made her forget her better judgment, she'd wound up giving up her lifelong dreams.

To keep reading, go to your favorite online bookstore or brick and mortar store and purchase *California Wine*.

The Story Behind the Story

California Sunset, my first romance, was written during a difficult personal period. My third marriage had shattered on the rocks of alcoholism, my child was in trouble with the law, and not too long later, I was laid off from my tech management job in the 2008 recession.

Like many of us, I wallowed in a pool of self-pity for a while, but eventually decided that wasn't doing anything constructive. A chance meeting with a psychic sent me on the road to recovery. The body work I received at the hands of a skilled practitioner helped eradicate some age-old wounds that had had me making less than optimal choices.

Looking back ten years at that time, I realize it had to happen for me to be able to fall in love again with a man who would support my dreams and work with me to make our marriage the best it could possibly be. And yes, he introduced me to Ellis Paul and a whole host of other folkies.

I hope you enjoyed the book and will continue on to the next in the series, *California Wine*, to be re-released in 2019.

Other Ways to Connect

Join my newsletter list on Stories About Love (www.stories-about-love.com) and get notifications of new releases.

Like my Facebook page (www.facebook.com/Casey.Stories.About.Love/ where I frequently post photos of nature and animals.

Other Books by Casey Dawes

California Series

California Sunshine
California Sunset
California Wine
California Homecoming
California Thyme
California Sunrise

Rocky Mountain Front Series

Home Is Where the Heart Is

Stand Alone Stories

Chasing the Tumbleweed
Keep Dancing
Love on the Wind
Love on Willow Creek

Christmas Stories

A Christmas Hope

About Casey Dawes

Real Life ⟨℞⟩ Real Problems ⟨℞⟩ Real Love

Casey Dawes has lived a varied life–some by choice, some by circumstance. Her master's degree in theater didn't prepare her for anything practical, so she's been a teacher, stage hand, secretary, database guru, manager in Corporate America, business coach, book shepherd, and writer.

She inherited an itchy foot from her grandfather, traveling to Europe and Australia and many towns and cities across the US while in business. She's lived in towns with a population of 379 and in an apartment complex on 42nd Street and 9th Avenue in Manhattan. She's dragged her belongings from New Jersey ... to Massachusetts, Michigan, Pennsylvania, Virginia, California, and Montana.

She believes in true love and the ability of honest, thoughtful conversations to solve most problems.

Her stories contain characters who have to deal with real life and real problems to find real love.

Made in the USA
Las Vegas, NV
17 December 2021